MW01686486

White Leather and Flawed Pearls

White Leather and Flawed Pearls

A NOVEL

Susan Altstatt

2017 · Fithian Press
McKinleyville, California

Printed in the United States of America

Published by Fithian Press
A division of Daniel and Daniel, Publishers, Inc.
Post Office Box 2790
McKinleyville, CA 95519
www.danielpublishing.com

Distributed by SCB Distributors (800) 729-6423

LIBRARY OF CONGRESS cataloging-in-publication DATA
Names: Altstatt, Susan, author.
Title: White leather and flawed pearls : a novel / by Susan Alstatt.
Description: McKinleyville, California : Fithian Press, 2017.
Identifiers: LCCN 2017034209 | ISBN 9781564746030 (softcover : acid-free paper)
Subjects: LCSH: Rock musicians—Fiction. | Mate selection—Fiction. | GSAFD: Love stories.
Classification: LCC PS3601.L8585 W48 2017 | DDC 813/.6—dc23
LC record available at https://lccn.loc.gov/2017034209

To Betty and Clarence Hoe,
who for years provided at "less than cost,
the greatest variety of marriage, the safest, fastest,
and finest marriages in the world,"
right across Curry Street from the license bureau
in Carson City, Nevada

White Leather and Flawed Pearls

Prologue

SATURDAY, MAY 3, 1986

GUEST STAR TOMMI RHYMER drapes Paul (PM Post Mortem) Merriweather's talk show couch in a pose so bonelessly lascivious it doesn't matter zip he's fully dressed, looking much the same as ever: hair so red, you kill the color on the TV or his head blurs to a fireball. Just a dirty knockout blow to the theory all men were created equal.

And inane old Merriweather welcomes the '86 Belshangles tour to the U.S., welcomes Tommi to the show, says he should've won Best Actor for Carlini's *Drake* and gets a giggle from him ("Rockers turned thespian don't win statuettes, y'know that, Paul"), flashes the *Snake Oil Salesman* album at his viewers.

As if there weren't monster 3-D displays and ten-foot stacks of it in every Tower Records: Initial of each word printed red and glowing, SOS. The band on a wagon like an old-time medicine show, pitching elixir bottles to a crowd of naked, gray, apathetic skeletons, off into the dark on every side. Subtitled *Songs About Love and Poverty*.

On the back, you see the wraiths who chug their bottles sprout angel robes and ostrich feather wings, and flapping into aerial formations, spiral upward toward the light.

"Tommi, you were telling me before the show why Belshangles didn't play *Live Aid*—"

"Well, it's no lack of feeling for the starving blacks in Africa. But with only so much effective sentiment to give, I'm afraid mine goes more to the poor black yobos looting stores and trashing streets in Brixton—"

"Charity begins at home?"

"—And white ones behaving much the same in Liverpool and Manchester and Birmingham. Y'know, our future Charles III has set up a 'Commission of Investigation'; he doesn't look forward to presiding over people whose ranking outdoor sport is doing skin-violence to one another. So far his experts tell him people do these things because they're criminals, and being incited from abroad.

"Now, I have a somewhat different perspective; I used to steal when I was young—like fourteen—and on the street. I stole food. And clothes when I hadn't any, and the tools of my trade for the same reason, and not a single foreign power bothered to look me up. I'd like my day in court to tell the Prince about it. Man to man, I'd tell His Highness of some other ways I found for staying alive."

"But, you were saying, you consider this present Belshangles tour largely as promotion?"

"Three hundred eighty-six years ago, a chap off Shakespeare's stage, a song-and-dance comic named Will Kempe danced a jig from London to Norwich. A hundred miles on the roads, took him nine days. He did it on a dare. They called it *Kempe's Nine-Days' Wonder*.

"Nobody's dared me, but I think I can go Will Kempe one better. I think I've found a profitable use for poverty and desolation in the streets: I'm going out to dance through it. Anyone who wants can come along behind me. Kids all over Britain are taking pledges for the miles they can stay with *Rhymer's Jig*, running, walking, pushing wheelchairs.

"Bit of a downer, going all those miles and ending up in Norwich; being a London boy, I choose to dance it the other way 'round. Friday, September twelve, four weeks after we go off tour, Belshangles will play me off the steps of Norwich City Hall. Ten o'clock in the morning, I head south with bells on.

"We'll have music every third of a mile—like marching bands passing a reviewer's box, only here the bands stand still, and I will do the passing by. We've got thirty-five flatbed stages that'll move each night, and all sound gear donated—"

"Are you talking kids' bands? Garage bands?"

"Some are, but we've some big names too. My only demands were that they *not* have been in *Live Aid* or the other charity circuses, that they submit original music I can dance to, that they can play an hour set, and that they put their energies into raising pledges from their fans or their districts. Man, we've *got* over three hundred bands, punk, heavy metal, ska, reggae, I've got Scottish pipes, you name it.

"Nine days later. Belshangles'll play me into the City of London, right up to the doors of the Lord Mayor's Guildhall. And we've got every sharp young filmmaker in the U.K. out there, and from the continent and the States, with the best gear donated, taking it all in. Rich man, poor man, beggarman, thief, watching the music come down the land. Your Lucasfilm in California's pledged the editing."

"Lucas did get his awards for *Drake*, didn't he? The screen editing on the Spanish Armada—"

"Like Harlan got his for the music."

No Harlan perched beside Tom on the couch tonight, whatever that means. Belshangles's always been the two of them together. They've never given separate interviews. Being the fan I've been, I know. But Merriweather doesn't pick up on that, notice; he's got lower digs in mind.

"Dino Carlini—now we've mentioned *Drake*—was practically

black-listed in the 'fifties for films with homosexual themes—back when 'gay' wasn't 'in'—I suppose everyone looked for it in *Drake*: such a womanless piece, except for that larky royal seduction—"

"Elizabeth did dine alone with Drake onboard his ship. That bit was history."

"But did she chase him around the furniture? Was Drake a gay hero in Carlini's mind?"

Tommi ducks his head, makes his eyes go twice as big and pale under the red forelock and the dark red lashes. "Wasn't cast in bed, if that's what you're after."

"Oh no! Not at all; I wasn't suggesting—"

"Old Dino was gay when gay spelled revolution. The terrorist's his man now, the citizen who declares a private war and drags his nation into it, goes from outlaw to hero, never changing course—"

"That's how Carlini pictured Drake?"

"It's how he was. As for the dinner with Her Majesty: which sets a common man higher? Being offered intimacy with the powerful, or once it's offered, being enough his own creature to say no?"

"Which do you think?"

"Well, I know what Dino thinks."

"But *Rhymer's Jig*, Tommi: where does that film go?"

"A first-run theater movie to begin, then video. MTV will get their separate bits. And all the proceeds, the pledge monies—my share of this tour as well—will go to set up the 'Rhymer Foundation,' like a nonprofit think tank aimed at re-transforming the U.K.'s involuntary leisure class into the working people they once were."

"I think Carlini's given you a few ideas."

"I may have given him a few."

"Do you have any contact with Prince Charles?"

"I've been 'presented,' for all that's worth. There's friends of his are friends of mine. I go to parties where he goes." (He gives it the scandalous, shy grin and flaming blush.) "The Princess asked me for a dance last Christmas."

"But not the Prince?"

(Still grinning,) "Hasn't come to that yet."

"Aren't you concerned that the Prince, or the palace anyway—someone might be offended?"

"He knows a proper crowd-pleaser when he sees one; his family's been in show business longer than mine. Well, fancy how he must feel—a figurehead useless as tits on a boar—at the small end of our national absurdity, with millions of unemployed poor at the other, and in between, this great unresponsive, dumb, bureaucratic—"

"Where do you place yourself in that society?"

"Nowhere. That's the point. My parents died and the schools gave up on me. I've been out ever since."

"Not to change the subject: rock musicians are in some odium in the U.S. now; Senate wives etc. lobbying for industry control of lyrics on Satanism, incest, suicide, masturbation—I know young Turks have a way of becoming elder statesmen, but Belshangles was the shock rock of the day not so long ago. Did you ever write a song about masturbation?"

With a look of dense slow-dawning wonder (Tom can play the cockney clown like nobody else), "*What*, you mean doin' it to *myself?*"

"Well, I suppose that's the usual uh—"

"Doin' it to myself?"

There a nervous network cued a deodorant commercial, leaving every family paper in the U.S. to print the rest:

"Y'know, I've always made a point of writin' personal stuff: one changes some things naturally (so's not to get sued), but apart from that, I write what I know. I would take lyrics of that sort to show an author suffering from a certain lack of congenial company. No, I'd be mortified.

"Or did *you* mean, *doin' it to others?*"

WEDNESDAY, JUNE 12, 1986

As motto to my senior picture, my last yearbook at Paly High, I put *"Ut videam."* The yearbook guys said, "Uh, *what?*"

"It's a quote," I said. "It means—"

"Sorry, no quotes. You know, copyright."

"C'mon, you guys! It's from the Latin Vulgate Bible! Who do you think is gonna sue, Saint Jerome?"

The blind man on the roadside said it: when they told him the noise he could hear was Jesus going by, he left off begging and began to yell, *"Have Mercy on me!"* And everybody tried to shut him up. Except, of course, Jesus, who came and asked, "What do you want from me?" The blind guy said, "That I *may see!"* (*Ut videam*) And then it goes, "—his eyes were opened, and he saw men like trees walking."

I would give anything there is, anything, to see men like trees walking. Dirty-clean like trees are. Rain- and wind-battered like trees are, on deep simple roots nothing can touch. And in defiance of all, still growing—not just up, but upright. Damn fool romantic nonsense, probably; then I always did get sex confounded with religion.

Anyhow, *"Ut videam"* made the yearbook. In English it would've sounded snotty and pietistic, worse yet, born again. In Latin it was merely arcane. I could relate to that; I didn't give a shit if nobody understood but me. And, being odd enough, I got away with it.

Chapter 1

SUNDAY, AUGUST 17

IT'S 10:45 A.M. and twenty-seven seconds. I begin my final approach.

Fifteen minutes finds me wedging the VW bus between delivery vans in the alley behind the Hotel Montor. Five more minutes has me edging through the crush of warm bodies at the main desk, praying, as Saint Stephen did just before the mob stoned him—

In manus tuas Domine commendo spritum meum.
Redemisti nos Domine Deus veritatis,
(Into your hands, Lord, I commend my spirit,
You have paid us out of hock, Lord God of truth)

—thinking what he probably thought, too: "Like everything else in this world, good or bad, it'll be over soon. And I can stop guessing."

Check my purse. Still in it: your ordinary slick gray British mailing-paper envelope. I say "ordinary." Three years ago the premiere arrival of such was like the first breath of life, an extraordinary heart-busting shock. But breathing itself grows ordinary. So I learned to depend on them.

In this last were tucked two others: a narrow, colored envelope such as concert tickets come in (now holding last night's stub of happy memory)—and a heavy, creamy-crisp expensive envelope, such as wedding invitations come in. An engraved invitation certainly, complete with wispy tissue insert to keep it nice, but what it said was:

Mr. Thomas Peter Rhymer
requests the company
of
Miss Miranda Dolores Falconer
At her earliest convenience
after the hour of 11:00 A.M.
Sunday,
the Seventeenth of August,
Nineteen Hundred and Eighty Six.
Admission by invitation only,
to be presented
at the main desk
of
The Hotel Montor
San Francisco, California
USA

It looked so real. This was no fill-in-the-blanks; my little name was all engraved, one piece with the rest of it. And nothing said about R.S.V.P. Look at the desk now. That's what I'm doing. Soft lights and efficient people behind a glowing sculptured brass and stainless steel façade. The people might as well be brass and stainless too; eighteen-and-female has small chance of snaring their attention.

And there's my contact: How could I miss him? Short wide man in glitzy suit, Belshangles badge prominent on the pocket. The hair on his head has failed him; in retaliation, sideburns overrun his big round cheeks in Babylonian profusion. He waits there at the far side of the desk for me, the chick with the matching glass slipper.

No good, man. Look me over, around and through, you'll never spot me in a million years; I look like this terrorist type who's hijacked a stewardess for her clothes, and spoiled the effect by sleeping in 'em.

Mama's blue-check Pendleton suit was liberated to my closet days ago. Under that is my white Esprit mini dress, which can double as a blouse and a change of clothes. I'm skinny, so the blue skirt doesn't sausage out over it.

Clever, think I.

Only while combining them in early morning stealth do I realize: the little white purse and little white flats I expected to complete the outfit are, in fact, my filthy little white purse and worn out little white flats. As insignia of a grown-up woman, a grubby purse with ink stains doesn't cut it. And now I can't escape myself: this hotel is walled in mirrors.

Look around.

A massively trendy hotel with a world-class rock band staying, holed up on, one might almost say *occupying* (in the military sense) the thirty-second floor. The lobby crawls with kids, gray faces, makeup smeared from yesterday's concert madness and a sleepless night. Others wear camera-bag wreaths around their necks: freelance photographers, not tourists; no Hawaiian shirts on these babies. And there's hotel security, discreetly squelching deals in bootleg Belshangles photos, etc., etc., while S.F.'s Finest maintain a walky-talkied presence near the revolving doors.

You can almost hear it, lust and love and hope and greed, despair and exaltation, wild curiosity and the promise of wilder pleasures radiating from that unseen point source high above, like sweet loud pulsing music.

"May I help you?"

Saint Stephen's first stone, right on target.

"I've been told to pre—pre-se—pre-sent this uh, at the desk and—I mean—"

Brief ordeal. The steel-and-cashmere Valkyrie behind the desk glances disdainfully from me down to my invitation, then back to me with different eyes entirely. "You're Ms. Falconer?"

"Yes."

"One moment, please."

Stepping behind her fellows, Desk Person conveys my invitation half-a-dozen yards to Bulky Man, he of the Belshangles badge and the burgeoning sideburns, who listens, brightens, turns, spots and comes for me, behind a kid's grin and an outstretched hand. The hand jammed suddenly into mine wears a big gold ring and lots of curly fur on the back.

"Well, Miss Falconer! Glad to meecha. Sim Garfein! Yeah! How'ya doin'?"

"Fine."

"Mr. Rhymer's been lookin' forward to this! I mean he's *up*, y'know?"

We wade the crowd together, toward the long glowing brass bank of elevators. I can feel the avid eyes and ears of the more observant Belshangles fans following.

Whizz.

Elevator doors switch off the white noise of the lobby.

"How long has ah—Yeah." Maybe Garfein always squirms that way, but I don't think so. I see somebody else having trouble with his mouth: not me, this time. "—How long have you—How long have you and Mr. Rhymer ah—hm."

"Three years."

"Ya don'say."

· — ·

CLICHÉ has it, that the really heavy secrets are forever clawing and digging to get out. In fact, that they *will* out, no matter what you do. My experience is the contrary.

I think, the bigger the secret, the farther down inside your mind it burrows like a mole, builds itself a house and pulls you in to live with it. And soon you go out less, and talk less, and eat less. And need less. All your personal pleasure is piled up there, inside that secret.

Tommi Rhymer told me to rent a post office box when I was fourteen years old.

Lots of kids spend years concealing drugs or liquor from their parents. What I hid were little packs of peanuts off airlines I'd never flown on, exotic bars of soap from luxury hotels around the world. That the Belshangles posters I collected weren't marketed in the U.S., and the Belshangles photos and memorabilia in the manila folder on my desk couldn't have come from *Movie Memories*, those were the secret "highs" I hid.

I sent him things, too. My school grades. Stuff that amused me from the local papers. Kid stuff, bits of my life, just as he sent me bits of his. We never wrote letters, exactly. In ways unexpected, he was a very cautious man.

· — ·

WE'RE almost at the top, when Garfein gets the gall to re-format his question: "Well how did you ah—ah—"

"I took a thorn out of his paw one time."

Whizz.

The obligatory big mirror, facing the elevators on the top floor. This one is gilded art deco, with a little table built into the front, and a beefy Belshangles guard lounging back on it, elbows planted behind him, jacket hiked to free the holster underneath. When he saw me on Garfein's arm, he grinned. When we trucked off down the hall, he followed.

The high-water mark of last night's partying remained in corners, a damp sea wrack of paper plates and napkins, orphan beer bottles in plastic cups. Behind closed doors someone of indeterminate sex (male maybe) was vocalizing, a bawdy operatic soprano shifting by stages into vigorous screams.

Other doors slammed open just ahead, and a man came out in his boxers: a state in which I'd never seen Belshangles drummer Rollo McInery; I knew who it was just the same.

Spotting us, he said one word: sounded like "Wotcher."

A rangy young woman in a bright blue teddy materialized behind his shoulder.

Whiffs of grass, taped music, and two bearded dudes in Levi's and Belshangles T-shirts drifted out the next door; a naked toddler with an older brother in pursuit fell out the next.

It reminded me of—well, I knew what exactly.

My mother is a circus nut. Every summer, sure as Ringling Brothers makes its rounds, Mama's got tickets. All the summers of my childhood, front-row seats, right down where you can smell the tiger pee and dodge the elephants.

She used to get 'em for Oakland or S.F.: Ringling always gigs on both sides of the Bay. One year she bought too late, and could only get Cow Palace tickets, way around the end where she'd never have chosen. Then we found, to reach *those* seats, you went along a section of the concourse the performers used also, between the arena and their trailers in the exhibit barns.

You could stand right next to those death-defying demigods of sequins and sawdust and admire them shyly. They didn't seem to mind. They laughed and went around in bathrobes and smelled of greasepaint and garlic and talked a torrent of Bulgarian.

Afterwards she never bought seats anywhere but there.

Like that now. Except that circus, however glittered up, is for children of all ages, sexless. And rock bands were designed for adolescents, to be the furthest opposite there is.

Like touring the halls with a fife and drum, the rate we're gathering volunteers. McInery's pal is still among the front-runners: she's popped a T-shirt over the teddy, the chest reads *"Love is Blind; Lust Doesn't Give a Good Goddamn."* We reached the side corridor at last, and a door at the end. The same as three years earlier? Memory crazes current events, an untrusty kaleidoscope. Same or not, Garfein coaxed it open with a key, and, ushering me through, rounded on our little mob of spectators. *"Now look 'ere!"*

· — ·

ALL I heard, because the door swung shut. That may have left me on the inside; but not, I discovered, alone.

Harlan Parr. Nemesis in a black silk dressing gown: sunk

deep on the back of his neck in the sofa across the room. Black hair spreading on the sofa back. Black inscrutable glasses fixed on the door, and me. Neat impeccably expensive shoes cocked up on the coffee table. The soles were that peachy virgin-leather color. They had never been off a carpet. Indescribably erotic somehow: the sweet glazed unmarred paleness of the soles of his new shoes.

Harlan got up, made me the smallest formal bow, and vanished down the hall. What I can imagine: the carpet smoking under his exquisite little feet.

Lord God, Father Almighty who made me—
Have mercy on me—

What I can feel building up inside, a good loud scream.

I am a latter-day Don Quixote, happy in my private landscape of windmills. Tom Rhymer is my Dulcinea; I have no intention of being put off, put down, or put out of the running by the extraordinary, any more than I have of letting some nice young ordinary guy come along and help me to forget him. I have no intention of forgetting him! He still fills my measure of "Beauty Incarnate"!

And it's not that I don't really know the worst about him; I remember the contents of my crash course in "Thomas Peter Rhymer, Human Being" very well. He laid it squarely on my head himself: into every drug in sight, designer and generic; into everybody too, male and female—What was it but the classic tale of woe that goes with his profession? I was fourteen years old. All it did was shift my emphasis, from the "beauty" part to the "incarnate." My hero had feet of clay, a great unexpected relief, and far as I knew, the material all human feet are made of. His were still the prettiest feet of clay around.

And the only person he'd ever loved—for *sure loved—*

· — ·

SO here I am, standing in Their Room. Thinking. About the May '86 cover of *Time* I pinned to the wall above my bed.

The caption: *Tommi Rhymer, Harlan Parr: Charity Rocks On.*

A gaudy artist's rendition of those two launching into their act, hitting the stage in a pool of white light, glued so close together back to front, the wonder was how Tommi kept his butt out of Harlan's guitar pickup.

Could be Harlan's down the hall crying his eyes out even now. Could be that's why he had the shades on. My stomach is beginning to churn. Harlan has the face of a Renaissance angel. Botticelli would have chased him down the street to use him for a model. How awful in the end, if all that beauty couldn't guarantee him endless love.

Lord Jesus Christ,
Who takes away the sins of the world
Have mercy on me—

Pretty soon, a second little niggling, giggling inner voice beside my prayer begins to chant, "I fought the windmills, an' *the windmills won!*"

Stop that! Deal with it. Look around.

Pray harder.

It *is* the same suite as before, and maid service hasn't gotten to it yet. I see pieces of clothing, the morning's newspapers with scissored columns, stray cocktail napkins, used olives and toothpicks in the ashtrays. Not garbaged out, but certainly the lived-in look. Lived in by *Them.* Time was, I would've ripped off tidbits of their trash and treasured it. Even now I feel the urge. After high school, one does not do such things. Eighteen is a woman, however green.

The room has a sweet scent. Subtle. Warm. Not pot smoke, but mind-bending. A scent out of imagination: drowsy sun on the King's strange garden. It gives me an unsettled head and heavy eyes.

A scrunch of keys in the door: Garfein again, nearly bashing me in the back, reconnoitering the emptiness.

"Nobody here?"

"Except Harlan. And he left."

"Aw Christ," he says, and lumbers off distracted toward the bedrooms. Down the hall, where Harlan went.

Bittersweet scent. Illusive. Playful. Clear fountains in blue tile courtyards. Plates of dried fruit. Lemon trees and water lilies.

But oh, talk about Earthly Paradise—on the table lately graced by Harlan's heels, between the coffee cups, sits a real one of those fancy, tiny mixing-and-dubbing decks musician mags all advertise ("Fits in your lap; carries on; do your composing on the plane—") plugged into a headset and a quarter-size sparkling white guitar. Harlan's toys.

Midway of the rug, I realize I'm moving.

Nearly to the couch now: it's the plushy, sink-in-to-your-hip-bones kind. Where Harlan had been sitting left a dent. I consider sitting in it. I consider sitting next to it.

God help me, and I've only just begun! It's much too soon to get depressed!

I sit in Harlan's dent. It is noticeably body-warm.

Actually, I'm not depressed. I'm scared shitless.

So damn easy to think up a vilest possible contingency, then a worse, like Dr. Seuss's "Glunk"—nearly impossible to "unthunk" once the old mind spewed it out. I *don't* think I'm about to die a horrible death—he might be into S&M, and kill me making "snuff movies," deep-six my body in the bay—that kind of thing. Nobody knows where I was going. I don't even think he'd throw me to his roadies and watch them tie me down and stuff beer bottles up me, like you read about in trashy rock mags. The Tommi I remember is a battered child-man with a gentle heart.

Lord Jesus Christ,
Who was once a human child
Have mercy on me—

But what if—what if he's just polite? That's the kind of possibilities my reason refused to unthunk. Polite. Invite me down to coffee. Say, "Gee, how awfully nice to see you. Let me take this opportunity to thank you; what's more, my lover thanks you. Now, what are your plans for college? You must fill me in on how you're doing, the next time we tour through."

Lord God, Holy Spirit, Comforter—
Have mercy on me,
Take away my pain.

I shut my eyes. Put my hands over them. Let the room get truly dark now, make it go away. (I either know a lot about answered prayer or even more about self-deception.) I wait while all the sparks and lightning flashes fade, and nothing shows but pure rich dark. Then I open them. Tom Rhymer is watching me from the end of the hallway.

White cotton shirt with no tie. Cloth shoes. Cream cotton wash pants. Ordinary clothes, right? Not on him.

I am thinking: what an insupportable, terrible tragic loss, if, in some dry season, my instant knee-jerk to this man should ever stop being *"Grab fast! Ask questions afterwards!"* and a mental memory dump of all the love poetry I ever was exposed to—this time, fittingly:

My Beloved is white and ruddy,
the chiefest among ten thousand—

(Ten thousand is like nothing. There'll be some beautiful kid in any high school who's chiefest among ten thousand. Ten million, and you might be getting there—)

His head is as the most fine gold, his
locks are bushy, and black as a raven—

But his aren't; Harlan's are.

Now I'm standing up. I shot up when I realized he was there. Not proper. Not grown-up in the least, or ladylike, or liberated, or—

—His hands are as gold rings set with Beryl:
his belly is as bright ivory overlaid with sapphire,
His legs are as pillars of marble,
set in sockets of fine gold:
His mouth is most sweet:
yea, he is altogether lovely:
This is my beloved, and this is my friend,
O daughters of Jerusalem—

Oh shit, and he's laughing at me, too: exactly the funny almost-lover I remember, under cover of the *Song of Songs*.

"Well," the man says, head on one side, "You didn't turn out half bad."

"You're no old bag yourself." Now we're both laughing.

"Where to?" I said finally.

"Y'want to talk about it?"

"Can we talk here?"

He thought. Glanced back down the hall. "Coffee shop."

(Now here's the place for my nightmare to begin—the "I thank you, my lover thanks you; now where will you be going to college" one—)

"Okay."

"Moment; I'll phone up the lads."

Tom loped to the bedroom. I listened open-mouthed. Phone dialing. What he said was short, and much too low to catch. (What "lads?")

But he came back with a smile and took my arm, and his hands were warm as—hands are as (Oh God, here we go)—

—gold rings set with beryl—legs are as
pillars of marble—mouth is most sweet—
yeah man, altogether lovely—this is my—this is my—

Out in the hall now. Not a soul in sight.

Until we rounded a corner and came to the elevators. Two black guys were standing there: two hundred fifty pounds apiece, and they weren't fat either; they were six-and-a-half feet tall. They were dressed in a colorful West African sort of way, and I noticed as we got closer, one had gold rings on his left hand and a gold earring in his left ear. The other's rings and earring were on the right. Apart from that, they were exactly alike. Mirror images. Tom grinned. "Hussein," he said pointing at left earring, and at right, "Hassan."

I bobbed and mouthed "How d'you do?" and regretted it.

They both made silent little flourishing salutes, right-hand fingers to the heart, the lips, the brow, and finally to me. They could have been the Sultan's deaf-mute eunuchs out of the Arabian Nights. They could have been genies out of lamps. Tom was a porcelain miniature between them.

Two elevator doors whizzed open: one on a fat old couple who gaped at Tom and his demon guardians in horrified awe. We got into the other. Nobody spoke. Hassan hit the down button. Tom leaned across, after the doors came shut, and kissed me, kindly, meticulously, and briefly, on the mouth.

He said, "Y'don't smoke, either."

"Is that bad?"

"Good: saves you the trouble of quitting. Never could abide the taste, myself."

Of cigarettes? Or smokers' musty mouths? I knew without being told. I felt all down my back pop out in a fine slither of sweat, my pulse keep rising and rising.

Across the wide brass-and-glass lobby with its indoor trees and flowering carpet, small groups of girls were keeping watch for Tom. They let off a kind of silent shrilling when he came in view, like supersonic burglar alarms. To the trained ear. Mine is infinitely trained. Look, you Daughters of Oakland, San Jose, wherever, I can relate: you've kept vigil, all night maybe, for your Idol, your Icon of Desire. Now, mid-morning, he finally appears, escorting some dumb chick in a suit. I half expect them to school Piranha-fashion and rush him, teeth gnashing.

But we're safely past them, Tom moving fast and me on his arm, the two huge Blacks in wing formation. Past the flower shop, past the Ticketron, homing in now on the dark mouth of the coffee shop, and the coffee shop hostess standing there, immaculate stack of menus on her arm. Latest lacquered hair, lacquered makeup, lacquered linen dress, a long slim shoulder-padded number divided diagonally, hem to shoulder, "smoke" and "champagne." No wrinkles across the crotch of that dress; being judicious, she has never tried to sit in it.

She doesn't see us yet.

Now she does. Her whole face comes apart in looks which have no place there: "Why me, Lord?" panic. Human awkwardness. Undisguisable terminal yearning.

I hear her whisper, "Oh, Mr. Rhymer—"

And we're past her too, into the shop, all tile and stainless '30s chic—headed full-throttle for a roped-off section of tables. The clip-clip-clip of her embarrassed little heels is loud as she scurries to reach the velvet ropes ahead of us and get them down. Tom spurns her immaculate menus, and salves her with a shy smile as immaculate. "Just coffee, love, be kind: it's the middle of the night for me."

He takes his seat in the very middle of the unused section, at least one row of empty tables between us and the world on every side. The "lads" have vanished, if anything that large aspires to vanishing, to a table on the full side.

All food-and-conversation noise in the place was squelched by our arrival. You can honestly identify the Mood Muzac, an early Belshangles tune blandly rearranged, disarmed.

Tom looked up at me. Dark red forelock, dark red lashes, pale, pale eyes. "I didn't ask if y'wanted more than coffee."

"No problem. Coffee's wonderful."

He waited for the noise level to rebuild, for Muzac to spin its next, with only the bass line audible.

"And are y'still virgin?"

"Uh-huh."

"All right. So what do you want from me?"

I opened my mouth; I thought about men like trees walking, and almost said "*Ut videam.*"

He laughed, and shut his eyes, put the tips of his long fingers together. "Let's start by saying, I owe you. Look at me: can you imagine? I've fans who write to say I look too healthy? I find that a bitter kind of love.

"—I've even come through without a bottle of Jack Daniel's growing to one hand, unlike some people I could mention. I don't drink at all. I'm wealthy, and perhaps a bit wiser than you saw me last. Lot of things to be said, maybe, for going through life radically anesthetized; but holding on to your money is not one of 'em. And if it wasn't for that little stunt you pulled on me, I'd be—well, I wouldn't be any of those things."

I guess I laughed.

"What?"

"Radically anesthetized. Only other place I've heard that was Greenpeace. The guys who skin seals admitted clubbing 'em first might not exactly kill, but left 'em—well, what you said."

"Listen, the way I was when we first met, y'could've had my skin off, and I might not've noticed for an hour or two—"

A man loomed over him, dressed in black so grand he had to be the *maître d'* from the nouvelle cuisine enclave across the lobby. The little hostess's immaculate stack reposed now on his arm. "Good morning, Mr. Rhymer, it's shortly before noon; would you prefer the luncheon or the breakfast menu?"

"I'd prefer my coffee, if y'don't mind; I never take food at this time of night."

"Very well, sir, as you wish." He bowed.

Tom gave him a little rock-royal wave of dismissal. He bowed again. Tom waved. He bowed. Tom waved. And when he was gone:

"—Say it was accident I finally crashed while you were watching: not somebody else. Say it was coincidence y'had your place to take me, and the means and the guts to take me there. Say it was pure beginner's luck I didn't die in your friend's car, and fool's luck of some kind I didn't kill myself, or you, or somebody, before I cleaned up.

"'Cause I've tried saying all that to myself, and more. Just too many fucking coincidences in one place, girl, if you ask me. There's got to be a purpose in it somewhere."

I remember every moment of it.

A very strange two weeks spent in his company, him getting cold-turkey detoxified, me staying cold-feet virgin. It was how I lost an Icon of Desire and gained a pen pal. Say rather, traded a false idol for the real old thing.

"—So, you have your free week that I promised you, three years back. Thomas Peter Rhymer, at your service. What do y'want me for?"

A really vast percentage of young girls survive their early years in love with horses. Then they discover boys, and the horses languish. Boys of a similar stripe pack their juvenile libidos into cars and motorcycles. Most withdraw enough in time to marry the erstwhile horsey girls. But some stick with the cars.

Boys of a certain other kind love heavy metal rock stars and read *Soldier of Fortune*. Most grow up, but a few go off to die in Africa. And girls of certain kinds love rock stars too. (Usually different rock stars.) When they get out of school they marry someone else.

Then one or two—much like their counterparts who really do make mercenary soldiers—one or two marry rock stars. A statistical necessity after all, since rock stars marry.

He snickered. "Bet that's y'mother's wool suit, too."

"Right. Let's drive up to Reno and get married." He was my enchanted prince, after all. If you rescue the prince, I've never read of more than one traditional reward.

The red brows arched. I'd agonized for three whole years, thought of every last contingency, and a telling comeback to each last thing he might say: each thing in fact but what he *did* say: "Y'asked me that three years ago."

"I did not! Well, not in those words!"

"I got it."

"I noticed you didn't say yes."

"Something else y'might have noticed."

"What?"

"Didn't say no."

"I noticed."

"Hey! I don't get serious proposals often as y'might think! Well, proposals, sure—but I mean, the kind that I might—well, y'know."

The coffee came. It was a guy who brought it, that was all I noticed, a white starched sleeve and male hand moving past my ear. But when the hand and cup came past Tom's ear I saw his pale eyes track it; once the cup was safely on the tablecloth Tom caught the hand before it got away. It belonged to a thin young guy, black hair, black eyes. Tom leaned back against his front, and smiled up at him.

"Lead or rhythm?"

The kid was practically gagging on his load of terror and shy desire. He managed to whisper, "Lead."

"Are y'any *good?*" A painful shrug. Tom still kept his hand, fingering it appreciatively. "Won't do, love, you mustn't give that answer. Are you any *good?*"

"Sure I'm good."

"Better. Bet that hard spot in your pocket is a tape, huh? Say 'Hendrix was a spastic' and we'll have a listen." He'd made him laugh, but given him the hiccups.

"Hendrix was a (hic) spas(hic)."

"Send it to the room."

He let him get away, turning back to his coffee, and me. "Fingers hard as a bone pick, and the tendons bowed right out across the knuckles. Only way you get hands like that's playing guitar ten hours a day. Y'look at Harlan's sometime."

I didn't want to look at Harlan's hands, or any other part of him. I didn't want to think about Harlan. His name vanished into my thoughts like a stone in deep water.

"Sure y'know what you're saying?"

"Uh-huh."

"A hot week at your cabin wouldn't do?"

"A hot month makes the barest start on what I want."

Tom inspected the bowl of packaged sugars and creamers

with great care. He looked up. Think about the white tiger at the S.F. Zoo: young male, one of only fifty-two on earth. He looks up from his meat with the same sterling silver eyes, and gravely lethal innocence.

"Is there nothing else y'want to ask me?"

"Unh-unh."

"Such as, did I go to the doctor and have my balls reconnected? That seemed of some importance to you at one time." He waved a long finger at me. "What would y'say, if I told you I'd not gone? Would y'still be offering to marry me?"

"I wouldn't be too happy, but I'd still want you. What if I'd told you I wasn't still virgin?"

He chuckled ruefully, licked the finger, and made a score mark for me on the air.

The fact that I was virgin didn't make virginity "my trip." Nobody ever explained to my satisfaction the supernatural virtues of the state: It was just a new womb, like that other place the Gospel mentions: "A new tomb, in which no one had yet been laid." I don't see dedicating my reproductive system to God by not using it, any more than dedicating my brain to God by not using it. But I saw a lot of sense in saving it, like the new tomb, for a proper occupant.

Every functioning instinct said this one was proper, proper, proper, from his head down to his feet. Beside the rank desirability of him, any drawbacks he might have were very small stuff. Papa always said, "Don't sweat the small stuff."

Now Tom was looking across the coffee shop in a deliberate sort of way. I followed his gaze, and saw a waitress being reeled in at the end of it, like a marlin on a 100-pound line. This woman was middle-aged, stylish, and fixy, but she wore the identical sleepwalking wounded look as any kid lurking in the potted palms.

Taking her hand when it came in range, Tom leaned back into her, the same small intimacy he'd used to waste the young guitar player. "Say, could I have milk for this instead of the non-dairy slop? It doesn't sit too well with me."

"Of course, dear," whispered the waitress. "I know exactly what you mean."

He watched her go.

"What if I said, 'We tried, and it couldn't be done'?"

"Same."

Yet another waitress brought his glass of milk. With her, a young woman in expensive meet-the-public clothes (the stainless warrior maiden off the front desk, in fact) brought a full candle glass, replacement for the nearly full one burning on our table.

I began to get the picture: a shock of ripples running through the hotel staff every time Tom left his room. Quick sprints down backstairs, whisperings, in-house phone calls: "Tommi's in the coffee shop. Run run run. Quick, grab the girls, find the guys, say, "*Love walks visible among us—*"

Build me a tower, forty feet high,
So I can see you, as you ride by.
As you ride by, dear, as you ride by,
So I can see you, as you ride by—

What an awful burden for any mortal shoulders, and his not the widest. He was a naughty little kid playing fantasy hero in one of the most beguiling suits of flesh-and-blood dress-up ever issued by a witty God. He waited patiently each time until they finished ministering to him.

"Well, I did go," he said when they were out of earshot. "Swiss clinic. The whole guided trip through the marvels of modern medicine." He looked down at the table.

"They wanted a biopsy to see if I was still good, but I didn't like the thought of that. I said, 'Hook it up, and I'll pay for it, no matter.' Then they wanted to do one side and the other later, but I saw no sense in being sore twice. And I had to heal up for six weeks.

"When I came back, they went through the whole story about the only mark of success being a sperm count. Which all came down to me having to do it in my hand, so he could look under a microscope.

"He left me kicking my heels in an examination room for an inordinately fucking long time. Couldn't tell a thing from his face when he came back, either: some bedside manner that was. Then he said, *'What I have to tell you Herr Rhymer is,* not only *have* you the sperm count, it is already in the normal range—'"

"More coffee?"

A dippy little girl in a bellhop's monkey suit was bending over him. Her hair was half as red as his own.

"Thank you love, but that's all, now. My time's gone." We waited while she poured, and poured, and backed off smiling.

"So how many paternity suits have you settled so far?"

"God! What d'y'think I am? It's only been three months! If I'd gone out and banged half of Geneva the first night, it still takes nine!"

"Did you?"

He giggled. "Hardly. Old Harlan's been almost happy with me."

"Are you—still—" "Lovers" can be a hard—next to impossible—word to say.

The pastry cart, also, was hard to ignore in its approach as a siege engine trundling toward the walls. The girl behind it was so tall. Lean, athletic. Long honey hair around a gentle stately face. Her bellhop outfit said more "Queen's Own Guard" than "monkey suit."

She eyed Tom soberly. He didn't crave sweets; she knew he didn't. He looked at her and saw that she knew. Put myself in her place, that cart of sugar crud my only link to Tommi Rhymer, one he didn't want. I had to look away, down at the tall girl's shoes. I don't get fooled about a person's sex very often, but the feet are the real giveaway. Those were a guy's feet, in a guy's big generous black shoes.

"Almond tart." A young guy's soft, unassuming voice.

"You make it?" asked Tom in a voice that matched.

That put him on the spot. He thought long. Downcast eyes. "Wish I had."

"I wish you had too." The answer was yes. Yes, yes, yes, I knew it was. And not just to the almond tarts. "You recommend?"

Now the boy had to raise his eyes. Sweet blue eyes. Thick, honey lashes. "Fine stuff," he said.

"Okay."

"All right!"

Tom, pointing to me: "She wants one too."

"All right!"

Simple as that. A man wooed by forwardness, and won by innocence. Wooed and wooed and won and won. Picture this sudden vivid vista of a life spent in his orbit, beating back a non-stop stream of earnest forward innocents. With a bat.

Lord God Holy Spirit
Who teaches me to pray
Have mercy on me.

The boy with the cart had left; Tom was looking at me gravely. I couldn't remember where our own talk stopped.

He said, "Harlan."

That was it, all right.

"If I could walk away from him, I would be nothing you might want. I could walk away from you, ten times as easy. I'm not that changeable. May be good for you I'm not. Very old-fashioned, in my way. My grandparents' marriage was arranged, I'm told. It lasted fifty years, and they died within the month of one another.

"So I don't see why, if I should put my mind to it, I couldn't call you my own dear love, and not be lying. Now, y'gave me to understand that you've got some religion. I've imagined y'were Roman, but I may be just imagining."

"You're not."

He had taken a bite of almond tart. He chewed and swallowed it in slow silence. Then he said, "Fortunate."

"Like not smoking."

"Right.

"I was raised that way too. And my head is Roman in funny places, though you might not think it. Can't be too sure what they teach these days, 'specially in America. But the Church taught me; the only right reason for marrying, is what they used to call the 'procreation of children.' Now I find that very sensible."

Another pretty person brought the check, black, this one, with Michael Jackson California Curls, and almost certainly a guy; he had a little moustache.

"Wait, love." He didn't look at the check; he put two twenty-dollar bills on top of it. "Never mind the change, we haven't time.

"—My idea would be, that if I should marry you, anyone who sees us should feel satisfied that we just got it on. And I don't intend appearances to deceive. I mean to be quite shameless in my marital bliss. If, say, that embarrasses you, better back off now."

"Foot of the Nelson Monument."

"You bet. I'll do it on the BBC if they give me an hour show. I've got my public to consider, after all. Wouldn't want them to think that Rhymer's faded. Just that he's all grown up and taken out a public license. Also. I have had my lifetime's fill up to here," he gestured, "with birth control. When you said years ago that what you'd wanted out of me was a house full of redheaded kids—remember that?—you don't know what you touched."

"I sort of hoped it was your heart."

He choked on his coffee. His face went scarlet with laughter, and he hid it, though he stole a glance at me.

A water glass appeared at his hand, fast enough for a magic act. I didn't look to see what brought it: I didn't care, so long as it got away and let him finish.

"Why Reno?"

"It's in Nevada. No waiting to get married. Every place else, it takes two weeks."

"You mean, married before a judge?"

"I guess I do."

His silence lasted. Finally he said, "I suppose what I'm wondering is, if you come from religious people, why you're not after getting married in a church."

"I am very much after being married in the Church. I just want to sew you up first, so I get the chance."

He was laughing and shaking his head. "You're too damn smart."

"I hope that's why you're marrying me."

"I hope so too," he said. "What d'y'think I'll need?"

"ID. Passport, I guess. Clothes for a week. The cabin's halfway between Reno and here. We can be back there married by this evening."

"You got your own car?"

"My mother's." No use lying to him. Just brazen it out. "You know. Like the suit."

"Does your mother know you're here?"

"No way."

"Do I take it that y'don't get on?"

"I love my mother; she loves me."

He looked away. Bit his lip. Looked back. Looked away again. "—Have to think about that one." His change came anyway, on a stainless art-deco salver.

"—Hey," I said, "years ago, the last thing you asked of me, the very last, was to give you proof that I could keep your secrets. I've done it all the way."

He started to snicker. "Wouldn't be too fair, I suppose, to start wondering, if you're that close keeping secrets *for* me, just how you'd be at keeping 'em *from* me, once we were—"

"No. It wouldn't be very fair at all."

"Didn't think it would."

A wallet came out of his inside pocket, and a roll of bills came out of that. He started to peel off tens. He made a little circle of them on the table, ten in all, like the spokes of a wheel with the candleholder for a hub. "Good service," he said, "appeals to me."

Chapter 2

SO KEEP IT TO A WALK across the lobby, and a demure jog (jogging with a purse) around the block. Down the alley with its loading dock and service doors, its kitchen noises and kitchen smells, I set the land speed record.

Inside those kitchens, even now, are people giving wired, inspired accounts of what they did for Love Incarnate in the coffee shop. How they danced attendance on him.

Love Incarnate isn't waiting on the dock.

So, what'd I expect? Give him time to reach his room; give him time to get his stuff. Time to say goodbye.

I reach the car, unlock and sit in it. The dock is quite invisible from where I am. My heart rate sags toward normal.

Lemme guess, he won't be there.

He'll have gone back to his room, thought it over, talked it over, and recognized the money and the misery and the bad PR it'd cost him to get out of this. Eventually somebody (that Garfein probably) will stroll down here and offer me apologies. Thank you, but no thank you. Fun talking to you, but. Maybe it wouldn't even be that kind. I'd wait and wait, and nobody would come.

I said I was going to Mass this morning.

So I wouldn't be lying, I found a 7:30 A.M. (Our Lady of the Suburbs), and went to it. A genuine California Catholic Church, designed to be a school gym after the real church got built. Which it never did, of course.

A hospital chaplain was the celebrant. Right at the climax of the Mass, the Consecration as a cosmic cue, his pager beeped. It sounded like the end of the world. For some unknown in Stanford Hospital, it probably was.

Father Chaplain clicked the ceremony into fast forward: ten minutes saw him off to bless the dying and comfort the survivors. Everybody else went home. Except me.

8:30 A.M.

Junipero Serra: dubbed by little rustic signs "The World's Most Beautiful Freeway." Forty-five minutes to an hour north (depending on your attitude), the Serra dumps you out in San Francisco: 19th Avenue. North of Golden Gate Park, 19th crosses Geary. Now you're pointed at the beach.

Out in the avenues, old Geary's lined with Greek laundries, Russian bakeries, and Filipino movie theaters. It goes residential at the very end, and splits into a Y. One half is called Seal Rock. That's where I parked, by a dry yard filled with succulents: aloes and agaves, pink and gray and green and striped and spiky. From Seal Rock downtown, Breakers to Bay, is a measured fifteen-minute drive exactly. Punctual's fine. An hour-and-a-fucking-half too punctual's got nothing to be said for it whatever.

Behind me was the last stop on the bus line: people who get off there are at their leisure, mostly, headed out to jog the sea cliff. Couples jogging by me, never any singles. Trim young couples with kids in pack frames, trim old couples in unisex warm ups. Trim gay couples, shirtless to show off their Nautilus muscles. I watched them bounce over the curvature of the street and disappear, down to where the sea lions bark, and the bright mist rises off the breakers.

Saint Francis, when he felt in need of input, used to play this game: shut his eyes, pray, open up the scripture or some other book, plant his finger on the page. And if what he read there bore no obvious application to his problem, he'd do the whole bit over: shut his eyes, ask for a clue to the first passage, random access the book.

I'd like to go through life that way: random access and refuse to edit. (People at school used to ask what I was smoking. Answer: *nothing*. I am entertaining myself.) Pray, "Lord, that I may *see*—" Then open the eyes, *bang*. And see what comes by, the most *amazing stuff*, not the dumb theories people make and like to call the really-real.

Theories are only suitcases; you cram in all the "real" you can, and cut off what hangs out. But it's the funny incorrigible things I always loved the most, the stuff that won't *be* suitcased, the things I don't know what they *are*. Antique whatsits with rusty moving parts. Holy medals to saints I can't find in the book. Little books about strange days, in languages I don't read. Matters that take penetrating.

Take the Gospel of this Sunday's Mass:

> —*You think I have come to establish peace on earth? I assure you, the contrary is true; I have come for division. From now on, a household of five will be divided three against two and two against three; father will be split against son and son against father, mother against daughter and daughter against mother, mother-in-law against daughter-in-law and daughter-in-law against mother-in-law*—

Which wouldn't be so wild, you see, except they tell you, "God is Love." Think about the five in my house: who would side with me if I managed to come home with Tommi Rhymer? Mother, father, sister, brother? Maybe it wouldn't be three against two, but four against one.

Another bus grinds to the end of the line. More pairs of pastel couples trot past laughing, seaward, over the brow of the hill. Well, for better or for worse, here comes the Lord of Love. Groovin' up slowly.

12:15 P.M.

So I've asked the man to marry me: my fantasy since I was twelve. I'm back in the car alone (nothing changed except the scenery), down in the musty deep between two city buildings. Thinking: what about a household of four? Is it two against two? Three against one? And a household of three?

Two against one, no choice.

And a household of two?

I fired up the bus, drove around the kink in the alley, and *Oh God,* there he was already. Same clothes. He'd added a white cloth English cap and shades. His left hand held a leather carry-on; a luggage-stickered fiddle case was in his right. Just delicious, thirty-two going on seventeen, fidgeting on the dock next to the garbage Dumpster.

He saw me, too.

A little run took him off into the air, heels tucked against his rear, arms flung wide with a bag in each hand, picture perfect, circa 1940s Hollywood musical.

When he'd made it through the door I hadn't unlocked, he said, "They must have rings and such in—where we're going, won't they?"

I ground along in low to the end of the alley.

"We could take whatever comes today," he said, "and do it right next week in London—"

"Next week's stuff may be terrific, but it can't ever be the *same*—" (God, why am I so stubborn? Why say that?)

"Or, we could do it here," he said.

Side by side, we peered from the end of our alley into downtown crowds, crawling noontime traffic, jackhammers, open manholes, torn-up streets. The real world.

"So what are y'doing now?"

"Thinking."

"Tell me."

Can't. Why not? *Don't know.* I have lived a short life steeped in secrecy, so accustomed to censoring my mind for public consumption. I'm marrying my fantasy confessor, the inhabitant of my dreams who always understood. I have to get used to his reality. He is not a dream. He is not a pet. He inhabits the front seat of my mother's VW bus. If he asks what's on my mind, it better be safe to tell him. Or I better find out now. "I like old junk stores."

He said, "So do I. Wanta know a secret?"

"Yeah."

"Never bought diamonds in my life. Not even for me."

"I like to walk in some old cluttered place and close my eyes and say: My thing is in here somewhere. God put it here for me. And wave my face around like a shut-eyed dish antenna, seeing if I can home in on it. *Don't laugh!* I can, too!"

"Hey, Green Eyes," he said.

"—And my favorite thing, you know what my *favorite* is? I've got like, this whole little collection of things I don't know what they *are*—"

"Now, now," he said, "I want to see you do it: I know some chaps've got grouse dogs that work like you."

A block or two from Union Square garage is this tiny little shop that does estate jewelry. It has one glass door and one glass window, and inside is so narrow, the counter sits edge-on to the street. I'd always been enamored of the jewels in there, slightly tarnished by reality. They had their histories and mysteries; they'd all belonged to Mafia Dons, or Edwardian Divas who blazed scarlet careers across the princes of three continents and ended penitent days in a convent.

It was just ahead; I could see the small glass door. Also the CLOSED sign through the glass.

Can't imagine a more embarrassing *bleak* impacted situation: shooting off my mouth and blundering around in search of special gifts from God, with my glorious white-and-ruddy Dulcinea like a dog at heel, *watching* me not find 'em. In present light, the weird old baubles in the window looked straight off the geegaw shelf at Goodwill anyway.

"Not fine enough, is it?"

"C'mon," he said. "They got the better stuff inside."

"Closed on Sunday."

"Somebody's in there."

Two somebodies, a man and a girl, bustling between the counter and a back room with lockboxes and ledgers.

"C'mon," I said, "let's go. Please let's go."

Tom already had a hand up, tapping on the glass.

I saw the man jump (he saw us), his lips form, "Sorry, but we're closed Sundays."

Tom fished inside his pocket for the wallet, extracted a hundred-dollar bill and flattened it against the window.

Watch the guy begin to waffle. He approached the door, unlocked it. He had a gray suit, gray hair, and gray eyes, and a sleek gray-lavender tint to his skin, as if his grandmother was a Rajah's daughter out of Ranchipur.

He said, "We're closed on Sunday."

"I'm gone on Monday. Would y'take a hundred dollars just to let us look? Who'll ever know?"

So he got his laugh, and got inside.

"All right," Tom had taken off the cap, put it in his belt; taken off the shades, put them in his pocket. Now he put a good preliminary grip on me: "I'm marrying her; she needs a diamond doesn't she? I want it to be like no one else's. Let's start with the most costly ring you have."

"For a woman?"

Tom looked suddenly very shy, about the most devastating trick he has. "Don't know. Whatever she fancies."

Store Man thought. His focus shifted; more people stood outside the window, a group of girls. And they weren't ogling the goodies in his case. Tom motioned at the door: "Y'might lock that up again."

"—the finest woman's ring I have just now, is, in fact *two* rings, and can't be disposed of separately. But should they be for you, the extra might be remade as a brooch—"

Two girls scooted off along the sidewalk, and reappeared with half a dozen.

"—The Dewitt sisters: Carlotta and Constanza Dewitt. Their parents were the pinnacle of Peninsula society in the '20s, and the girls were twins, identical. They dressed alike, did *everything* together: they made their joint debut, a legendary blowout; they both chose extremely decorative and totally worthless young gentlemen (Tom laughed quietly) to marry, and were married together, double ceremony. After a few stormy years on the Grand Tour—"

"Matching divorces, right?"

"Right." He opened the fragile leather box. Two objects of pure fantasy glowed in a green velvet heaven.

Tom made a noise of appreciation, a kind of cockney fishwife squawk. "That's diamonds, is it?"

"That's diamonds."

"What color would you call that, now?"

"I believe, officially, they're canary."

They were Day-Glo orange if anything. They were little alien spacecraft with rows and rays of glowing lights, two genuine close encounters of the third kind.

"—The twins never remarried," he was saying. "They were fixtures of the San Francisco scene for, oh, years out of mind—I can remember them from the '70s, tottering out of their limousine in Union Square, still wearing the most stunning identical couturier outfits. The matching engagement rings remained in the estate. The nephew, or grand-nephew, placed them here."

I made so bold as to take one from its velvet. Antique things are dainty and tiny: I couldn't wear one away, even if Tom bought them; it'd need a piece spliced in—

"—They're an old-fashioned cut of course, what's termed 'Mine Cut': less valuable, sorry to say, than if—"

It fitted like a custom job.

"The Dewitt sisters weren't as tall as you, but certainly more—what? Zaftig."

Tom picked the extra little apricot spacecraft from the velvet tray. He slipped it on his own ring finger with a kind of shy finality.

Tom's are magic hands, immensely long and fine, like the outsize hands that bless and gesture across old mosaics. My hands are square, capable, I always thought embarrassing: hands of a twelve-year-old boy programmed to be a very big man. Who could have guessed at all? I was crying, and I hoped nobody noticed. Then Tom was poking something soft into my other hand below the counter's edge. A Kleenex.

I have been playing 21 with God. Not just asking, but begging, weeping, bullying a silent heaven to deal me *one* particular card out of the deck. And now it's dealt, it's face down on the table, I'm easing up one corner just to look—Jack of Hearts! All at once, a second card, uncalled for—not by me, at least. Ace of Diamonds.

"How much?"

Swift figures written on a pad, and held up where I couldn't see. Store Man seemed almost apologetic.

"Right," said Tom.

"Well, they're *not* the most expensive item in the safe by any means."

"What is?" said Tom.

"You mean, in the way of rings?"

"In the way of anything."

"Ah." Store Man cogitated; tapped the counter glass. "Oh! Of course. Marilee? Madame Hoang's bracelet, please. Marilee's head hung through the curtain from the back room: a piece of taxidermy, glass eyes fixed on Tom. "Yes, just get it out. As you'll see, much more than starving fishermen came out of Vietnam. Ah—I think I'll do as you suggested—" He locked the door. Kids scattered back, closed in again. Bolder ones began to tap the glass.

Marilee's head disappeared from the curtain. Her father

pursued it to the back room, and, after much whispering, brought out a safety deposit box. A metal case inside that opened with a combination. A leather one inside that took a key. A shower of white spangles made good its escape, and rioted across the walls and ceiling.

"About to ask a dumb question: that's not diamant?"

"Oh no! Oh no no no, God no. They're perfectly matched blue-white diamonds, modern cut, over two hundred of them."

"Sorry, but I've been used to wearing things like this on stage, and they *were* diamant, and some of those could cost three hundred pounds—"

"Oh doubtless."

"May I?"

"My daughter, who is better acquainted with such matters, tells me you're an entertainer."

Tom grinned, and the white fire in his hand cast fairy lights across his face. "I do get paid for it."

"By 'Bill Graham Presents'?"

"For one. But *this* came out of *Vietnam*?"

"Madame Hoang spray-painted it flat white, and wore it out on her own arm. A real estate consortium has it from Madame and the General now, down payment on acreage, roughly the size of San Francisco, near the Mendocino coast."

Tom, bemused, amused, and thoughtful, was turning it in the air. He draped its flaming length across his wrist.

I tried to image Madame Hoang. The original Dragon Lady? Or an antique fragile matriarch, and the General was her son. Or she could be a leggy Swede with platinum hair, kept by her oriental warlord in secluded kinkiness.

"—It would make a proper piece for the stage," Store Man was saying, "if expense meant nothing, and you didn't mind the risk. Most women are intimidated. This is what you call a serious piece—No one would ever expect to find this here—I don't have an international clientele—"

"She'd expect it." Tom gathered me in tightly, "She's got a gift."

Wait a minute! I didn't pray this out of thin air—I *didn't* know it was here, I knew the store was here, I like to window shop—I'm accepting a hero's medal for a rescue I never pulled, for great deeds only contemplated—

"—if I hadn't gone to Stanford with their mother," the man is saying, "provincial loyalty, or what have you. Sotheby's appraiser's coming, possibly tomorrow. It's my hunch this will end up broken and reset—"

Tom dropped back to the real world. "No it shan't, I want it whole. I believe I have the perfect use. How much for the three? The two rings and the bracelet?"

Hardly the time to tell him I'm not a holy hero. Store Man wrote again. All delicacy aside, I *craned.* A definite six figures; was it seven? They were too fast for me.

"Right," said Tom. "Believe I can still manage. I'll need to call my road manager, get him down here. We're on our way to—where is it now?"

I said, "Reno."

"Right. Reno, and—"

Beaming, Store Man pumped my hand. "Congratulations!" He did the same to Tom, adding, "God loves a cheerful giver."

A telephone was served up on the counter's warm glass top. Tom fought his patient way past information, the hotel desk, and a clutch of unwanted Belshangles personnel.

"No, you won't do. I need Garfein. I love you, but y'won't do." Listen. "God, Margot, I don't care where he is, have him open a crack, and pop the fucking phone in with him. He can manage the two at once." Pause. "Sim. Bless you."

Longer pause. "I've just spent a lot of money. Yeah. Right, love. Like *a lot* of money. Right. Like London, Switzerland. So get off it, and get down here."

He turned back to us helplessly. "Where am I?"

· — ·

FINALLY Sim arrived.

"My road manager."

"Beautiful."

"Sim. We're taking the rings; the bracelet I'm leaving with you. He'll explain. One thing, you're not to show that piece to Harlan. I don't want him to see that toy, or know that it exists. Okay?"

The answer to my question I supposed, a chill and sobering answer, about Love's entry to the household of two.

"Got it," said Garfein.

"Ta," said Tom.

Halfway to Union Square, he stopped, dismay all over his face. *"We still've got no wedding rings!"* Most of the store crowd had gone, but a few stayed watching. Their patience was repaid when we plowed in. *"Wedding rings!"* said Tom.

"To complement your apricot extravaganzas?" Store Man didn't look surprised. Sim looked frazzled: if he'd had more hair, he might be tearing it.

"A plain gold band like old country people wear: that's what I want. And I mean to leave it on, until at last it won't come off at all."

So I said "Same for me."

Tom put his arm around my hip, not the waist, the hip, as I'd seen guys do in the Castro (each with a hand down the friend's back pocket), and yanked me hard against him. I nearly fell over. I didn't have any back pockets, but he did. My hand went in as far as the ring.

· — ·

TOM slid down, till the back of his head engaged the car seat and his knees were wedged against the dash. His white cap met the top of his dark glasses; not much of him was visible. His sweet cream cheek. The brash little tough-kid thrust to his jaw and lower lip. He said, "I've known for two years I'd get married." Most Americans say married "marr-ied," almost "mare-id." Whether it was the Londoner in him, or just the *him* in him: he said "ma-rried," dainty and precise, a small boy making his cautious curtsy to an adult explosive word.

I didn't know what to say. So I didn't say anything.

I knew why I was marrying him: a Grand Passion, conceived

in childhood, nursed in solitude, pursued with total lack of self-preservation through adolescence.

Yesterday, this is what I did.

7:00 A.M.

I turn up in the kitchen dressed for action, and wait for Mama to say, "Where to?"

So I can answer, "Mountains."

"Alone?"

"Kaye Lyttle would like to go with me." Which is true; she's said so many times. Didn't say she *was* going with me.

"*May* I have my old key to the cabin back, please?"

"Baby, I still don't think that's safe. Besides," she adds tellingly, "I don't know where it is."

"I am eighteen, and it's in Papa's dresser drawer, like everything else he ever took away from me."

"Three years," she says. "You've known where it was—"

"Hey, I'm honest."

"Wouldn't it be better if we all went? That way you'd have people to cook and wash up for you—" Very long-suffering.

"I have my own food."

"You've only been eighteen for a week and a day."

One year's all that anybody's got to be eighteen in: not exactly a discipline you can give a lifetime's practice.

· — ·

ONE week earlier, caviar and champagne for me at Saint Ann's after Mass. I mean Beluga and the French stuff, too. My parents and their crew don't mess around. There is always a spread of food in the Newman House after Mass. For birthdays, weddings, baptisms, and major feasts there is an unconscionably ginormous spread of food. The Saint Ann's High-Mass crowd take those scriptures about the "Heavenly Banquet" and the "Supper of the Lamb" quite literally.

So I can observe from where I stand, two Benedictine monks smearing Brie on baguettes and laughing, three tenured professors, one doling out Russian caviar, sweet butter, and minced onion in minute, sacramental amounts (*mine* being the only authorized seconds: *my* birthday)—and any number of emeritus professors, visiting professors, foreign students, graduate students (not all Catholic, but getting there), parents, wives, husbands, lions and lambs together, everyone drinking wine and eating cold roast beef with horseradish sauce.

Also lots of kids. Saint Ann's High Mass must have the highest infant baptism rate of any Sunday service going.

And here I am, dandling my solitary glass of French champagne (I asked about seconds there, but none are forthcoming). "You know what I *really wanted* for my eighteenth birthday?" Great line to put the dampers on a celebration.

Papa (one of the tenured) lifts champagne bottle-mouth from glass in sparkling mid-pour.

"For you guys to truck down to the Savings and Loan and redo my bank account so I can draw money out of it."

"You need money?"

"I'd like that little passbook in my purse to say 'Miranda Dolores Falconer,' not 'R. Falconer or M.F. Falconer as custodians for M.D. Falconer.' It's the principle, that's all."

"What's it doing in your purse?"

"Getting dirty, mostly." I earned half that money myself. Minors are the world's original second-class citizens.

But my setup is complete.

All that's required now is to mouth *"Cu-s-t-o-o-d-i-ans,"* two or three more times in as loathsome a manner as possible. And pray: "Lord, 'subtle as serpents' is okay, so long as 'innocent as doves' goes with it. I've known I was devious since before I could talk. Just don't let me be dishonest."

The contents of my prayer life get a little odd. *My* contents are a little odd. I figure God knows that.

Papa waves the champagne bottle at my chest. "You realize, if you manage to blow your college money, it's *you* that's going to miss it at Berkeley in the fall?"

"Uh-huh."

Sad, because I aced the SATs with scores impressive enough

to show what a lazy clot I'd been at school. I got accepted into Berkeley, no sweat in the least, when lots of poor hardworking hot-to-study types are headed for the Junior Colleges. Sad that I'm a rank impostor. I never intend to go. And so far, nobody knows but me.

That was a week ago last Sunday; when the punch line of the morning's Gospel was "Wherever your treasure lies, there your heart will be."

· — ·

FRIDAY afternoon, here I go, off to the Savings and Loan. All by myself. A first. Food for a week for two is what I need, opulent (this time) but non-labor-intensive food for a week. I think about a hundred dollars. Gas money also, cash to reach the mountains maybe four times, up and back and up and back, untraceable. Thirty dollars a crack. To be safe, I took three hundred dollars. Put it in my little white purse, right in the envelope with the tickets and the invitation.

Saturday morning. I got in the old VW bus, and before Papa could stroll down the drive and request my flight plan, I roared away.

· — ·

OREGON expressway to 101; 101 south to 237. Crossing below the marshy lower end of San Francisco Bay, I pick up northbound 680 on the other side, through the first range of summer-yellow hills. High above the freeway canyon a red tailed hawk wheels toward her nest, bearing a very long, very limp snake in her claws. I take it for some kind of omen.

Livermore valley. It was eighty-five degrees on our front porch in Stanford. Hot. Here a roadside time-and-temperature display stands proudly at 102.

The second range of hills.

The San Joaquin. Wide hazy valley, fertile and sweltering: orchards, alfalfa, corn. The food of a nation wells from here, as far as the eye can see. Dim black pillars around the rim of the world, the occasional inevitable grass fires, pour their summer donation of smog into the sky.

A place named for Joachim, husband of Saint Ann, father of Mary. The barren man who prayed so hard, and so hard and *so hard*—he got more than he asked for. San Joaquin, Grandfather of God.

Off the last freeway now, onto Highway 88 east of Stockton. Here begins my provisioning (farmers are opening their road stands for the day) with melons so fragrant they perfume the car, fresh sweet corn, some white, some yellow—and better yet—some bicolored. Viny tomatoes, still hot from the sun.

Into Jackson on the far side of the valley: time for a lightning pass through the local Safeway: bacon, eggs, bagels, cream cheese. Salad stuff. A twelve-pound slab of New York steak, still in one piece.

One more stop in Jackson. Main Street: where the curbs are two feet tall, and a sidewalk plaque commemorates the last public hanging. The last whorehouse got shut down in the '50s, Papa says.

Old saloons have metamorphosed into slick boutiques, but in among the ticky-tacky is a cavernous dry goods store that still sells gold pans. Also the Jackson Bakery, home to glorious fat flaky turnovers. I buy all the blueberries they have plus raspberries to make a baker's dozen, just as my mother and grandfather always did before me.

Still on the early side of noon, I begin my leadfoot run up the mountain. Five thousand feet. Six thousand feet. Where the granite bones of the world begin to show, and the sky gets darker blue, and the trees all smell like bitter incense. Meditating, as I go, about the food I've bought. All very homely and American. But so am I. The food is like me.

What if he doesn't like it?

God, what if he doesn't like *me?*

Why would he have sent me mail for three whole years now, if he didn't like me?

· — ·

MY sister and I ran age group track for years: national level competition. Papa maintained a certain distance from the whole affair; it was Mama who drove us to practice and drove us to meets, and drove us up the wall. And as long as she kept after me, I excelled. The 1984 Olympics didn't seem so far away. When I got too big to intimidate, I went down like a rock.

Hormones. I quit; fell in love with a Rock and Roll Star. Not supposed to work out that way, is it? Growing up means getting serious, *taking charge of your life*. The 1984 Olympics came and went. I never turned the TV on.

But Mama had a sort of system, a ladder of degrees to rate performance, from lousy to sensational. The bottom rung was "Don't run last."

And man, was I happy to be through with that forever.

Now here I go, rating my own chances from the bottom up: if Belshangles had played Oakland and Tommi didn't contact me at all, that would be running *dead last*. Doing better than that already. I got tickets and an engraved invitation.

But to what event? Though Mama might not equate my bedding Tommi Rhymer with "Finishing in the Medals," I had been prepared to grab for any level of intimacy I could get, depending on a whole galaxy of unknowns. That was yesterday.

And now, twenty-four hours later, I teetered on the last, the ultimate plateau, corresponding to Mama's "Win." I had my fantasy lover headed for Nevada; I was wearing his Day-Glo diamond ring, and he had on the matching one. So far it was working like a charm. The real question: why? What made him so unrealistically tractable—a matching Grand Passion?

He knew what the Grand Passion trip was about okay, and had embarked, I guessed, on one such journey in his life, but certainly not for me. More poetry surfaced (learned at school, would you believe—)

He hangs in shades the oranges bright,
Like golden lamps in a green night—

Andrew Marvell's *Bermudas* is what it was:

—He makes the figs our mouths to meet,
And scatters melons at our feet,
But apples plants, of such a price,
No tree could ever bear them twice.

Passion fruit. Somehow, I wouldn't even want to make Tom bear those apples twice.

But he was talking again. "Up till now," he said, "well, up till now I've not been old enough. Few years from now I'd be too old, and it wouldn't be seemly."

I couldn't think of any answer, plain, ordinary, conversational. I ached to stop the car, rush around to his side and crush him to me. Cover him, hide him, so he couldn't ever be too old. I found the mental address where I'd left *Bermudas*, and vanished into it. Excellent way of keeping sane. See how much I can remember.

Where the remote Bermudas ride
In the ocean's bosom, unespied,
From a small boat that rowed along
The listening waves received this song—

What should we do but sing His praise,
Who brought us through the watery maze
Unto a land so far from home,
And yet far gentler than our own?

Where He the great sea monsters racks
That lift the deep upon their backs,
He lands us on this grassy stage
Far from priests' and prelates' rage—

I'd made it past the fruit, right down to the end in fact—

—Thus sang they in the English boat,
An holy and a cheerful note,
And all the while, to aid their chime,
With falling oars they kept the time.

—before he spoke again. "I don't have AIDS."

The car hummed along.

"Well I *could* have, you know that."

We'd been on the road exactly one hour, tooling along through Vacaville now: dry gold hills and dusty oak trees all around, the little airstrip on our right humming with tow-planes as they lofted one sport glider after another. An affluent swarm of multicolored dragonflies circled on the thermals overhead.

Lines of an old T. Rex song ousted *Bermudas* from my mind, something definitely *not* learned for school: Marc Bolan calling himself a sexual glider, imploring a current lover to be his plane in the rain.

Except there wasn't any rain. Smoggy, brassy-hot California valley August. We drove along.

"I went and had that blood test done. They say I haven't even seen the bug."

"I'm not questioning you."

He swung around on me with a shrug that almost looked like desperation. "Shouldn't you? *Shouldn't you be?*"

"No."

"Why not?"

"Because you told me you were well."

Silence closed in again. The last of the coast hills dropped behind. I started the long straight run across the San Joaquin. This far north it's properly the Sacramento Valley, but I still think about it as the San Joaquin, Spanish for Saint Joachim. Hazy fertile summer place.

"Maybe I was lying."

I didn't take him up on it.

· — ·

ISRAEL waited for a Messiah in Saint Joachim's day, with the pious all set to go in their assemblies of tens, hundreds, thousands, and ten thousands, all shined up and ready for the great Assembly of Heaven, the coming of the Kingdom of God.

The Dead Sea Scrolls tell all about it.

Women weren't allowed in that assembly. Neither were men with problems. Not just the reprobates, but the deaf, the blind, the retarded, the sterile, men who stooped from age, men missing a limb or lame in one—even men who were scarred in their hands or feet. "Because," they said, "the Angels of God will be there, and it wouldn't be *seemly*."

So the irony was, when the Messiah came, they nailed Him through the hands and feet, and banned Him with the other undesirables. And kept on waiting, waiting—

I see Him like the kid in *Alice's Restaurant*: sittin' there with the mother stabbers and the father rapers, laughin' and havin' a wonderful time and playin' with the pencils on the GROUP W bench. Joachim was His grandfather.

Joachim and Ann had no children, and the dumb priests wouldn't let him worship. A man was bound under the Law to worship God and get children; if he couldn't do one, he wasn't counted fit to do the other. So Joachim ran away. He sat out in the hills and prayed. I guess he must have known the moment his grief was lifted; he went off leaping, back down the mountainside to town. Ann must have too; she left home and headed for the gate.

It's just a legend, an old story. I never met anyone who believed such stuff but me. Most of the things I love are apocryphal. So they met and kissed in the public road under the city gate, kissed in front of everybody. Mary was conceived from that kiss.

What a kiss that must have been.

Thinking about that and driving along across the summer valley, it all drifted with the heat into the end of *Alice's Restaurant*, where the crazy Sergeant reads off his paper to the litterbugs, mother stabbers, father rapers, etc., on the GROUP

W bench, declaring them unfit for the draft: Then, on the other side—right in the middle of the other side—away from everything else on the other side, it said:

"Kid: have you rehabilitated yourself?"

· — ·

THE old VW hummed along. We passed the flood plain west of Sacramento, arched above the slow brown river. Capitol and State buildings paraded by at a leafy distance.

Unruly suburb infiltrates the miles of gold-dredge tailings north of Sacramento, baking scrubland stripped and jumbled in the last century, disguised with tract houses in this. But at Auburn, oh, at Auburn the road swings east again. Triumphant mountains which you never saw approaching are suddenly under your wheels.

We had been two hours on the road.

· — ·

"WELL what if I *did?*" He burst out finally, "What would you *do?*" Remembering the question wasn't my problem. Knowing my answer wasn't; I just couldn't say it. Silence didn't stop him this time. *"Get the hell away from me, that's what you'd do?"*

I said, "No, I wouldn't."

Silence. Up and up.

Oaks give way to fir trees. Grass gives way to rock. Valley smog becomes Sierra blue sky. And the blue gets darker, and darker—

"So what would y'do? Hold my hand with rubber gloves and watch me die?"

"If that was my only option left, I guess I would."

"Well, I'll just say in advance, I want no part of it. Besides, I already *got* somebody with a pretty firm commitment to that job."

"If you went first."

"What?"

"I said, if you went first. What if it was him? Hey, what are we talking about this for? Is he sick? Is he exposed to AIDS?"

The white cap shook emphatically. "He's got no chance

of not having what I've got. Or of getting what I haven't, for that matter. Which, right now, thanks to no virtues of mine, is nothing."

"So?"

There's a fine, fine art to getting up a long grade in an old VW bus. You have to stay above sixty-two miles per hour. So plan ahead, stand on it well before the grade, get the old momentum up.

Then hope like *crazy* nothing makes you brake, for if you do, and backslide off that cusp of speed, then it's slower, slower, helplessly slower—gear down, move right, until you're laying down a trail of oil, sweat, and tears: twenty miles an hour in the far right lane all the way to the top.

"—So it seems I've gone looking, and put myself in the goddamn middle of every 'high-risk identity group' I can think of, 'cept for being Haitian. Little late for that."

"You're no hemophiliac either."

"No, thank God I'm English!"

"You could buy property in Port au Prince."

"I'm not laughing! Couldn't you just imagine me as AIDS Poster Boy of the Year?"

"Don't do that to me!"

"Say, don't do it to *you? I don't wanta do it to me!* I don't want to die of that stupid, goddamn ignominious disease! *I don't want to die at all!"*

He was going to freak. I didn't know what to do.

"If I lived in L.A., I'd be dead now!"

Headed up the grade to Donner summit at sixty-two miles an hour in the next-to-the-fastest of four lanes of traffic. I didn't know what to do. Think about Saint Francis and his random-input enlightenment method. I bet old Francis never did it on a freeway. I shut my eyes anyhow, and prayed to *see.*

Instantaneous response: a screech of alarm from my passenger, *"God! Look out! Bloody fucking car!"*

I have entered the Realm of Seeing. Some big American tank with lots of chrome, stuck behind a yet slower vehicle in the right-hand lane, pulls ponderously in front of me at thirty miles per hour. Prominent on the born-again rear end I'm about to impact is a bumper sticker: "JESUS GAVE ME THIS CAR."

Input, if I ever saw it!

So Jesus Gave Me This Man!

(Breaking as hard as I can: sixty miles an hour!)

He can't go bad on me: I prayed for him!

(Fifty-five mph!) He's *mine!*

(Forty-five!) *No backsies!*

(Thirty-five!) Gear down, oh help, *oh God*, I'm so close on the guy, even his bumper sticker disappears from view!

Like it says: You love your kids; would you give 'em scorpions if they ask for fish, or stones instead of bread?

(Thirty.) The bumper sticker reappears, and placidly, unmindfully, begins to pull away.

You gave him to me; God doesn't give no trash!

He looks as good and edible to me as loaves and fishes!

Be *damned* if I'll believe he's scorpions and stones!

No scorpions! No stones!

Good San Francisco French bread, a nice long baguette, fresh and warm, sweet as anything. And rich mahogany smoked salmon, straight off the North Coast!

No switches and ashes in my Christmas stocking!

Etc., etc.

· — ·

"I'VE been thinking and thinking now, all the way here, how it was I ever planned to cut the coat I covet out of the cloth I've been given. You know—" he said, beginning to sound horribly tearful, "—in San Francisco, when Sim came down to fetch you from the lobby there? He got me out of Harlan's bed before he went. Anybody looking for me who knew me at all'd try there second, and if he *really* knew me, might just look there first. I've almost no conscious cruelty in my nature, and I would call it more than cruel, not to make positive you understood that."

"I think—" I said, "I think I understand that."

"Well I don't think you do!"

"What I'm *trying* to say: sooner or later I'm afraid you'll end up by despising me, and maybe sooner is better than later. You think I'm joking, but I'm not. You'll get inside, and see it's all for real. You'll say 'Why didn't you tell me?' and I won't have any answer. Then you'll want to get the hell out, and you will."

He made it all sound so final.

Competition left me a very dull kid in some ways. Isolated, too. Capable of being single-minded. I have the personality of a snapping turtle: grab on, and not let go till it thunders. The only coat I'd ever coveted, I was wearing. I had no apprehensions about getting it out of the cloth I was given. God wouldn't *almost* give him to me, would he? An earthly treasure too far gone to wear? Just to prove I'd got my values on all backwards, a prize past mending?

Prayer fails; it fibrillates: then it tumbles in upon itself, a black hole of the spirit contracting so fast under its own gravity, no sensible word escapes.

My sister raised rabbits for a while, and my brother, age four, was forever grabbing and messing with the baby bunnies, in spite of threats and paddlings, until he managed to pull the tail off one.

Here he came, holding the tiny lifeless tag of fur and bone in one hand and the ruined baby in the other, his face a mask of dirt and tears, crying, "Glue! Glue!" That was going to be me in a moment, weeping like a child at the insupportable ruin of things: broken things I didn't know how to reassemble.

Glue, glue. Cosmic glue.

I had crawled—like the sinners up Dante's mount of Purgatory, each heaving along a heavy boulder on his back—to the very summit ridge of the Sierras to the place John Muir called the Range of Light. Shows all *he* knew.

I saw a sign for the old scenic route down to Donner Lake and Truckee, and took it. He really was beginning to sob. And so was I. Then it was "VISTA TURN OFF—¼ MILE."

"You can keep the rings—" he said, "—something decent to remember me by."

I slammed the van into the turnoff, into a parking slot against the vista rail, yanked his faery-canary diamond *thing* off my hand, and shoved it at him. It came off easy.

"Don't *want* your silly rings."

"Ah *please*, don't make it worse and worse—"

"Not without you, I don't!"

"I bought them for you—" He snuffled stubbornly.

"You'll find somebody else to give 'em to."

"No I won't—" He started to work the gaudy cluster off his own ring finger. It stuck fast at the knuckle. His hands were bigger after all. "—I shan't try this again—"

"You must know hundreds who'd be likelier than I was."

"I wouldn't say that: ones I do, I can think at least a hundred reasons each for my not marrying. Don't know hundreds, anyway."

"You mean the magazines are wrong."

"What?"

"Talking about your AIDS-risk people."

"What?"

"Twelve hundred lifetime partners."

He looked absolutely aghast. He even stopped tugging at the ring. "What d'y'think? I haven't spent my *entire life on tour*, y'know! See? You've begun on me already! I—I just don't think this is going to work, that's all. I'm afraid, *plain terrified it isn't going to work!"*

"I don't give a shit if it works or not!"

"I wouldn't say *that*, either!"

There was the view, rocky heights horizon to horizon, and Donner Lake dimpling and flashing in the trees below. Stout people in bright cotton clothes were using it for backdrop, taking snapshots of each other.

A small breeze wandered whistling past the windows.

"C'mon girl, what I'm trying to tell you: you can still get out. You don't want to live with my problems?"

I felt ready to explode.

"What kind of shitty question you call that? *Of course* I don't want to live with your *problems!*" He looked tearful and taken aback. "Do *you?*" I went on talking much too fast. "Listen, you know what all this reminds me of? A dumb story in a book back home, made a real dent in me when I was about fourteen: there's a little coastal steamship going up the Irish Sea or someplace, and it's coming a god-awful storm.

"Well, this young sailor starts to freak, screaming, 'Captain, Captain! We are going *down!*'

"And the captain—you know what he says? He says, 'Didn't ye *know* that ships go down when ye first hired on?'

"'Yessir!'

"'Didn't ye *know* some go down every year?'

"'*Yessir!*'

"'*Weren't ye hired to go down?*'

"'*Yessir*!'

"'So *go down* like a man, *and to hell wi'ye!*'

"That's much the way I've felt about a lot of things. I always figured I was hired to go down."

Silence.

We sat in the car and looked out over the windy sliver of Donner Lake a mile below—the meadow at the far end, where the Donner Party sat, and starved, and cannibalized each other one whole winter long, because they hadn't had the smarts to mark the snow drifts where their oxen froze. All around the lake are summer homes and boat docks now. A miniature ski boat with a pair of tiny skiers sliced its silver surface, soundless, effortless. On the far side, a train was hauling up the sheer eastern face of the Sierra, four big diesel engines pushing and four pulling, through the endless snow sheds. Chinese coolies died to build those sheds a hundred years ago.

Tom got out his shades and put them on. "So who did y'say composed that little moral tale?"

"I didn't. It was Yeats, I think."

"William Butler Yeats?"

"That's the one."

"Goddamn Irishman. You know, I don't *like* that. In fact, I don't like it at *all*. I never hired you on to go down. I hired you to float high. And if you don't, what use are you to me? What the fuck: I never hired you anyway!

"Turn the car back on. C'mon."

I drove the long, slow way round the vista parking lot, avoiding children and the overflow from litter cans, arriving at last, unavoidably, back at the highway entrance.

"Which way?" I said, "San Francisco?"

"Hell with that. I said you're going to float. How far is ah—"

"Reno?"

"Right."

"'Bout half an hour that way. Are you floating too?"

He shook his head. "I suppose I must, if I'm to keep an eye on you."

· — ·

I SCRIBBLED a phone book list of wedding chapels at the gas station in Truckee. Really freaky for a California kid: the whole of Nevada fits inside one phone book.

After Truckee, California goes away. Nevada comes on hot and heavy, fast enough to give your eyes rope burns.

97.4% GUARANTEED PAYBACK!
NOBODY TURNS IT ON LIKE ONSLOW!
98.5% PAYBACK!
WINNERS PLAY HARRAH'S!
RENO'S BEST ODDS! 99% VIDEO POKER!
NEXT EXIT FOR FUN!
2000 CAR GARAGE!
HAM 'N' EGGS 99¢ !
HOSPITALITY AND ALL THE REST!

The roadside hype goes up ten decibels with every elevation line you drop. Then California is a mile-high wall of shadow, gray stone, green forest, little fastnesses of August snow, all behind you. Simmering ahead, a tacky mirage in a shallow desert bowl, is Reno.

The Reno chapels cluster on Virginia Street, from

SWEETHEART CHAPEL OF LOVE
CORNER OF N. VIRGINIA ST. AND I-80 EXIT 13!
OPEN! COME IN!
COMPLETE WEDDINGS, CERTIFIED LEGAL!
FLOWERS, RINGS, GARTERS, GOWNS!
VISA AND MASTERCARD!
SE HABLA ESPAÑOL

to

GOLD RUSH WEDDING CHAPEL
IN OUR HOTEL-CASINO
CONVENIENT LOCATION—UNIQUELY ROMANTIC
2 BLOCKS FROM THE COURTHOUSE
RELIGIOUS OR CIVIL CEREMONIES
INDOOR OR OUTDOOR
FREE VIDEO AND VIEWING
FREE CHAMPAGNE! FREE TRANSPORTATION

Tom was riding with his eyes shut. He opened them at the corner of Virginia Street and I-80 exit 13. On the right side stand a motel, a wedding chapel, an RV storage lot, and another wedding chapel. On the left, a hair salon, a wedding chapel and a fast food joint.

The two on the right are former storefronts painted sugar-frosting colors, strawberry, grape, vanilla, lemon-lime. In California they'd be card parlors, and the signs would say PAN-POKER-LO BALL. The windows of the first are masked in pointy plywood arches, cupcake pink: pure ghetto-fantasy Arabian Nights. The second's windowless but wears the same kitsch arches all around: shadow boxes framing red plush hearts. The left-hand chapel's in a bungalow. Between its windows and their lacy tiebacks interpose the arches, screaming yellow.

It took a minute, but I figured it. They weren't *supposed* to look Moslem: Moslem reads heavy sex in the harem. *Gothic* reads church. Church reads *wedding*. Ghetto gothic. Drive by slowly, people already honking at my rear. Quick, glance at Tom's face and wish I hadn't: it wore a *look*. Really betrayed disbelief.

Drive on. Next block began the high-rises. Casinos. Lighted signs. Flashing lights. Harrah's. Circus Circus. Signs hyping casino entertainment: that elephant graveyard where old '50s TV luminaries in sequined caftans go to die.

DISCOUNT SOUVENIRS, WORLD'S LARGEST
SLOTS AND SODA WORKS!
99¢ T-SHIRTS!
NOVELTY SLOT MACHINES!
LEATHER AND LACE!
CASH FOR DIAMONDS AND GUNS!
BUY —SELL—TRADE

Beyond the crush of cars was a steady two-way flow along the sidewalk. Obese, permed women jostling by, and raddled, faded men, so many purposeful ants on their way to the garbage. Onto this swarming walk the casinos spilled directly, no formality of doors or walls, huge many-layered galleries a-whir with coins in machines, *chicka chicka chicka chicka chicka.* The buzz inside the hive.

Ahead, a steel and neon message spanned the street with flashing stars: Dante's inscription over Hell Gate wouldn't have surprised me, the one that ends, *"Abandon hope, all ye that enter here."* Just about everybody's heard that end; but you know how it begins? It starts *"Love made me—"*

All that this one really said was

RENO! THE BIGGEST LITTLE CITY
IN THE WORLD!

Casino Canyon isn't long; it empties into hot sun, open space, wide stone walks, stone parapets. The Truckee River hustles through the middle of town, still singing to its stones about the California peaks they washed from.

Here squats a big stone building, abashed and patient, very closed on Sunday. The Courthouse. Must be: the next alley is Court Street. I took a right into its dark mouth. The Courthouse bulk made up one side of it, the other was like big motels, lobbies on the street level, rooms on the next level, parking on top, and signs that said

QUEEN BEDS
U SET TEMP
DIRECT DIAL PHONE
COLOR TV
MARRIAGE SERVICE
LICENSES AVAILABLE 7 DAYS A WEEK/ 8AM TILL MIDNIGHT
SMALL FEE—VERY PERSONAL—SIMPLE FAST SERVICE
CIVIL MARRIAGE COMMITMENT
NO WAITING.

They didn't actually advertise "Best odds in town" and 99-cent ham 'n' eggs available with each and every wedding, but I bet you anything they had slot machines.

Into the sun again, no waiting, and there, a block behind the Courthouse, sat a brick colonial building; in California it would have been a funeral home.

Here it was a duplex; one half said MORTGAGE INSURANCE, the other MARRIAGE CHAPEL. Parking lots at either side said MORTGAGE PARKING / MARRIAGE PARKING. There was a wet green lawn out front, a sidewalk, and, gracing the curb, a ten-wheeled limousine forty feet long.

"Wait!" said Tom.

I put us on the Marriage Parking side.

The back of the limo had a removable roof. Removed. And obvious why: closed up, it would have rained in there. The whole rear end was an eight-foot hot tub, bubbling away in gold-flecked fiberglass. Then came a pulpit (complete with reading light and fringy frontal), plush pews, a bar, refrigerators, and finally, a place for the band.

Music stood open on the stands: if I went around the street side and shaded my eyes, I could just make out:

"One Hand, One Heart"

Tom had loped on down the sidewalk. Now he circled back along the gutter and met me next to the music.

"What's it for?"

"I believe people get married in it."

"Drivin' *around?*"

Somebody guffawed.

Chattering, *Español habla*-ing people cascaded from the marriage side of the building, down the steps, and onto the lawn. Big plushy people, two big families, lots of brown friends, and brothers in rented tuxedos, sisters in pink satin, an abundant fluffy bride in a veil.

Tom hit the asphalt with the professional aplomb of a commando under fire. He let his back slide down the limo; I descended in his lap. He laughed until he cried.

Thomas Peter Rhymer in the desolate Nevada street where I'd transported him: thin, frightened, desperately fragile. Working-class English. Thirty-two and aging. Wearing the plain scars of every kind of hard knock and tough scrape I could imagine. I wanted to put my arms around it all, bury my face in him until I couldn't see anything else. So I did, down behind the limo. The side of his collar smelled like fresh bread.

Very hot and private on the concrete. The people on the lawn couldn't see us, and there weren't too many driving by. Who cares what they thought anyway? Just one more weirded out couple embracing in the gutter. The limo's shiny oyster flank collects the sun, flat black tire rubber gives off heat. I peep at grit and glitter, pebbles and glass bits on the pavement. Somebody's marked-up Keno card.

"So, girl," he whispered, "I didn't come up here to be

your ninety-nine-cent souvenir. I know too much about that trade."

"How about my ninety-nine-cent ham'n'eggs?" I asked his collar.

"Now, I might just go for that. But isn't there some other kind of place here, a town hall or the like, where men and women marry in a bit of dignity?"

Every last desire, fantasy, hormone that I owned nuzzled up close to him and lay content. T.P. Rhymer, clinging smartly to the tag end of his dignity.

I liked him, too.

Well, I did know where there was a town hall, but it wasn't Reno. Forty clean miles of desert south. And we'd have to pass that way to get back to the mountains. Describing Carson City to his collar I found far easier than looking him in the eye. Such a funky little place, state capital or no, that, as my grandmother would have said, "If there was a boxcar on the siding, you missed it."

Her father had run a mining company railroad, which left a certain railroad color to her vocabulary, like the gem she insisted was the company motto of the Southern Pacific: "Uphill slow, downhill fast; tonnage first, safety last."

That set him off again, laughing till he couldn't breathe: *"Oh God,"* he gasped, "Oh God. The same as *us*. So—" (he got a first good breath) "—is it going to work out like the rings?"

"What?"

"This morning, you were having me believe God leaves treats around for you to find—"

My faith lay damp and macerated as a tired pound of hamburger leaking through its paper. Nevertheless, if Grace (or similar entity) had led me safe this far, it did seem inconceivably senseless that Grace might not intend to lead us home. "Okay," I said. "Okay, it's like the rings."

"You *promise?"*

"I promise." But I wasn't sure of anything.

We got up, leaning on each other.

As I cranked the van, his left hand slid across the hot vinyl till the back of it lay comforted under my thigh. I looked at him to find out how to take it; he wouldn't raise his eyes. There were still tears in the lashes. But the hand stayed where it was for the rest of the ride.

Chapter 3

I-80 INTERSECTS 395. 395 South springs away mercifully fast at first across the top of Reno, as the big signs say

WE HAVE A SLOT FOR YOU!
NO LEASE REQUIRED:
WASHER, DRYER AND FIREPLACE!
WE'RE THE CREAM: $435 A MONTH!
FOR SALE, FOR RENT, VACANCY, VACANCY—
FREEWAY ENDS—1¼ MILE.

And so it does, in a surly tangle of paving machinery, on an overpass to nowhere. Ground level now, still headed south from Reno, down the backside of the Sierra Nevada.

In Nevada, there are no zoning regulations. Or it's difficult to figure what they are. In Nevada, three quarters of the people live in trailer houses. In Nevada the '60s never happened. There is no rock music, only star-spangled country western. In Nevada, all the highway signs are dimpled by shotgun pellets, and all the private signs say

STEAK, LOBSTER, RIBS, DRINKS!
SALOON, SLOTS, TRAILER PARK!
WIN GOLD, CARS, TRIPS, SPAS—PLUS CASH!
TAHOE LAKESIDE—YOU HAVE FRIENDS IN HIGH PLACES!
ZERO TO $650,000 IN 6 SECS!
IT'S WHAT YOU COME TO TAHOE FOR—
RIGHT LANE ENDS.

Fleeing south now on a two-lane road. California's mountain towers march along, a cool inviting presence of sanity on the right. Hype recedes to forlorn little messages: "FOR SALE BY OWNER—" *But then*, just as the desert seems about to win, and tumbleweeds begin to stack against the fences:

CARSON CITY 32 MILES!
BE A WINNER!

Tom was riding with his eyes shut. "I don't think there's anybody," he said suddenly, "if they had a choice, who wouldn't want to be conceived in love."

Here we go again. *In manus tuas Domine commendo spiritum meum.* "Oh," I said, "I bet *you* were."

"Like to think I was." He was warming to his subject. "—But I can't ever *know*. People lie to each other. They lie to you. Especially about—well, matters of that kind."

I couldn't say a *thing*.

"—You *see* so many couples, man and wife, spend their whole time in slagging and belittling," he said. "Distaste. Disaffection. Disgust. Disrespect. Well, I suppose that God makes all, but still, if I knew my flesh had been made up of that, I'd have trouble holding up my head.

"I decided, any kid of mine ought to know right off he was conceived in love. Never need to make up pretty stories to keep himself warm. And if I hadn't that to give them, I'd have none. Have myself fixed so I couldn't.

"Don't know if that makes sense. But I'd feel being born of a passing pleasure made me pretty light stuff too. Like cheap ready-to-wear. I'd be the last to say that passing pleasure can't be very pleasant, but I wouldn't want my flesh and bones made up of it. It wears thin."

Now the big signs march along competing with the mountains:

$50,000 KENO!
400 SLOTS!
CARSON NUGGET 17.5 MILES!

"God, I was worn thin. So thin when we first met. You could see light between any two threads of me. Larger and larger part of my time was bein' spent using up strangers. No matter whether or not they wanted to get used: because they did. And they do. But I was getting used up fastest of the lot. One day all the fun was over. I just woke up, wanted to pack it all in and go home, take him home with me. Only I hadn't any home to take him to.

"So I just went on and on. The drugs and liquor don't help, but at the *time*, y'know, it seems they might. So it was on and on: nobody caught me at it. Like I was hoping someone might catch me at it. Nobody caught me at it. Except you."

"I didn't catch you at it," I said, tears approaching surely as the next casino. "I never saw you do anything."

"Maybe not, but *you* did something."

"It was all an accident."

"Don't believe in accidents," he said.

ORMSBY HOUSE!
FOUR RESTAURANTS, TWO SWIMMING POOLS!
2000 ROOMS!
ENJOY FREE DINING!
CHILDREN'S LOUNGE! 12.5 MILES!

"Never gave the future much thought. Could be, I supposed, I'd got no future coming. But thinking about—well, about Harlan with no future coming—that was just something I could not support.

"I'd gotten so I understood losing my own family; they all died. Wasn't anybody's fault, not even mine.

"But losing his family, now that I did for him. I ought, I wanted to be, his roof in the cold. Crutch for his weakness. Medicine for his pain. And if I hadn't been a very good boy, wasn't because I didn't know what I signed up for.

"Worse yet, only way I saw of doing it was to make some viable future for myself. Y'see what I mean?"

I nodded silently. There were connections in what he said, which I could hear but wasn't getting, or which some part of my mind was getting very well, just refusing to share with the rest. The car buzzed along.

Suddenly he snickered. "Wouldn't want to have popped out of a turkey baster, either."

The car hopped over a desert rise onto the main drag of Carson City. And main was almost all the drag there was. Out on the edge sprawl shopping centers, new and tacky, flat ground-gobbling buildings: land is cheap. None look over five years old, or built to last more than ten. Auto dealerships, RV sales, pizza, Taco Bell. Food, gas, diesel, bait. Then the motels.

Then a sign: CARSON CITY URBAN AREA: what used to be the town, bulbous neon casino signs—24 HOUR POKER BAR! SHRIMP COCKTAILS $1.00!—and old brick buildings housing multiple pawnshops, THE PONY EXPRESS HOTEL, CHINESE FOOD, IRENE'S BAR, VIDEO POKER! EASY SLOTS!—and—

Tom elbowed me. The Salvation Army Store: showcase windows, and six high-mileage, bouffant hairdo mannequins standing shoulder-to-shoulder right across the front! They all were wearing wedding gowns. "Want to get yours there?"

"Nope. Got mine."

I punched my seat belt loose, let the VW coast, lifted my

butt free of the seat, slipped the wool skirt down around my ankles, and quick! Whipped it off and stomped the gas before the car stalled.

Wide-eyed and unguarded, Tom appraised me. I had molted. The damp white mini dress was a little crunched just now, but like a dragonfly's wings, sun and breeze would bring it out.

"Hey! That's it!"

A little green sign arrowing off to the right:

MARRIAGE LICENSES

⟶

PARK IN REAR

Too late to turn. I hung a big U around the neoclassic bulk of Ormsby House, a Proletarian Pleasure Palace built for giants, and drove slowly in the opposite direction, one block closer to the hills.

Main Street was a countrified midway. Then came the state buildings, leafy and sedately out of place with their historical markers, their cannons on the lawn. One block to either side lived in a different century.

Drowsy, desolate, full of small secret life. Pigeons courting on the buckled sidewalks. Tall old cottonwoods: crows in the tops broadcast their views with all the force of radio evangelists. Tall old nineteenth-century mansions, some for rent. Vacant lots, desert-bright, where mansions used to stand. Nineteenth-century cottages housing—

Wedding chapels.

Well, at least these didn't look like card parlors or funeral homes; rather like gypsy spiritualists instead:

MADAME LEONA WILL READ
THE FUTURE IN YOUR PALM:
LOVE, MARRIAGE, MONEY,
BUSINESS, PERSONAL.

You know the look. Lace-curtain nefarious.

I put us in the middle of a vacant lot. No Trespassing signs hung from a chain around it, but the chain lay in the gravel. Lots of tire tracks wandered in and out.

Next door a big Victorian and lesser antique structures rimmed a square of grass. A faded neon sign on a pole in the middle of the grass said Serendipity Square.

It was a place divided like a nursery school into play areas or fantasy locales, only here the daydreams were for older children. Right from the sidewalk I could see The Livery Stable with Ye Olde Hitching Rack in front, a Photographer's Shoppe, with racks of frills for dressing up in, an arbor arched above a swan boat from The Tunnel of Love—and in between it all, beds of black-eyed Susans, herbs, marigolds, and leggy old roses nobody pinched the hips off. Along the edges of the walk, onion plants produced fat yellow onions at their bases.

The shed nearest the street was Rhett's Stage Stop. Sidewalk changed to boardwalk in its shade. A real live wedding was going on inside, but you couldn't see in very well because of the rococo message painted on the glass:

Office for Chapels
← Follow Footprints

Your Choice of Four Chapels in Serendipity Square:
Scarlett's Chapel (Elegant)
Rhett's Stage Stop (Western)
Wedding Parlor (Homey)
Garden Chapel (In Season)

Special Offer to You: Less than Cost
Greatest variety of Marriage
Safest, Fastest, and Finest Marriages in the World.

OFFICE
←

Hopeful white paint footprints pace the boardwalk, but they're not going our way.

Across the street, the State Building wears the dowdy and abandoned graces of a 1920s city high school: same huge, somnolent rumble of air conditioning, same chain link around the light wells. In the shadow of its wings lies a little gravel parking lot. On its rustic stone hang four green signs and a white one: the white one says

DO NOT PARK
IN THE
MIDDLE OF THIS LOT

The green ones say, in order, left to right

CITY PRISON VAN
STATE PRISON VAN
CITY DELIVERY VAN
MARRIAGE LICENSES DOWNSTAIRS THIS BUILDING

Down, down two steps at a time, to blond wood and gray linoleum, the standard institutional smell. There was a chest-high counter and desks and file cabinets, and two women clerks. A little prop-up sign on the counter said

LICENSE FEE $25.00
CASH ONLY
THIS LICENSE MUST BE USED
IN THE STATE OF NEVADA
CORRECT CHANGE IS REQUIRED
AFTER 4:00 P.M. AND
ON WEEKENDS AND HOLIDAYS

"Hullo," said Tom.

The papers seemed perfectly straightforward. There was nothing reasonable to prevent anyone at all from getting a marriage license, and no place he could use it but the State of Nevada. Even the ballpoints on the counter worked. Tom paid the clerk too much, and told her to keep the change.

He said, "I'm about to ask a dumb question. Have you a paper handy with the wording of your marriage vows?"

"Oh no, honey," said the older woman. "Each one of those J.P.'s just has his own he likes to use."

"J.P.'s?"

"I'm sorry, honey: Justice of the Peace. Get so used to people knowing what I mean."

"Could I speak to him?"

"Well there's no J.P. *here* Sundays, you know, that's the problem. Used to be they took turns on the holidays, but with the budget like it is—"

I would have said about now, had anybody asked me, "It isn't going to turn out like the rings."

"There's the chapels of course—" she said, still flustering with his money "—right across the street and they're every one open till midnight—"

Good thing nobody asked me.

"—Come back Mondays through Saturdays now," she called after us. "You could just step down the hall—"

The boardwalk led around the Stage Stop. There the footprints descended, onto the cracked and grassy walks of Serendipity Square. And it was hard not to follow that row of white prints around the corner once the suggestion had been made—very hard—in fact, it must have been too hard.

A well-dressed man shot out the front door of the big house and almost scampered toward the Stage Stop. He froze when he saw us, as a squirrel does, noticing it's not alone.

Tom waved.

"May I help you?"

"Depends," said Tom. "We were hoping to get married."

"Did you have an appointment? Trouble is, we're so insanely busy—Weddings in three out of the four already, you know—There's no Justice over there on Sundays—"

"Right. Well, we were leaving anyway."

"No, no! Wait, why don't you see my wife? She's just inside—" pointing behind him to where painted footprints marched up wooden steps.

"Hullo, ma'am."

To the left inside the dim house a long velvet room (obviously Scarlett's Chapel, elegant) bulged at the double doors with a wedding in progress. To the right, closed parlor doors (homey) and muffled voices.

The woman at the desk raised faded eyes.

"We've no appointment I'm afraid; we didn't know—" Tom tucked his head, studied his shoes. It was an almost scandalously foregone conclusion.

"Oh dear, oh dear, are you sweet people all the way from *England?*"

"Your husband said there might be some small something y'could do—"

"You know, the *papers*, the newspapers do pieces on us *all* the time, why just last Sunday—I've got Xerox copies, I should give you one—the *years* we've done these chapels, we've had couples from *thirty-five different countries* —"

Tom's eyes moved up to hers.

"From *England,*" she murmured. "What a long way."

"Yes ma'am, it is."

"Oh *dear*."

· — ·

IT was built of lattice, held firm by a hundred summers of white paint. It crouched in a narrow side yard, an old iron fence between it and the street, like it was playing hide-and-seek and we were the first to find it. Leaves fluttered down around it from the cottonwoods. Crows cawed lustily. White butterflies visited the grass. A white wicker table and chairs furnished its insides. The chairs had plastic cushions puddled by a sprinkler. Another wicker object might have been an altar or a buffet, depending. Around the sides on pedestals were wicker urns of plastic flowers, aged and sunburned to a median orange.

"Wait," called Tom. "One thing, are those removable? I'm sorry, but I can't stand plastic flowers. They make me think of cemeteries."

The stands were lashed to the lattice with electrical wire, but the plastic bouquets came off. When they were gone, the little garden chapel stood even more dreamlike and forlorn, a childhood place: not even your own childhood, Ray Bradbury's childhood, maybe. Old and thoughtful. Spooky-gracious.

Its floor was all uneven, with half bricks and homemade concrete pavers set in it like precious stones and painted glossy red and glossy green, as if your grandfather did it himself and Grandpa was more loving than handy. Here came the woman with her husband and another man, very tall, very old. He wore a hearing aid behind one ear and gold rim glasses. His black suit had a green patina. Ray Bradbury would have loved him.

Reverend Such-and-Such I didn't catch (retired) shook both of our hands. His own were slow and warm, withered as the desert evening. Tom asked his question about the wording of the vows. He'd clasped me firmly from the back, both arms, just as he'd done when asking after rings.

"The State requires me to determine of you both your true intent," said the Reverend Such-and-Such, sweet old ponderous pulpit-voice punctuated by the click of dentures, "and if your true and uncoerced intent is to marry, that I pronounce you man and wife in the name of the State—"

"That's all?"

"Whatever else you wish, if you wish to be more—"

"No," said Tom emphatically. "That's what I wish. Exactly that. No more."

"And your given name is Thomas?"

"Yes, sir. Hers is Miranda."

"That's all I need."

"Thank you, sir."

The old man draws a long formal breath.

"Now understand," says Tom, "I've no objections to your mentioning the presence of God, so long as y'make it short."

The old man opens his mouth.

"—Short and *kind*," says Tom.

"Dearly Beloved—"

"And *dignified*," says Tom.

The old man smiles at him. "Dearly Beloved, we are gathered here this evening for the purpose of uniting this couple, before God and man, in the loving bonds of holy matrimony (take her hand)—"

"Right."

Tom slips his left hand down to find my left. Late sun bores in sideways, molten amber casting silver shadows, but where it shines through the orange diamonds, blood-red light-drops spatter both our arms.

"—Thomas, do you take this woman, Miranda, to be your lawful wedded wife, to love and to cherish as long as you both do live?"

"Right. I do."

The old man smiles at Tom again, before asking me the same. "Do you have rings?" (plain gold ones, like old country people wear—) "Repeat after me, 'Take this ring, and wear it as a symbol of my lasting love—'" (—the kind that, if you leave on long enough—)

"Take this ring and wear it as a symbol of—"

"By the authority vested in me by the State of Nevada, I now pronounce you man and wife."

· —— ·

I WAS sitting in the car.

Everything was dizzyingly dazzlingly hot. Trying to remember now, how to put the key into the lock. Almost went to sleep standing up, there in the summerhouse. Tom kissed me. Warm arms, warm front, warm mouth, sweet breath, sweet dark. Sleep forever. Then he let go, and I had to stand on my own. Remember him handing out hundred-dollar bills.

Tom said softly but distinctly, "Goddamn bloody frigging fucking hypocrites."

I must have jumped a mile. I'm sitting in the car.

"Oh, not those people—they're honest people—It's the government, that's what it is."

I find the lock, and put the key in it.

"I hate the government: license me to love, will they? *I could be lying! Do they care?* I could be planning to unload you in a year: they'd help me to fill out the forms for it! And *you* could be planning to shake me down for mental cruelty and half of everything I own! *You could!* Nothing easier: just tell 'em everything. And would they mind? God, no, so long as you paid the taxes on it. But license me to cherish? *What the hell do they know?*

"Harlan and me—do you realize, that if one of us had sex change operations, they would let *us* marry? *Think* about it. I think about Harlan—he has the most beautiful body—I have ever seen. On man or woman either. He wouldn't strip, or show it off on stage, Oh no. It's not in his nature. I don't know if you can understand, he's very—"

"Chaste," I said. The kind of information that I don't forget. It stopped him open mouthed.

"After his fashion." (Now he's forgotten that he told me.) "Takes a clown like me to do that.

"Every cell in his body is male, believe me. And I love it. It's not just that he's got—that he's—Well he does, y'know. And I'm very fond of—about the dearest thing I know, feeling him get—when I—Ah *God, I don't want to talk to you about that!*

"God made him right the first time!

"And if he would go in a clinic, and have himself cut, and take those shots; if he would go through all that pain and shame to make a sideshow travesty of himself, your government would write him out new papers saying he was female, and a license saying he could be my lawful wedded love in public! They'd laugh at us, of course, but they'd pat us on the heads and say 'All right!'

"And he wouldn't ever *be* a woman.

"I couldn't ever have children from him, any more than him from me: he'd just be my Harlan ruined and wasted—he'd be an abomination, and so would I if it didn't give me the horrors to touch him! But your *fucking government would call that satisfaction from us!"*

He looked away out of his window, wiping his face where I almost couldn't see it. Defiantly, he turned back eye-to-eye.

"Sooner do it to myself. Much sooner. Well what are *you* crying for?"

"I don't have Harlan's looks."

"Who does? If that's your only problem, you're in great shape."

"You do."

"Sorry. And I thrive on flattery as well as the next. Nothing wrong with your looks, anyway."

"I'm flat-chested. I've got no hips!"

"Well, it's better than having too many! Now, I quite like the way the way you're built."

"You would. I'm built like a guy!"

"Oh no you're not!"

"Besides, you couldn't marry him if you both had fifty operations!"

"Yes I could! It's legal!"

"No you couldn't!"

"Why not? You tell me why not!"

"Because it's bigamy! That's why not! You're married to me!"

We sat in the front seat of the old VW bus, in the vacant lot where some grand house once stood, in dusty furnace-hot Carson City, Nevada, and stared at one another.

His silver eyes were wide with amazement, and filled around the edges with fresh tears. One loose tear, forgotten, found an escape route down his cheek.

I wanted to touch it. Wipe it.

I wanted to touch *him*. I wanted to pull him right inside of me, and never let him out.

Tom gave a kind of delayed strangled screech. He grabbed my waist in both hands and bounced me bodily up: my knees smacked into the steering wheel and my ear grazed the roof; I was traveling a perfect arc, over the back of the driver's seat, into the mid seat of the bus. *Touchdown: the Eagle Has Landed.*

I did some fancy screeching of my own: The sun shone on the seat, the vinyl was hot enough to fry eggs. But Tom was coming down on top of me—He *was* on top of me, and he was hotter than the seat by orders of magnitude.

· — ·

YOU know all that trendy business in the schools, the rah-rah programs to molest-proof kids? They had the nerve to tell us, "You have to learn you are free to say no."

I made radical trouble at that point, and a really evil name for myself, by raising my hand and saying, "We *aren't* 'free to say *no!*' Not unless we're also free to say *'yes!'*

"What a bunch of hypocritical schlock! We're *required* to say *'no,'* that's what you're saying: we're under obedience to our parents, the schools, the cops; we aren't allowed to be sexual. What's with this 'Free to say *no*'?"

Ground Zero, you guys!

Free to say yes!

Has anybody thought to teach me *how*?

All I know is, if I raise an eye, I'll find the entire van surrounded by raunchy paunchy Nevadans in iridescent mirror shades and cowboy hats.

But there wasn't any crowd of strangers watching. I was the only stranger watching. And *watching*. Watching me and watching him. *Ut Videam*. I didn't know how to stop.

Suddenly, a tenable reason why we shouldn't get it on in the parking lot. I tried to wriggle and say, "No!" Only the wriggling worked; my mouth was occupied. And wriggling is subject to misinterpretation.

Wriggle and squirm and go, *"Mmwpf!"*

Wonderfully unsuccessful. He was stronger than I was.

"Wedding night!"

"Don't shout!"

Silence. The still, hot, drowsy car knew one sound, heavy breathing. His. Mine. We were wound up in each other like a bucket of snakes. "Sorry," I whispered in his ear. "What I meant to say was, I only plan to have one wedding night, and I would very much like to do it right."

Tom sat up, and I sat in his lap. There was no other car but ours in the entire blazing vacant lot. "I can understand that," he said.

I watched a lizard scoot across the gravel. Another followed it.

"Fact is, I can understand quite well. Furthermore, I know exactly what to do about that. C'mon."

· — ·

BACK on the main drag, headed south. Married. And getting close to the edge of town. But the middle of Carson City is close to the edge of town.

"Hey."

We were passing a sun-blasted shopping plaza, around a Skagg's market. A sign on the market's front said LIQUORS.

I parked against Skagg's plate glass. All across the store, just inside the glass and long before you came to the food, stood a phalanx of slot machines, and before every one stood a middle-aged woman in polyester, pulling the handle, letting it go. Putting in money, pulling the handle. One left empty-handed; a sister took her place.

Tom also came out empty-handed.

We saw one other liquor store, featuring slots: Tom did such a fast in-out there it amounted to a rebound. "You'd think," he said, "a place like this'd want more liquor to get by."

True: there would have been a Liquor Barn on every block in California. Now we were on the edge of town. We passed an empty field, a well diggers' supply, a feed-and-grain. Then a little pink house made over to a store. The sign said MARGE'S LICKER LOCKER.

Hold it.

Marge was pushing fifty, bare-armed and burly. She tendered Tom the wistful once-over some people save for brand-new Cadillacs.

"I've just been in two bottle shops," he said, "and asked them for their best champagne. The clerk said this, and I said 'Wrong,' and he said thus-and-such, and I said 'Wrong—' I found nothing there worth over twenty pounds! I must not be expressing myself too plainly in the local patois. What I *meant* to put across: I want the best all-out fuck-'em-dead champagne in the state of—"

He looked perplexed. I said, "Nevada."

Marge's eyes bounced back and forth from Tom to me for several seconds, like a spectator's at a tennis match. She shook herself. "Hold on, now." She gave a last speculative look at Tom over her shoulder. "You're English, ain't ya?" She went, and from the back came splintering crate sounds, popping staples, ripping cardboard.

Tom shook his head. "Feel really foolish never remembering the name of this place: must put me in mind of something I don't want to think about—"

"'Neva' is Spanish for 'snow'," I whispered, and regretted it: his look could have withered trees.

"Didn't have to say that."

Marge came back with a bottle. Instead of a paper label, a name was painted on the glass in art nouveau sinuosity: "Perrier-Jouet, la Fluor de Champagne." While on every side, white painted opium poppies swayed and danced against the green glass bottle, and hung their drowsy heads.

Tom's eyes kindled. "All reet petite. Why didn't y'say so in the first place?"

"—'Cause I don't carry this, is why. It's special for a lady out of town. One of her friends from the coast is partial to it."

I reached up, and whispered, "Whorehouse," in Tom's ear. He gave me a startled look. "Legal in Nevada."

"Like instant weddings?" he whispered back.

"More like slot machines."

"God." Then to Licker Lady, "How much are you asking?"

"—Now she don't like people to mess with her orders. Still, I suppose one of these babies could get broken. Never has, but you know it's always possible—I just know that I remember you from someplace."

"How much?"

"One hundred dollars."

"Oh God!" Tom squawked. "What'd y'do? Pack it in on native porters?"

"I'm a businesswoman, be fair: I gotta charge something for a breakage fee." But she threw in two cheap glasses and a cooler of ice. Her last words, plaintive, longing, drifted down the steps behind us: "You wouldn't be on the *soaps*, would you?"

· — ·

THE desert softened; it reverted to the nineteenth century with a sigh the minute Carson City fell behind. There were katydids singing in the grass. Dead skunks on the road. Lights coming on in squat, substantial farmhouses. And squat, substantial steers and quarter horses standing up to their bellies in sweet pasture.

Down behind the mountain, but still making himself known on his long retreat to the west, the sun spouted an amazing baroque fan of coral rays into the sky. The nearest ridge was gray-brown burlap stitched black for thickets and ravines. The one behind was flat dark purple, a cutout in wool felt. The height behind that was mauve, and behind that stood another, palest lavender; absurdly, almost tearfully like that place in the song:

Oh beautiful for spacious skies
For amber waves of grain (oat hay in this case)
For purple mountain majesties
Above
the fruited
plain.

Getting atop those mountains from the fruited plain is a two-hour's drive on the California side. Fifteen rock-hard vertical minutes does it from the east: up Woodford's Canyon where the West Fork of the Carson tumbles down its shadowy chute into Nevada.

The old VW lugs on up and up the darkening grade. A doe high-steps her twin fawns through my headlights. Our first California sign says "TOIYABE NATIONAL FOREST: LAND OF MANY USES."

Above lie Faith, Hope, and Charity: three high valleys, shallow granite sky-bowls spilling evening light. Mormon settlers named them, clambering up this way with their pushcarts and their piety. The one the road runs through is Hope. And just beyond that, at the very top of Carson Summit, is a sign reading "AMADOR COUNTY LINE."

People notice what pertains to them. Like say, an Australian aborigine can spot a kangaroo in the bush a hundred times faster than a white guy, but the white guy's faster at coins on the sidewalk. So here's this sign. I saw Tom's head crank right around to follow it. "That's 'Lover County!'"

"Well," I said, "they try to make out like it means 'Love of Gold,' but that would have been 'Amor d'Oro'—"

"It's plain 'lover.' A weekend on Ibiza will give y'*that* much Spanish." He shut up like a trap.

Caples Lake slips by in the twilight, followed by the looming mass of Carson Spur. Then Silver Lake, twinkling yellow nostalgia from store and lodge and campground. Our highway roller-coasters down the ridges; headlights turn approaching trees to ghosts. The sun has danced away over the edge of the world, "laughing," as the Psalm puts it, "like a giant to run his race." One last persimmon smear out by the coast still marks the way he went.

· — ·

YESTERDAY afternoon, and far out there, I pursued that westering sun across the San Joaquin. My cabin chores were finished, I'd powered up pump and water heater, stowed my groceries, put fresh sheets on my parents' big bed. Checked off my list of Tings 2 Do.

Getting on toward 3:00, I launched myself downhill for Oakland Coliseum and Bill Graham Presents. *Ut videam.* Well, I was going to see all right. Hope, depression, fatigue, and adrenalin began to fight it out. Almost an hour from the cabin to the highway, an hour down to Jackson, an hour from Jackson to Stockton across the Valley, pit stop for gas, two cups of coffee, and a fast trip to the bathroom. An hour from Stockton to Oakland Coliseum.

Smog, heat, crawling traffic, sinking sun. Belshangles won't be on stage yet; your main attraction waits for dark. The Red Hot Chili Peppers might be doing their thing about now.

I abandoned the VW at the rim of the Coliseum lot. One last Ting 2 Do, find a good home for my extra ticket. I have an appreciation for fanatics. Sure enough, on the asphalt by the box-office window still lounged a line, two dozen of the hardcore ticketless. I applied myself to the end of it.

Ahead of me, a tall skinny kid was rattling around in new black Levi's two sizes narrower than mine. He had blond hair and he'd dyed it black, then he'd dyed it red and it'd all grown out and gotten cut off in patches: it was really decadent if you took a close look. If you didn't, it looked like mange. The front of his shirt said Psychic TV, and the back, "Brian Jones Died For Your Sins."

We started to talk. Not that much younger than me; sixteen maybe. Not going to school. Playing guitar (sort of) and looking for a band (sort of). Living in Vallejo. He said his name was Joshua Sweet. I'd known at least a dozen of him. He was cute and sad and last in line. People at the head had hope even now for returns. He didn't have a prayer. Thought to myself, I've found my boy.

I said, "I've got something that might interest you."

We hunched over my purse, away from predatory eyes of types who hoped this was a drug deal they could join. There was the dog-eared envelope with the British stamps, inside that, the colored envelope, inside that, two precious strips of multicolored cardboard:

> Bill Graham Presents: A DAY ON THE GREEN
> Sunday August 17: BELSHANGLES
> and special guests
> Reserved Seats
> Row Number:

Joshua Sweet gave it the long perusal of a kid who set great store in cool. "Ting, tang, walla-walla bing bang."

"You might say that."

He walked me further from the line. "How much?"

"Somebody gave 'em to me. I'll give you one."

He thought. "What for?"

"Fun."

He thought some more. "I can live with that."

"Look at it this way: I can't sit on both of 'em."

The line grew shorter by two bodies. Joshua Sweet and I loped toward the stadium. One last mysterious barricade of fear, that the tickets were a hoax which everyone would spot but me. Not to worry. The takers took 'em, tore 'em, and turned us loose, up the long concrete stairway to heaven.

J. Sweet's practiced cool evaporated. He'd wanted to see the Chilies. I would've liked that too, but you can't have everything. He'd writhed in helpless torment, hearing the thunder of their set from the Coliseum parking lot.

He'd wanted to see if Kiedis and Flea had the nerve to (or if Bill Graham let 'em) pull in a stadium what they usually did in clubs: get naked for their encore, with a gym sock apiece on their privates.

I went to hear them last October: crushed in the front row of a local club with an idiot crew of dudes who repeated like mantras every last word to the Chilies' songs, and whose epitome of wit was to shout, *"Whazzat in yer pocket?"* and make a flying grab at the other's shirt, to frantic evasion attempts and shrieks of *"Fuckitman! You leave my goddamn tit alone!"*

Or to bellow *"Penis!"* back and forth at one another.

I wanted to shout, "*Shut up!* You guy's have all *got* 'em; be a whole lot funnier if you didn't!"

Finally, there was Anthony Kiedis.

God help us, what a stage presence. He stalked and strutted, swung punches, fondled his crotch, flung himself into the crowd. It was a great act: obnoxious as hell, but great. Male authority at the sub-basement level, like a bull ape hooting and putting on the primal Ritz to the delirious wonder of his tribe.

Then the same stupid thrasher stepped on my head twice in

successive kamikaze rushes to the stage. Nobody needs that. I headed for the tables and chairs in back. The whole back quarter of the audience was male. Guys who'd come with guys. The few chicks who'd gotten in the wrong rooting section beat a huffy retreat during the show.

And Kiedis kept egging his audience on to fuck each other (assuming *of course,* he said, that it was true love), and when that didn't meet with much compliance, he ordered 'em all to *kiss* each other like crazy, and they wouldn't. Somebody shouted that he didn't want AIDS. I saw the sexual revolution ending, in much the manner T.S. Eliot says the world does.

The man on stage shouted back, *"What d'ya mean it isn't worth it?"*

They stared up at him with little kid's adoration—that said in every line "*Look,* just look up there! He's *our beauty!* That's what we are! We'd all be lean, splendid, fearless, *just like that,* if only you could see us right—"

Even then, nine months ago, they'd bagged the "sock" finale. Kiedis climaxed by binding himself, knees to nipples, round and round, with a roll of silver duct tape. A techno-punk Statue of Liberty he stood, and showered his screeching vicarious lovers with "canned confetti," that spews out wet and white as semen, and dries to papery colored strips.

Nevertheless, J. Sweet kept asking kids he met about the socks. Legendry dies hard, I guess. It did appear the answer was "no." I could have told him.

People flowed, each head a living corpuscle in the great slow veins of the stadium. Arteries pulsed up and down the concrete stairs. Small streams filtered through the toilets, past sticky soft drink outlets, and hotdogs duded up in catchy hues of mustard, ketchup, and relish. Past bazaars all rich and titillating with their heaps of T-shirts, pins, and programs. Capillaries fed them back into the seats. And the field below, what was that? The pumping heart of the matter, so full of celebrants, they compacted to a solid single flesh.

The crowd amused itself, and waited for its heart's desire.

Recycled soft-drink cups, big tall ones, eight or ten inches of wax-coated red-white-and-blue commercialism, industriously smashed flat, make splendid disposable Frisbees. Collect several dozen, you can fly 'em off the stands at once, joined by hundreds of others' zealous collections, and the air grows full for a moment of flying jubilation, like a swarm of bees in May. Fifteen minutes, the collectors will have done their work again: gathered up all their waxy colored fliers with newly flattened reinforcements from colas bought and guzzled in the interval—up they go.

We'd put ourselves in the reserved seats, and they were splendid, perfect comfort, perfect view. J. Sweet emitted all the small talk he could think of, and a distinct impression he wasn't happy sitting there with me. I knew what he wanted to do, go down and mingle. Hack, stab, kill, and bullyrag himself through that human flesh-flow covering the green until his belly touched the stage front.

The man I loved had put my name on the seat I was in. Nobody gets that kind of treasure and the stage front too.

"Who'd you say gifted you with these fine seats?"

I said, "Tommi Rhymer."

"Himself?"

"Himself."

"Right. Well that was really—ah—*kind* of him."

Well do I know the look; he thinks I'm crazy or druggy or both. "Yeah. It was."

"Be sure to thank him for me."

I said, "Will do."

"I suppose you wouldn't very much mind—"

"No," I said, "Feel free."

Last seen bouncing down the stands, he vanished at the bottom, a grateful fish into the human sea. Darkness falls sedately and seductively, ten thousand wisps of pot smoke rising past it like the sweet odor of evening sacrifice.

Think about the person who marries Tommi Rhymer. What will she get for her portion? Backstage, for sure. In his dressing room, in the limo, in his bed. But never front-row center anymore. I hadn't penetrated the outmost of those places: and here already, a wave of nostalgia for front-row center. I felt remote and solitary as the moon.

Canned rock thunders from the speakers. Monster video screens flash bright seductive images above the stage. Down on the field a dude is getting tossed in a blanket: popping up from human anonymity with arms and legs spread wide and flailing, into the festive summer evening. And see there? Halfway across, another spread-eagled body accelerates into view! Competition! The first bounce takes him maybe two feet over people's heads, the second three, the third five—

The fourth should orbit the guy. Instead it lands him off the blanket, body lengths away in the crowd. Now the first crew's found another human volleyball and started up again. They're joined by a third. And a fourth.

And the moment finally comes—time is splendid and inexorable—Bill Graham in the spotlight, a little thinner and weirder than last season, still sharp eyed, sharp edged as an aging buccaneer. "*Ladies and Gentlemen*, for the first time in three years—their seventh American tour—their third *Day on the Green*—from London, Rollo McInery, Nicki Cavanaugh, *Harlan Parr, Tommi Rhymer! Welcome Belshangles!*"

A sudden onslaught of sound and vision: a light blast exploding out over that compact forest of upstretched human arms and hands, sweeping the rosy waving flesh like a bed of coral polyps at the bottom of the sea.

Wish that all the lovers
I ever had were you:
Well I wish that all the lovers
I ever had were you.

What's fast is too soon past
And the past turns future fast—
And it's much too late for gettin',
But you must admit the wishin's new.

Wish you were the only
Traffic on my road:
Well I wish you were the only
Traffic on my road:
For you its concrete eight lanes wide
Top speed four lanes to a side—
Little red flag behind you
Sayin' Caution: extra long load

So on down to the very final chorus, as the whole great crowd, holding up the appropriate fingers, chanted with him:

—MACH ONE!
MACH TWO!
MACH THREE—
Just SO long,
SO long sweet lover
As you don't mock ME.

Time hastens. All the best shows are too soon over. The crowd shuffles out onto the concrete ramps, dazed and lowing like thirsty cattle. Knowing pain, withdrawal, loss for which there is no cure.

This young guy stumbling along behind me is practically shouting to the sky, *"Oh God, I've seen what I wanna be when I grow up, and the job's already taken!"* You think that's a funny line? Turn around and check his face. Not funny. *"There's gotta be room in the world for more of them! You think they could use a road company?"*

I made it home and into bed unchallenged, and greeted in the quiet my usual concert after-symptoms: the high steady singing in my right ear and a kind of shimmery rustle in the left, like distant tambourines.

· — ·

I DON'T make the turn too elegantly; a steep left hairpin down into darkness. Then a tooth-rattling eyeball-bouncing cattle guard (Tom sits up rigid, like somebody goosed him), and a row of little white diamond-shaped signs with inspirational messages:

> Side View of Chainsaw, MUST USE SPARK ARRESTERS!
> Side View of Motorcycle: MUST USE SPARK ARRESTERS!
> Side View of Cigarette: CRUSH ALL SMOKES!
> Side View of Nothing: ENJOY YOUR NATIONAL FOREST!

Twenty miles to go. Down the ridge I stutter in the log truck ruts and across the dam. Buck and sideslip up the far ridge, jitter down. Along Bright's Creek, and across the bridge. El Dorado National Forest: Land of Many Uses.

One of the many happens to be logging.

The past two summers' Federal Timber Sales have butchered half the woods between our property and Bright's Creek. Big diesel Cats hauling off corpses of trees I've personally known since childhood have chewed all bloody hell out of the place. I wonder what the puzzled roots think, left in the ground. The bark still grows and tries to heal on them. The sap still flows. Death comes slowly.

Certain whimsy to National Forest signs: right out at the back of beyond you come on cryptic little wooden strips:

> LEECH LAKE TRAILHEAD, 2.7 MILES ⟶
> UPPER FRANCHIERE (SITE) 3.8 MILES ⟶
> ⟵ SNATCH SPRINGS 7 MILES

Well here, in the middle of what looks like World War I, one of those small ecologically inoffensive strips says

> PARDEE CAMP (PRIVATE) 2 MILES ⟶

We are farther from the world than we were.

They blocked our road at the timber sale boundary with cratered earth and splintered logs. We have to drive off south around a ridge and back, and join the stub of our past below the meadow. Fewer people come here by mistake.

Congress swelled Mokulumne Wilderness Area by 15,000 acres; it rubs uneasily against our eastern property line, as logging does against the west. Fiddler's Lake is closed to vehicles now. One guy who'd fished in there for years defied the signs and drove in anyway. They made him take his jeep apart and pack it out.

Congress could take Pardee for wilderness, Papa says. And will, some year. Private ownership, like private love, doesn't have much impact on their planning.

But the trick is, none of that really shows from Pardee Meadow. A quarter mile of our own trees stand tall between. *Tom doesn't know.* And like a peculiarly modern Quasimodo, crying "Sanctuary! Sanctuary!" where there is no sanctuary, hauling my Esmeralda (for the second time) up a bell tower the Church condemns for demolition—

I think that I won't tell him.

My sanctuary is the Forest of the Night: less a tower than a journey underground. Here tree trunks grow to secret columns between floor and roof. Darkness amputates distance; there is no sky. Young trees crowd to meet us, combing their spikey hands along the car. Suddenly, we've arrived.

"You know. I got a question I'm afraid to ask." Whispering on the porch. "How'd you get me in here? The time when I—y'know."

"Carried you."

"With your friend?"

"All by my lonesome."

"My face is red."

"Doesn't look red from here."

The rickety front porch at Pardee is black, moonless subterranean as the inmost gallery of a mine. The meadow is a vaulted hall; I see glowworms on the ceiling.

"Y'have the keys?"

"Oh, sorry."

He told me to prop the door. Then he boosted my rear to the porch rail, and gathered me into his arms.

And I'm remembering something (he circled around in the dark close room) about being borne up on eagles' wings—until his shins came up against an old sofa. We tumbled onto it: instant replay of the backseat in Carson City, only this was the remix, the extended play.

"We haven't had our champagne yet!"

"Don't shout, I'm right here, y'know."

Together we went out and carried in his bag, his fiddle, our champagne, to where the kitchen light made an almost infinitesimal puddle of home comfort in the enormous blackness of the woods.

Papa eases his champagne corks out a micron at a time. Tom comes from a different school of celebration I can tell; he fires his off the ceiling.

"Have you a hammer in this place? Come on, I bet y'do. Nails too, what?" He took the hammer and a nail selected from the can, and climbing sock-footed onto the Formica table beside the fizzing, fuming poppy-painted bottle, surveyed the ceiling. "There 'tis." He bent his knees and bit his lip, and ceremoniously nailed the champagne cork into the dent it generated. I admired the droll figure that he made, all long spidery arms and legs against the kitchen light. Taking a gold pen from his breast pocket, he wrote, there on the ceiling beside the cork:

Thomas Peter Rhymer
Miranda Dolores Falconer
August 17, 1986

One glass for him. One for me. Second glass for him. Second for me. Third glass for him. I'm gazing up into the light. Wonder how it feels to be a moth and spin around it.

"Problem?"

"I've never split a bottle of champagne."

"You want I should finish that?"

"Thought you didn't drink anymore."

"A man can't be stone cold sober on his wedding night," he said. "Well, it's not proper. Y'got to pay tradition *some* respect."

It was all gone, anyway.

"Y'want to stay here, or camp out like we did?" He waited. Except for light that flowed in from the kitchen, the little bedroom was broom-closet dark. "Whose bed is it anyway? Your parents'?"

"Grandparents.'"

"Well that settles it: we stay here."

I'm thinking. My grandmother hauled it from some old body's attic when she was a bride, butched the legs and painted it (walnut country gothic was out as out in 1929), and then, when they bought real furniture, it came up here, and since their time my parents slept in it—

"Y'know—" he said, "—been eying the cut of that dress all afternoon, conjecturing—" He slipped his thumbs inside the neckline, just above both collarbones, and popped it deftly outward off my shoulders. "Ah."

I said "Whoops!" or something like it, followed by "Wait! Wait!" The bra straps followed the shoulders they were pinned to. The sleeves were peeling inside out now, two long reptilian sheddings: soon I'd have no hands for anything. It all went down as far as my waist, and stuck.

I got inside the front; unsnapped the bra. "There."

The thumbs continued their smooth passage down my sides. When they reached the waistband of my panty hose, they simply slipped inside. Every hair all over my whole body stood on end.

Dress, bra, hose and two quiet hands progressed toward the floor. When the thumbs reached the top of my briefs, those joined the party and went on downward with the rest.

Tom knelt, freed my left foot, naked, from dress and hose and briefs and shoe, kissed and set it naked on the wooden floor. The right followed, neat and clean and kind. It made me want to cry. If only he could get those thumbs inside that straightjacket euphemism of modesty, and slip it simply to the floor as all the rest.

Tom stood up and said, "Now me."

It was a proper giggle; it was better than the wine. Standing naked in the dark, playing Easter hunt for little pearly rounds on a smooth cotton front. The last two were down inside his belt. I had to tug his shirttails out, steam pressed from being next to him.

Without the belt the cotton trousers found the floor all on their own. Kneeling on a pile of my own clothes, I picked his feet up like a pony's and slipped away the cotton socks.

His shoes were under the kitchen table. His hips were a slender silhouetted blackness inches from my face. If he had on any briefs, I couldn't see where they began or ended.

A vertigo'd mountaineer discovers going down and going up suddenly, and equally, unfeasible. Arms around his legs I clung, cheek pressed abruptly tight to body warmth, silky skin, hot clean smell.

"Well," he said, "I thought you were going to make love to me for real this time, not just in your mind." He waited for something to happen. "It's easy. It comes with the body."

With his, maybe: not with mine.

"Problem."

"Yeah."

"What."

"I don't feel like much of a woman."

"Why not?"

"I don't much *feel* like one."

"How do you feel?"

"Like something else. Don't know."

"What."

"A mind with eyes."

"Huh," he said, hoisting me by the elbows. "Let's have a go." The go he had was extensive. "You feel like a woman to me. Well, don't you suppose I'd *know?*"

I *did* suppose. His whole front was up against my front, warm as summer and much more tangible. And I *didn't* suppose he was faking. Not exactly. Oh, if only I could wrap him all the way around, and go to sleep inside.

"You feel *exactly* like a woman. Say I'm telling you the truth. C'mon. Saying's easy."

"You're—telling me—"

"—and you taste just like my woman, and you—"

"What."

He planted his nose against me and drew in, as if he could inhale me to the bottom of his lungs. If I were inside him, he would be my outside. I'd be wearing him. My battered but beautiful coat of many colors.

"—Smell exactly—like—"

"Like."

"Like you've got the hots for me."

Ridiculously true. No room at all for disagreement. And he did have briefs, because he found my thumbs and hooked them in the waistband.

"All right. *Now* say, you're going to make love to me, because you've wanted to forever; longer than I've known you were alive. Say it."

"Can't."

"Say it."

"Can't."

Is saying easy? Is it? Is it? What I wanted, the *only* thing I wanted, was to submit to him. And now it seemed, even saying that might be impossibly difficult.

Whereas, *in reality*—it wasn't hard at all.

MONDAY, AUGUST 18

Black dark. The moon had come and gone.

He reached out, keeping one hand on my wrist, and groped a light on. Scars. Two deep grooves below the wrist, growing shallow down the outside of my arm.

"I put myself through a glass door once."

He raised a face of pure dismay.

"I call 'em my suicide scars, but it wasn't on purpose. There's a number more: it all took fifty stitches."

Dismay mellowed to relief, and relief to cunning. He switched the light off. Some time later, a finger planted on my forearm. Back on with the light.

"Uh-huh. That's one."

The little shield-shaped scar, where one long sliver stuck straight in. He eyed it silently, a marred place on his property. Lights off.

Close to morning he turned it on again; he'd found the ziggy lightning bolt scar on the heel of my right thumb and the "zipper" down the middle finger. He turned my brown hand over in the light, surveying for more damage.

"That's it," I said, "You've seen the lot."

He found the small white line that rings the outside of my little finger, from ball to nail.

"That's not one, I did that to myself the first time I saw oysters growing wild; I was prying 'em off rocks with Papa's jackknife and eating 'em on the spot, up to my knees in water and nobody anywhere around, and the knife closed up on me. I cried; I thought I'd bleed to death, but the oysters were such fine little things, I kept on prying."

That got the slow grin, and the lights out, finally.

"Hey—" he said, "We're not so very different, are we?"

Chapter 4

THE MOCKINGBIRDS DON'T COUNT; they sing all night. But aside from them, the earliest risers are the hermit thrushes. A little five-note rising, slurring phrase in the half-light—with my preoccupations, I always heard it as the first two lines of "(I can't get no) Satisfaction"—repeated endlessly, first high, then low.

Liquid. Deliberate. Mischievous. Daybreak in the woods. I decided he was set to sleep all morning.

Well, those *were* his hours. That was what he did, sleep all morning. Somebody would have to get up eventually. Get up and make coffee. In England it might arrive at his bedside on a tray. Get up and make breakfast.

In other words, get up.

I extricated with the greatest care. He was a nameless lump under the comforter. My bare feet whispered on the dusty wooden floor. I'd gotten as far as the little hall when he hit me from behind. Still quite naked, but he had the comforter with him. He popped it over my head like a sack.

Through the kitchen, the front room and the front door he

half-propelled-half-carried me, wiggling, giggling, blind inside the comforter.

· — ·

THINKING, about a campy nineteenth-century poster that used to grace the inside of my bathroom door: the scantly clad shepherd boy and coy cozy shepherdess running from the rain under the billowing protection of his cloak. I used to have a pad and pencil on a string below it for friends' captions.

Well, that's how we look, only barer: the comforter flapping and batting around our heads; and there isn't any rain; only autumn sun and we're running from it, clear across the meadow, dodging willow clumps, water spraying where we hit the marshy places.

In the aspens' golden fluttering shade, between plump boulders scattered like hospitable gray granite pillows in the green shag meadow, he spun the comforter out wide.

He spun ourselves out wide on top of it.

"You'll get it dirty!"

"So I'll buy a new one!"

Then to be quite fair, there was silence in heaven for the space of half an hour.

But eventually the old wheels began to turn, *thinking*, how similar being really beautiful was to being super rich. You get one lover dirty, finding fresh ones was trivial as new bedding. They were lined up at Tom's door. Thinking, how truly odd of providence to have put me in that queue at all: but at the *head* of it? Wondering about Harlan, how Tom had got him dirty. Hard to accept. Harlan and Tom together *were* Belshangles. Their music had been my lifeline once. But more than that—I realize he's looking at me.

"One place on you," he says, "I haven't gotten in yet—" (with some alarm, I can't imagine where). He plants a sleepy finger just between my brows. "—I mean to get in *there*."

"Maybe you just think you haven't."

"*No*, no. Oh, I can hear the action going on, like a party happening down the hall, and I wasn't invited."

Funny. My feelings about him and Harlan once. They were at a party in each other's heads; I wouldn't ever be invited. But Tom had always been the guest of honor at my mind's party, maybe the only guest. Curled with him in the comforter, below the meadow flowers, I wondered about Harlan's party, whether all the fun was over.

"Like just now," he said. "What were you thinking?"

"This moment?"

"This very moment."

"Just *now?*"

The lush and weedy meadow stood up all around, leaned above us eager to hear: fragrant white cotton balls, tiny white lace balls, ragged purple star balls, all smiling and dancing on grassy stems, bowing to each other.

"I was remembering," I said, eyes shut, "the other time when you were here. How we sat that day and talked. And finally I asked you. About Harlan—" (I choked on the name as always) "—And you gave me that long story, how you were nineteen and playing in the street for a living, and after hours in this club, and how this gorgeous person started showing up each night to listen, and got you scared he was a ghost or something you'd dreamed up from being lonely.

"And how, one night afterward he came with a guitar and played this stuff that he'd written to fancy up your pieces, and wound up coming to your room, and you gave him your bed and slept on the floor, and then he just stayed and you were sleeping on the floor, and you were ashamed to touch him.

"And then he was showing you something, playing four-handed guitar one afternoon, and he kissed you. You kissed him back, but he got scared and you had this awful fight, and wound up, and wound up—"

"Look," he said, "I *know* how we wound up; you don't have to—"

"—And you had to go downstairs and play, and when you came back the lights were off. And you were scared he'd split. But he was asleep. And you just got in with him."

No answer but the birdsong, and the wind. The bass mumble of gigantic striped bees, bending each chosen flower nearly to the ground with the weight of their attentions.

"I was wondering," I said, "what went on next morning."

"What *for?*"

Pausing to check us out for edibility, a dragonfly balanced on cellophane wings.

"Comparison's sake?"

All around, a flotilla of its kind rowed the breeze, tiny aerial pirate galleys, just above the grasses.

"God! I don't want to talk to *you* about—any more than—*Well why would you think—"*

"You started it."

"Would I know you'd be thinking about *that?"*

"Uh-huh."

"Nothing happened, anyway."

He'd turned away from me. His breathing steadied, grew long and slow. End of story, I thought. Refuge in sleep. The sky was warm and humid, full of slow clouds. It lay on the blooming meadow like a kind lover. But I was wrong.

"Well, I woke the next morning," he said to the grass, "and there was his head on my pillow with me. I was looking him in the face. I never saw a girl was half so beautiful.

"All hot and damp from his sleep. Skin like an ivory rose with dew on it. And his beard beginning to come through. Ivory with black glitter on it. To show he wasn't any girl at all. I must have lain and looked for hours.

"Then his eyes came open. It was my part to say something: he was waking up naked in my bed. I couldn't think of anything right. At last I said, 'If you were a bottle of champagne, I'd want to drink it all.'"

I managed a whisper, "Was that right?" Somebody's simple sleepy nakedness had excelled all luxuries.

"I guess it was. It must have been. He cried."

I was crying too; I wished I hadn't asked. I would want it forever now: somebody else's very great praise.

"I don't know," he said, "what happened after that. Well I

don't! What d'y'think, I have total recall or something? 'What happened after that?' We got on with the rest of our lives, that's what happened: learning to live together, learning to play the fucking instruments, learning to keep our faces fed—"

Wait! Roll over, sit up. So I'm crying, so what? So is he. I'm naked. So is he. In the middle of someone else's praise, I think I've just heard *my thing* go by.

"*Would you like your face fed?*"

I'd hit upon a very potent commonality. We'd had an almond croissant, two cups of coffee, and half a bottle of champagne each since this time yesterday. He'd taken a big breath, but no more words came out. He had tears on his cheek and a startled expression. "You mean—food?" Clearly a dim word from a distant past.

I bundled up the comforter. It wasn't really damaged. He walked in naked from the meadow as slender and gaudy and shameless as the flowers that brushed his legs.

TUESDAY, AUGUST 19

Aside from the obvious, this is how he meant to use his time. Have me drive an indicated six miles, and flag the place. Bring the car home. Put on his Walkman with one day's tape of the hundred-mile jig. Dance his twelve miles worth of music, out to the flag and back. I could jog with him or drive behind. He wanted me close, in case. He'd done the same, he said, every day of the tour that wasn't concert prep, a concert, or a travel day.

Having learned my lesson, I wondered, but didn't ask, if Harlan jogged with him. I jogged with him.

But he danced by himself, through future crowds and English afternoons. He knew that whole road in his mind: the factories, villages, grimy housing projects, the woods and heaths and desolate country places. He knew where each band was. You could see him pass from white boy's rock to black boy's reggae, and never need to hear the music.

This is what he'd learned to do: run up trees.

He'd be bopping along, and pass a big tree. A sudden acceleration toward it, he'd leap, dig his heel into the bark, take another long stride up the trunk and kick away, arching into a back flip, or straight up, rocket fashion. Far out in the road he'd make a gymnast's rebound and keep on dancing.

Usually the Walkman stayed on.

"How can you be sure of a tree in just that spot?"

"Rather sure there isn't," he shouted back. "It's a bloody village High Street. Got to do *something* for distraction." He did another splendid aerial off a fir tree. This time the Walkman parted company. He let me listen: a kids' god-awful metal band called Copper Shrift.

"Well, it works on walls if they're rough," he said. "Works on cars too, but the paint suffers."

Sometimes he carried the fiddle on his arm, and played his own tune like an old-time dancing master. When our way was through the clear-cut places, he looked, and thought, but didn't ask. I guessed he'd learned his lesson too.

After his daily miles, while I was wrestling with his supper, he sat out in the meadow lost in grass, singing and playing to himself. Then the range cattle that graze loose in the forest around Pardee would wander in, bells dinging and donging, and listen in a circle all around him.

· — ·

DISCOVERIES.

Submitting was *not*, in fact, the only thing I could do to him. There was a seemingly limitless number of other things, and he vastly enjoyed almost all of them.

Everything I was taught in school, almost everything my peers whispered, almost (but not quite) everything I ever fantasized concerning sex was wrong. Almost (but not quite) everything I'd gathered off Tom's records was real.

The books in that much-hyped sex-ed class said, "If you don't enjoy it the first time: don't worry dear, You're *normal*." If you looked in the back of those books, you found they were funded and published by the companies that make sanitary napkins. Sex takes a little stretching out, but so does any other brand of athletics. And I haven't coveted normalcy since the third grade.

Sex is not mind blowing. We are talking natural function

here, pleasant. Pleasant like fine food and long unhurried sleep. Tom was just a very natural, bodily person.

He did it in bed.

He did it in the barn.

He did it in the bathtub.

He did it in the living room.

He did it in the car.

He did it in the meadow.

He did it behind trees.

He did it on top of huge, sunny boulders.

He did it in the road (as in the song, no one watching).

He did it on sleek granite just above the foaming, ice-green runs of Bright's Creek. And some people came out on the rocky bluff above us. Well, he'd promised me public procreation; why be surprised to find him good as his word? Like: Land of Many Uses! Enjoy your National Forest! And you don't need spark arresters. I think they went away.

He tried doing it in the creek. That was too cold for even him to get it up. So we dried off, severally danced and jogged the miles back home to Pardee, and started over in the bed. We were each other's sweet amusement park: we went on all the rides.

Thought: if he goes on so enthusiastically fitting him and his into me and mine, in the end I might contain him all. I would be his outside then, his garment, his cloak of invisibility.

One kind of little birds in Pardee meadow: the male is gaudy and bright orange, and he sings from the tips of willows. The female doesn't sing a note. What's more, she's brown. She watches. But inside their little bodies is one flesh and bone. Their desire is for each other.

WEDNESDAY, AUGUST 20
Tom's birthday.

As the apple tree among the trees of the wood,
so is my beloved among the sons.
I sat down under his shadow with great delight,
and his fruit was sweet to my taste

He brought me to the banqueting house,
and his banner over me was love—

(Thus far the Song of Songs.)

THURSDAY, AUGUST 21

Learning was about the shape of it: to live together, to play the instruments, to keep our faces fed. Shyly going through each other's stuff. His suitcase said a lot about him. The clothes were neat, even the well-worn ones, as things bought new from the store.

The man lived in a pair of Levi's. I never would have guessed. Split across the knees seam to seam, and across both thighs in back. I remember sexy shameless guys at school who used to wear the butt-split jeans. You'd see the pockets hanging down inside, never any underwear. That's why they did it, so you'd sit and puzzle if they wore any. Always that nice expanse of sinewy male thigh, discreetly furry. Tom had very little body hair, but the back of his thigh was a downy Hawaiian sunset. And the rips were just right for a lover's hand to slide in when he kissed them. Didn't he know.

But the Levis were clean to the point of sterile. So were the two pair of super-expensive marathoner's shoes he alternated for his jig, the white briefs, white socks, white cotton sweats, and white Lycra running tights.

Under the clothes was the music for the hundred-mile jig. Eighteen tapes, two a day: three songs from each band, one for his approach, which they'd play until cued that he'd come in range, then the song he'd chosen for his pass-by, and a third for his retreat. I listened to nearly half. Some were famous bands (as he said), some splendid songs I'd known for years. And some were just sweet kids, earnestly awful.

Underneath the music were the pillboxes. A rainbow of pills: red, blue, yellow, green. Clear gold gelatin footballs, two-tones, lots of different whites. No way to tell what any one was for, parceled out in daily dose containers.

What could they all be? Health supplements, vitamins, that kind of thing? Stuff to keep him off drugs? Medications? Was he sick and lying to me? He was dosing himself up like a heart transplant.

Maybe they *were* drugs, and he was lying to me. One item in the neat utility of his suitcase, a flat white plastic jug, still wore its prescription under tape. Three pieces of significant info: the name of a London chemist, Tom's name, and PABA. He caught me looking.

"Came back the time before all-over freckles. Old Harlan didn't like that." I got the quick apologetic bob that went with Harlan's name. Getting quicker (and less apologetic) every time. "Well, I can't take the sun. Back when we were playing in the street, I'd go all red. He made me get this stuff. Never gone without it since, except for that one time." Now it was the old shy-grin-and-flaming-blush trick. It made my heart swell up and pop, as ever.

"Prescription sunscreen?"

"Unscented."

"You don't like perfume?"

(My observation: most men don't. It's the women who mythologize their body parts with perfume; and guys at best ignore the stuff. At worst they're like Papa, who'll come into some perfumed presence with an enormous rhino sniff, and the query, *"What stinks?"*)

Tom said, "Like to choose the ones I live with, anyway."

His shampoo was a botanical with hardly any scent. His soap was Turkish: it smelled like sunny green-gold virgin olive oil in the bath, and on his skin like nothing.

But the sunscreen made fascinating business. He wanted it frequently, all over ("Sun comes through cloth, y'know,"), and he wanted help smoothing it on. Helping him was risky.

Times were, we never made it out into the sun at all.

It occurred to me to wonder whether Harlan wore it too.

FRIDAY, AUGUST 22

He hadn't ever said how long he meant to stay. A week would give us till next Monday. I'd hoped somehow it might be forever. But he began to look restless.

"What else is around here?"

"Just more of the same."

He wasn't a big eater, that's for sure. Most of the steak stayed frozen. Some of the salad drooped. What he did like: fried egg sandwiches with bacon and lots of Dijon mustard. He also drank me out of milk. The closest place to buy more was the "lodge," at the far side of the dam.

I took him to the lodge. Dusty little place: flat spots for trailers, a boat launch, and a log cabin store with flush toilets, video games, a telephone, a coin-op laundry, and a hair salon. All the domestic female-type comforts.

Some weekends in summer, a local western band gigs on the front steps. Izzy and me and friends would have fished and gone swimming on our side of the lake. When evening fell and the bats came out, we'd float the dark waters in a rubber boat and listen to the night-music, the whump-bumpa thumpa-bump electric bass and twangy country voices drifting over from the lodge.

· — ·

ALWAYS lots of kids around the lodge.

Tom stood at the counter with my eggs and milk; the girls behind him had a raft of diet sodas. The woman rang Tom up; he handed her a hundred-dollar bill.

"Nothing smaller than this on ya?"

"Not that I go flashing around."

It was the *way* he said it. One six-pack of sodas hit the floor. Tom got his wad of change, and turned. Girls ringed him, silent as a pack of wolves. Tank tops and tube tops, French cut T-shirts saying, "Where the hell is Panther Creek Reservoir?" Wide open mouths, wide open eyes. Levis and feathered hair. Another six-pack dropped.

He didn't quite run, just a long flat lope. I ran. I barely cleared the door ahead of them; he was at the car. Now I had it started. They were massed outside his window.

I banged it into reverse. *"Lock your door!"* I flung it backwards, past their toes. *"Roll up your window!"* I saw the mischief flash across his face, and thought about fireworks on a summer night. He rolled his window down.

"Actually," he said, "I'm not a thing like him."

I could see them in the rear-view mirror, pelting along in our dust till I turned the bend onto the dam.

He was silent for the rest of the ride.

I switched it off. We sat there in the car, at the top of the path that leads down to the cabin, as close as you can get and miss the sand.

"Sorry," he said.

"Don't need to be."

"Try to understand, your place here means health to me. There've been some black times when it was all the health I could remember. I wanted to come back; see that I hadn't imagined it." I looked at him sitting there. He was still holding the eggs and milk. "It's just that, like—this—" he indicated Pardee Camp, meadow, cabin, barn, with one long finger, "—would be your fancy private clinic. But I'm half well. Patient can't take the clinic home with him."

"Ah, vhat you vant, Herr Rhymer, is outpatient health."

He giggled in spite of himself. "Let me tell you," he said, "about Real Life. Place I quite dread to take you. One hotel room's like another if you keep the shade drawn. Dressing rooms are all alike. Same things go on in the back of this limo as did in the last one. And the airplanes, and the stages, they all look alike. The kids all look alike. Those girls back there are a big part of my life. I knew them faster than they knew me. And if I'm to make *you* part of my life, I must go home, and fit you in among the other pieces." He shook his head sadly. "Y'know, it's not going to be easy."

"I didn't think it would."

"If you want me—" he said.

"I want you."

"—Please take me home."

"Okay."

He grinned at me. "Amador County."

"Right."

"I do remember some things."

"Yeah."

So we did it in the front seat of the bus.

· — ·

AMAZING how "unlike" a treasure in the hand can look from one approaching, a kind of psychological Doppler Shift. Imagine being on a quest, a lifetime struggle, years and years, to reach that pinnacle where Dulcinea holds the magic treasure, the Grail of Love—whatever—in keeping.

And you make it. Sure enough you do. But when you get there, Dulcinea is changed before your eyes into a sweet human lover stuck on his own unlikely quest. That pinnacle was a slight rise in the ground. Its only treasure is this view: another wide, empty valley, and the real heights dimly visible beyond. On the road again. Moving right along. Only this time, Dulcinea's going with me.

· — ·

HIGHWAY 88. Waterloo. The cheapo gas station got torn down a year ago, and with it the Holy Phone Booth where Tom once called to see if Harlan was alive. An incredibly garish McDonald's stands in its place.

The new phone hangs in a little plastic hood outside; no privacy of any kind. Tom had his arms around me; we could feel my heart hammering. It's my call this time.

Mama answered.

"Hey."

Silence.

"Andy?"

"That's my name."

"Are you all right?"

"Relax. I'll be right home."

"Wait. Before you say anything, listen."

"Okay."

"Your father has ideas that are—what's the word—"

"Set-in-cement?"

Tom choked quietly.

"—About certain things: such as liability—"

"Okay," I said. "Go on."

"As soon as you left, it occurred to him, if you were taking a girlfriend on a long drive, you'd probably share the driving—" (It would never have occurred to me. I love to drive; I hate to ride. I fear for my life. I also get carsick.) "*So*, to make it short, he called Sam Lyttle—" (Be advised: that splattering sound you hear is, without a doubt, the shit hitting the fan.) "—You'll be relieved to know, Kaye's lavishly insured whatever she drives, their car, our car. She's also a summer assistant at a free vet's clinic in Cabo San Lucas."

"Now *you* just wait; don't jump to conclusions—"

Click. The other extension coming off the hook.

"Hello?"

I felt Tom stir against me.

"Listen, Papa, I'm not in any trouble."

"Doesn't sound too likely. Why don't you start at the beginning?" About that time Ma Bell required more money for her services. Papa said "Operator? Can you switch this to a collect call?" They dickered for a while. I took the simplest out, hung up and called him back collect. "Never mind the beginning. Start anywhere."

"I have been to the cabin."

"Okay."

"I've also been to Nevada and gotten married."

A long silence. Tom listened intently. I could fairly plot Papa's mental course past all the teenage guys I'd ever brought home to the family table for inspection. Most unlikely, any of 'em. Some of 'em downright bizarre.

Finally he said, "Anyone we know?"

"Tommi Rhymer."

"This is no joke!"

"I'm not joking! You were always the one who told me to 'form my own conscience' and 'keep my own counsel.' Well this is what you get! A close-mouthed self-directed kid!"

Gently, Tom removed the phone from my hand. "Professor Falconer, sir. Tom Rhymer here." Minutes buzzed by like cars on the highway. "I don't know about that," he said. "She could hardly mount my head for a trophy on her wall, could she, if she'd enlisted your aid bagging it. Well, yeah. Not sporting. You got it." He listened.

"Three problems? Which three, sir? Aside from what you call your 'credibility factor,' which our arriving there in person should—"

"But I do. Sunday's our flight to London. We're to be married at Westminster Cathedral, that's the Roman Cathedral of London—Ah, you know—Saturday, September 27 at 11:00 in the morning—"

Wait a minute. What if I'd never showed up at his hotel? So what if I hadn't asked him to get married? Was he going to ask me? What if I'd *said no?*

"Oh *God,*" he said suddenly. "What is this? How many hours? Eight? Eight *weeks*? Marriage Preparation Seminar. From the Diocese of San Jose. Approval of the bride's diocese. God. Well, what are my options?" He listened.

"*Outside* of joining another church. Now wait, Professor Falconer, they *don't* want the likes of me in their little public classes. I assure you they don't. Isn't there some way y'could explain the matter?" He listened. "I would be most everlastingly grateful. Now you spoke of a third—"

He listened, and silently handed me the phone.

Papa said, "Unless you've been a whole lot swifter than I know, you don't have a passport."

" ."

"All right, granted, you've obviously been swifter than I know, but *do you have a passport?*"

" ."

"You can get one in 24 hours, that includes weekends, *I think,* if you demonstrate need. But the passport office is in San Francisco, the foot of Market, Market and Second, something like that. They're open weekdays, nine to five."

"Yeah."

"This means they *close* at five o'clock."

"Yeah."

"They open again at nine o'clock, *Monday morning.*"

"In other words, I'm not going to London Sunday unless I get my ass in gear."

"You got it. I trust we'll be seeing you soon."

"Very."

"'Bye."

"'Bye."

We climbed back into the car. As we were hurtling around the cloverleaf to southbound 99 he said, "Some family."

"Yeah. Mine."

· —— ·

MY stomach writhed sourly and sickeningly upward, arriving, a dead-heat photo finish with the elevator, on the thirty-second floor.

Gotta lie down. Gonna be sick if I don't lie down. Tom's understanding was perfect. He ran me down the empty hall (no guards), had a key in his hand before we reached the door, rushed and cuddled me across the room (nobody there) into a dim bedroom and a clean fresh enormous hotel bed.

"Aspirin."

"Right."

· —— ·

I DROVE and drove and drove, seventy-five in the fast lane, eyes fried by the sun, switching lanes, wriggling between enormous trucks, failure pop-riveted to the back of my neck. Three thirty. Three forty-five. Four o'clock. Four fifteen. A lane closed somewhere up ahead. Crawling traffic, Smog, sun, exhaustion. The VW thumped like a cripple over buckled pavement. Four-thirty. Four forty-five. Four-fifty.

"Vitamin C. Tums."

"What?"

"Antacid."

"Afraid I haven't any."

"In my purse. Decongestant—sinus pills—pink jobs in foil. In the purse. Two of each. Water."

"Right."

Four fifty-five. The first signs for the Bay Bridge toll plaza. Five o'clock. Five after five. Five ten.

He brought it all. I sat up long enough to gulp and swallow. My eyes squirmed in my head.

· — ·

SOMEBODY said, *"I got tickets to Bora Bora!"*

Altogether weird: unattached to anything. I felt around for Tom; no Tom. And the dimness of the room wasn't thick drapes anymore; it was night.

"Well y'can bloody cancel 'em!"

That was Tom. The bedroom was dark but the door was open; light and noise wandered from the living room. Assessment of my condition. Meds have done the best they can. All I need now is the front of Tom's shirt, and it is involved in a fight down the hall.

"I'm takin' a guest!" That was the man with tickets.

"Bugger your guest!"

"He intends to, love," said somebody else, "in a little grass shack on the beach in Bora Bora."

A thud, knuckles on flesh. And a woman's voice, really screaming: "Tom, she's got a *family*, for God's sake—"

Tom, screaming back, "*—First-time married for less than a week, and you're asking me to pack her back to mother, is that what y'want?"*

She could yell right along with him. "What about *us*? How long did it take us to get the boys into that school? You think they'll hold a place for trampy music-gypsies' kids if we don't show? They've got a waiting list as long as—"

"—She is going to stay *here* at this fucking hotel, on my fucking money, and one or more of you are *fucking staying with her!"*

There was a lull. Somebody else said, "Well you got pussy-whipped in a hurry, didn't you?"

All hell broke loose. A good heavy crash, breaking glass, a

lot of swearing and demands that various people cut out various activities.

I loved Tom. I loved his band. I didn't know if they fought all the time, but fighting over me was bottom-line unacceptable. God help me. I got to the bedroom door. I got to the end of the hall. Tom was straddling a hassock on one side of the room, everybody else was on the other.

I couldn't bear to see him like that: slight and lost, no breeding, no education, off his balance, past his youth, and down to his fists as a last defense. I liked the man he was. I wanted to cover him, comfort him, give him back his glamour and his airs. He needed them and so did I.

I stumbled toward him, head thumping like a drum machine, over the furniture and people's feet, found the front of his shirt, and burrowed into it. If I was really flesh of his flesh, he could button his jacket over me and nobody would notice. Better than "seen and not heard"; not heard and not seen either. He wrapped his arms around me.

Somebody said, "I'll stay with her."

Silence. God. Maybe everyone was staring at me. Tommi Rhymer's married this unknown chick, and there's an enormous row, and she comes staggering out with a blind headache, looking like a refugee and curls up on his front.

"What?"

"I said I'd stay with her."

Real silence. Total. Tom's heart beating, nothing else.

I must be going back to sleep. Perhaps I'd never waked. His shirtfront smelled like cold sweat and other people's cigarettes. This was a lousy dream. A wash and bed was what he needed. I was supposed to be his medicine, not part of the sickness. Medicine needs its eyes open. I opened my eyes.

Tom (like nearly all the rest) was staring, not at me, but at an arm, a neat white sleeve, and a hand raised, orderly schoolboy fashion, on the far side of the room.

"You were going home with me," said Tom.

"Why?" The hand was Harlan Parr's. "I've nothing at all to do with the planning for your jig, until we play you off the steps at

Norwich City Hall three weeks from tomorrow. I can play any set you want on twenty minutes' call."

"You really mean it?"

"Of course." Harlan sat up out of the couch. "My pleasure." He took his shades off and stuck them into a pocket. "I'll catch up on my writing."

A warm spot started under my nose, in the middle of Tom's shirt. I felt it grow and grow, routing the fear smells and exhaustion smells, till it filled his chest and flooded down his arms. "Thanks, old man." He said it so softly, I could barely hear him.

Sudden cheers. Hampers of turkey sandwiches had made the scene from room service. I ate half of one and nearly heaved. Tom ate my other half. People *ooh*ed and *aah*ed over me. I heard a lot of names and remembered few. The woman with kids was the tall blonde in the "Love is Blind" shirt. Not a groupie after all, but Shan McInery, Rollo's wife of ten years. Sim Garfein had the tickets to Bora Bora. Nicki Cavanaugh had a fat lip where Tom slugged him one. He was filling his face with sandwiches and beer, perfectly placid. Everybody's problem seemed to have blown away except mine.

My last sight of the tribe, as Tom led his dried tears and my green flourishing headache off to bath and bed: Rollo McInery cackling and elbowing Harlan in the ribs. Harlan, grinning, elbowed back.

SATURDAY, AUGUST 23

The Diocese of San Jose did *not* want Tommi Rhymer in its Marriage Preparation Seminar. Papa explained it to them all right. Scared to know just what he said, I didn't ask. Things seemed to be out of my hands.

After noon, Tom had me climb back into the old VW and drive him south. He slid his nice warm hand between my leg and the seat. I wore the white cotton knit mini. Most of the cabin floor had shaken off it. The rest of the band and hangers-on followed, pulling onto the shady rear of the Stanford campus, filling the end of Salvatierra Street, a royal progress in three limousines.

My brother opened the door. My brother weighs all of fifty

pounds. Opening the door and coming face to face with Tommi Rhymer, and being always one for subtlety, he hollered, *"Chee-ee-eez Lou-ee-ze!"* and ran.

Papa's turn. Papa is a well-built man; he was stocky facing Tom. Stocky and speechless. His glasses mirrored. His beard stuck out. Who Tom was was so unquestionable, I felt with a pang, my own identity might be the only thing in doubt. At last he shook his head.

"I don't know what I could possibly say."

Tom gave him the shy, sideways grin. His red hair fell in his eyes. "'Well *hello*, son,' might cover it."

He was in like a burglar.

Mama was too dressed up, and was running around making too much food. All he had to do was hug her.

Izzy was there too, my sister Isabel the pre-vet major, all sun-bleached, freckled, and strong-armed from wrestling stud horses around the vet school barns at Davis.

And Russell of course, her Aggie boyfriend, the rancher's kid from Likely, California, who says almost nothing and sees almost everything with quick brown eyes. Those two are into 'fifties movies, and *le Jazz Hot*.

And Skye Milligan. Where the carrion is, there will the eagles be gathered. Still *bitter as hell* she had to help me kidnap Tommi Rhymer, and worse yet, had to keep her mouth shut afterwards. She's taking feminist journalism or equivalent at Mills, dressing for success, and is, at present, a Laurie Anderson fanatic.

I'm the only one who's stayed where I was. Same place. Arrested development. In love with the same frayed and torn man and his sweet loud music since I was twelve.

The house is full, the yard is full, I'm wandering around. The dining room. Papa's talking to Tom. "—Got *somebody*, Monsignor Shanty Irish, on the phone: he said what the Diocese usually counsels, you know, where the kids have run off and had a civil ceremony, is that they wait a year before they even consider marriage in the Church—"

"Meaning," says Tom slowly, "if it's a bad business they can still get out of it?"

"Affirmative. Garbage in, garbage out."

"This is the *Roman* Diocese?"

"Affirmative."

"God. And what'd y'say to that?"

My room. Mama's in there, looking with new eyes. "Okay," I said. "All right, the signatures on the posters and photos are all real, done in pen, take a look. That red fly swish thing on the wall behind the door, with the end bound in silk thread and sealing wax? When Tom cut the long part of his hair for *Drake*, I was where he sent it—"

She said: "Why couldn't you have told us?"

When she was halfway down the hall I said, "I guess because, if I'd been you, I'd never have let me do it—"

I've got no place to land in my own house, doomed to keep moving, like the Flying Dutchman.

Papa still. "—Every other rock personality I read of getting married makes this spectacle of bashing cameras, shouting *'I am a very private person!'* You seem to be operating in a different mode—"

Tom grinned at him. "Ever seen those T-shirts that say 'Life's *not* a cabaret—'"

So they were getting along. Wasn't that all I *wanted*?

"Right. '—It's a fucking circus.'"

I moved on fast, but Tom's voice carried: "You're looking at the Singing Ringmaster. If there's any part of me is private, it's so private that I haven't found it yet."

He was lying. There was always the thing he didn't mention, Tommi Rhymer was a fictional address. Of course it wasn't private, nobody really lived there. Tom's heart beat invulnerable in Harlan's chest, a private place indeed.

I went out into the yard.

Izzy's holding forth on horse breeding, as usual, and ignores me: "—Nobody wants their million-dollar stud all gashed up by some twitchy filly, so they've got these, like, sex surrogate stallions they call 'teasers.' Can be anything, pony studs are hornier 'n hell, and they cut 'em some way so they can't *do* anything really, but not enough so they won't be sexy, and let them work the fillies over till they get all warm and runny; *then* they bring the real stud in, and his job's easy."

Skye says "Hey, I know some real studs use rock singers for the same thing." They all three pulled these big, wry "*OhmyGod* I didn'*say that*" faces.

I just walked away. It occurs to me for the first time, looking at them, lined up shoulder to shoulder on the wall under the pear tree: I may very well have done the unpardonable. I've made fantasy flesh, and dwelt among it. A voice of pure fantasy rises in song from the kitchen. Rude as old stone, sinuous as wind across the hillside.

A sailor courted
a farmer's daughter
Who lived contagious
to the Isle of Mann,
Wi' warblin' melodies he
did besought her
To marry him
before she should marryanyothersortofaman!

That brings a whoop of raw delight from Mama: a scholar's infatuation for a newfound species. Well I *wanted* her to be delighted, didn't I? She has a doctorate in the legendary ballads of the British Isles. Tom's grandfather was a famous singer; the name of Thomas Rhymer figures in her sources more than once.

I round the corner. Tom's sitting at her table, eyes closed, hand cupped behind his ear, a spirit medium giving substance to a dead man's voice.

The farmer's daughter
had grand possessions,
a silver teapot
an' two-pound-ten in gold—

Harlan was there too, competent and witty in the kitchen, quietly helping Mama with the coffee, the white wine, the little quiches, little meatballs, lemonade, and cookies—I wanted to rush in shrieking, "*No!* Don't let him! He's contaminated!" which wasn't true, and, "How does *he* get off being so damn domestic?" which wasn't kind, and left holding a lemonade instead.

Some colleague had given Papa this set of tumblers with the Seven Deadly Sins etched on in Churchy Gothic letters. Cute. Only old sins come in sets of seven; glassware comes in eights. We were wondering, as he unwrapped, what minor vice they'd elevated to the list with *Pride, Lust, Envy* etc. It was the one I've got, *VIII: Choosing the Wrong Side.*

My all-time favorite.

The garage. Papa's out there now, enlightening the McInerys about the lack of rust on California vehicles. "—This is where your British collectors come to buy old British cars—" Somebody's under the gray Porsche on the mechanic's creeper, making first-hand acquaintance of its rust-free pan. I recognized the shoes and left. Harlan is a black magician. Harlan has the power of bilocation. Harlan is all over my house, like a swarm of bees.

I put on my own running shoes. Nobody saw me go. I jogged the whole circuit of Campus Drive in the hot still Saturday afternoon. Quail in the thickets by the Stanford tomb. Lovers on the grass. Oak moths fluttering. Girls playing radios. Guys playing Frisbee. I didn't get home until the limousines were leaving.

Only Tom remained, with his sterile little suitcase, slender and battered as he was. Papa put Tom in his old Porsche—before he could shut the door I jumped in like a dog—and drove him out where Redwood Priory perches secretively on a canyon side among the dark trunks of its namesakes. I huddled against Tom's seat back, arms around his shoulders, indulging myself while I could. He held my hands down warm against his chest.

Father Malachi taught me catechism. He's agreed to spend twenty-four hours with Tom and vouch we've both had marriage preparation. Irregular. But acceptable.

Father Malachi is a Hungarian refugee. Papa defines a Hungarian as a man who goes in the revolving door behind you and comes out ahead. All the older monks at Redwood are revolving-door Hungarians. Father Malachi's taught boys all his life. I've suspected sometimes that he thought I was one, and that was why we got along. He also counseled at Juvy Hall. I was never able to shock him.

Up till now.

What about now?

SUNDAY, AUGUST 24

Ring. That's how it would start, the late-night phone call. Not Tom, not Father 'Chi, not for me. The Prior. For Papa. "We cannot sign this paper; we will not be made accessory; we see *impediments* to this marriage." A term I never contemplated, embedded now in one of my more painful sectors like a broadhead arrow.

Morning.

The last thing Papa said when he put Tom out of the car was, "You might take a look at those guys' chapel floor; there's a crack you can put your foot in, and the whole back end is sliding down the gully."

"Right," said Tom.

My own father.

On the way home he said "How long is it since he's been to church?" Twenty years, maybe. "You know they'll ask him for a lifetime confession."

Maybe the Priory's phones are down. Temptation to ring out there myself, hang up if anyone answers. So I'll know. Some younger monk drove in to sing the High Mass at Saint Ann's. In place of Father 'Chi. He wasn't very good at it.

> *Try to come in through the narrow door. Many, I tell you, will try to enter and be unable. When once the master of the house has risen to lock the door and you stand outside knocking and saying, 'Sir, open for us,' he will say in reply, 'I do not know where you come from.' This is the Gospel of the Lord.*

Home at one o'clock, I locked my own door, pulled the covers up, prayed sad prayers (my passport), and dreamed bad dreams (Tom's lifetime confession: I pictured it about the size of the Congressional Record) until seven o'clock. As our usual crew was showing up for Sunday dinner, Tom's empty rented limo came.

I rode out to Redwood in it. Father 'Chi was waiting on the steps below the monastery, in the green shadow. He has this whinnying laugh, the greeting of a friendly horse. "Your husband has told me much about you that I do not know—He is a very beautiful young man." That's all. He started back up to get him.

I called after him, "You don't think he's too old for me?" and meant something much scarier than that.

"Maybe you're too old for him! He is like your posters, yes?"

Surprise, surprise. What could Tom possibly have told him? What did he tell him about Harlan? Certainly not the stuff he's dragged out of his heart with me.

Or?

Maybe it isn't so bizarre a situation; maybe half the guys Father 'Chi comforted all those years at Juvy Hall were just like Tom inside. Just not as pretty outside. The griefs were all the same; only the gifts were different. And nobody paid anybody off, there were no hypocrites and liars, the truth itself was not unmentionable, and the priest had heard it all and worse a hundred times. The Church could love Tom as he stood. Maybe.

There is Tom, talking to Father 'Chi. Suddenly I see him kneel on the gravel walk and hide his face against the old priest's habit. How easy it would be to laugh and turn away. Who kneels to anybody, after all, these days?

But Father motions, so I run up the stairs instead and kneel beside him, embarrassment suspended in a cool black woolen evening. Father put one skeletal fine brown hand on Tom's red head and one on mine and blessed us—with all the real old stuff too, my being like vines on the sides of his house and his seeing his children's children to the third generation—until both of us cried.

The Church is a clone to the Federal Government in so

many ways, you really have to think the Holy Spirit bears with it as advertised, or, like Papa says, the whole mess should have crashed and burned a thousand years ago. The Church has said an awful lot of stuff beside its prayers.

But how to image that indwelling? Is it, as they'd like you to suppose, hard-ass human folly at the bottom, and a trickle down of Spirit? Spiritual Reaganomics?

Or insidious Spirit infesting high and low, subtle as a virus spliced into the gene code of its host? Surviving in the same illusive habitat the Psalmist says His Mercy does, "—from generation to generation of those who fear Him?"

Undetectable, indestructible, incorrigible Mercy.

Thank God I'm never likely to know everything.

· — ·

KNOWING more might be a help sometimes.

Sight isn't always hooked to understanding.

Airport security blocked off a waiting area for Belshangles. We were in it. Tom had been kissing me goodbye, peaceful, as if no one else existed in the world and well in advance so his public would be sure to notice. No great mob of fans beyond the barriers, but the favored few had cameras. I asked him if he wanted to do it in the middle of the airport concourse. He whispered "Better house at Heathrow."

Tom left me and went to Harlan by the windows. The plane flashed in the dark outside. The interminable fuel and luggage was all on. Tom said something to him, ashamed, I thought, apologetic. For what? Saddling him with me?

Harlan's reply was steady-eyed and much too glib.

I saw Tom wince. Fear moved in like San Francisco fog. I hadn't wanted to stay with Harlan when he and Tom were on the best of terms. Tom tried again. Harlan glanced carefully both ways along the concourse, and made one brief suggestion.

I thought Tom was going to hit him.

Instead he wheeled off, angry, nervous, striding up and down. Harlan at his elbow matching words as quiet as shared thoughts, shared hurt that clings like acid in the face, and if you try to wipe it, transfers to your hands and burns in two places. A movie camera might have caught the body language. Still snapshots would only show their smooth, hard public faces. That pair could die in public and make it pass for part of the act.

Tom left him and kissed me again. I felt, rather than saw, a percussion accompaniment of flashbulbs. Then an airline person came, wings on uniformed chest, to usher Belshangles onboard discreetly, even before the handicapped and travelers with small children.

Another detained Harlan, murmured, "This way, please." Taking my elbow, she steered us down the gray metal, gray plastic, gray indoor-outdoor carpet ramp after the rest. Wild surmise for a moment. We were going too. Fame and money could buy anything.

We reached the curved door of the plane. I could see into the First Class, see Tom at the far end laughing with Nicki. But there beside us was another door, and a metal stairway down to asphalt, flashing lights, diesel stink, and screaming turbine roar. We picked our way down, leaning on wet wind. A ground level door took us back through baggage areas, straight to the escalators for the parking lot.

No fans followed. We hiked the length of the indoor parking. Harlan had a rented car, a blue Nissan Sentra, as are all rented cars. It wouldn't start. He popped its hood, swearing with quiet interest in what, from total otherness, I fancied must be Arabic.

I watched his coattails and narrow little rear. The rest of him was under the hood. How tempting. Up with his silly Italian shoes, pitch him into the engine, and slam the hood. And run. Yeah.

He convinced the rent-a-Sentra with regrettable ease. His hobby was sports car racing, after all. We drove from airport garage to hotel garage in silence, rode the freight elevator in silence, walked to the suite and our separate rooms in silence. I recognized the landscape: what Tom called "Real Life." Only Tom wasn't in it. There was fresh cold hotel linen on the bed. It didn't smell like Tom's love anymore.

Chapter 5

MONDAY, AUGUST 25. 9:00 A.M.

A MARITIME SUN sheds salty light and little warmth, while wind and trash and seagulls whip around the corners. It makes a body feel like running, but we walk, half a mile down Second from the rented car (parked under a Bay Bridge on-ramp), to the corner of Market and *the building*, great gaunt futuristic overwhelmer, stainless steel, black tile, glass as black as Darth Vader's goggles: a sci-fi locale for social injustice. Things get marginally more humane above the escalators.

There is a photo place; we pass it. I already have mine.

School pics were handy for turning into manifestos, about the only fun I ever saw in the whole exercise. For senior yearbook all the rah-rahs hire their own photographers to take these glamour shots. So I went to the school hack with the rest of the guys, wearing one of Papa's shirts, loose tie, big hair and a truculent expression, like some lanky little deathrock person dressed up too civilly for his convictions. Not very satisfactory at the time; it turned out much too normal. Just (in fact) like a passport photo.

But imagine our entrance now, Harlan in his tweeds, hair neatly minimized, me in my black Levi's, black Nikes, and dead-black Pendleton with the holey elbows, into that office: into a compacted jam of third-world bodies, a winding queue, a human Wall of China, confined by vinyl ropes on weighted stainless stands. At the tail of the dragon, a pushy red-lozenge sign demands, ENTER HERE. Another reads,

> U.S. PASSPORT FEES:
> ALL MINORS UNDER 18 MUST USE
> DSP 11. FEE IS $27.
> 15 YEAR VALIDITY.
> ALL ADULTS USING DSP 11
> FEE IS $42. 10 YEAR VALIDITY.
> ADULTS QUALIFIED TO USE
> DSP 82, FEE IS $35.

So I fill out my DSP 11, growing aware meanwhile of certain stock dialogues happening at the head of the line:

"Do you have a departure date in mind, sir?"

"Oh, I don't know yet, how long does it take?"

"Two to three weeks—"

"Are you *sure* you don't have a certified copy? How about your parents? This was Xeroxed from a certified original, I can see the seal—"

"Do I sign this?"

"No, you sign in front of an agent. Have a seat."

"How long is the wait?"

"I'd say about forty minutes—"

"Where is the original of this, from Florida?"

"That's it. That's all they send you."

"When were you leaving?"

"Friday!"

"The agent on the other side will probably request you get it certified—"

"Okay, your passport should come to you in the mail in about four weeks."

"I'll send you over to the agents to see if they'll accept this for identity. Take a seat, please. You are number ninety-four."

I am not a number. I am a free man.

Above the agents' desk, on the far side of the room, an electric sign shows the number being served: 28. While I'm looking, it lets out a buzz, and goes to 29. Buzz, 30.

Harlan doesn't have to stand through this whole line with me. I don't plan to need his services; I can fill in blanks as well as anybody. He is doing it anyway. Outside the plate glass is a view of canyon streets: parking garage signs, double-parked delivery vans, jointed buses crawling centipede-like between them. The street sign I can see says, BATTERY. DO NOT ENTER. So the one I can't reads, MARKET. What fun if it said ASSAULT, instead, and this was the corner of Assault and Battery? At the end of Battery a mid-air segment of Embarcadero Freeway cuts across blue sky. More wind, more seagulls, San Francisco Bay.

The two ahead of me have reached the counter now, a dark Hispanic type in turquoise rings, and a very tall girl, skin as pretty as *café au lait*.

DARK MAN: "I have lost my naturalization papers."

MAN BEHIND COUNTER TO TALL GIRL: "This birth certificate is not valid."

WOMAN BEHIND COUNTER TO DARK MAN: "Where were you naturalized?"

TALL GIRL: "It's the only one I have!"

DARK MAN: "Here, in San Francisco."

MAN BEHIND COUNTER: "This is a Xerox copy, it isn't certified."

WOMAN BEHIND COUNTER: "Go to the District Court on such-and-such street, floor such-and-such, obtain a certified copy of your naturalization records, bring it with two photographs—"

TALL GIRL (now wailing): *"It's the only one I have!"*

WOMAN B.C.: "Next, please." (That's me.)

MAN B.C.: "Then you must *obtain* a certified copy—"

I hand the woman my DSP 11, driver's license, and birth certificate, familiar items from all those years I had to prove my age at track meets. I fingered the Santa Clara County seal chomped into it to show that it was certified.

TALL GIRL: *"I haven't a faintest idea how to do that!"*

WOMAN B.C.: "Is this your identification? Your form is filled out in a different name."

"I was married last week."

WOMAN B.C.: "Then we'll need a certified copy of your marriage certificate."

"My husband has the only copy, he's a British citizen, he's in London; I'm trying to join him—"

WOMAN B.C.: Then you must obtain a certified copy. Were you married in the State of California?"

And I stand there, remembering Tom's hurt at little things, remembering, through a haze of sleep, the endless time it took the wedding chapel woman to write out that certificate, "The Pretty One" she'd called it (from the minute bit of gold illumination): "Now *this* one isn't certified," she said, "It has to be filed and recorded, and they won't be open till Monday, then your official copy will be mailed to you, it may take as long as twelve weeks—"

Tom's mailing address was London.

HARLAN: "Pardon me, but Mrs. Rhymer's husband is my business partner. Would my statement under oath—"

WOMAN B.C.: That might be allowable under certain requirements: you must be an American citizen, of legal age, and present at the event witnessed. Of course (back to me), you can always make the application in your maiden name. Is time important?"

· —— ·

I WROTE my letter to Carson City on hotel stationery and mailed it from the lobby. Harlan had nothing, nothing, nothing to say. Upstairs he traded his tweeds for jeans and a turtleneck, and selecting a guitar from a corner of the strangely lifeless living room, sat down to play.

So, I'd been put to the test when I hadn't expected it; and, like your ordinary teenage dumb-ass, I'd fucked up. I glowered at his self-absorbed and unresponsive back in blind frustration. Directionless fury. Directed fury.

What an uncompromising little back, slender and muscular as an otter's, a likeness his silk turtleneck did nothing to diminish, glossing him wrist to shoulder, chin to waist in rich black sheen. And the jeans artistically ripped fore and aft, very much like Tom's. Only on Harlan, no skin showed.

Black silk long johns to match the shirt.

He had me toying with a kid's story, half-remembered, witches or aliens who looked okay because they wore these indistinguishable masks, but when the masks came off, the faces underneath weren't human. Suppose the silk was his skin, sleek black pelt all over. The hands were gloves and the face an ivory mask. If you yanked it off, underneath would be darkness. He'd been playing guitar for almost an hour.

"So *damn it*, what *should* I have done?"

"When?" (playing on)

"Back there. It was a toss-up between joining him with my maiden name on, or waiting here till I could prove I had a right to his—and I could just *see* him—if my passport for the next ten years had got my maiden name on it because he'd gone off with the marriage certificate, like he hadn't known how to care for me or something—I could just *see* him freaking out—"

"Oh," he said, "especially—since, as far as you're concerned—after what you did to him before—he remains so abnormally—trusting. You're the little miracle worker."

I stared at him in utter amazement. He went on playing. It was too much for me. "So what are you suggesting that I did to him?"

He played a bluesy phrase, acid and simple, it repeated, and repeated—"Isolation—" he said. Now the phrase acquired a slow disconsolate variation. "Loss of familiar environment—" The original phrase sunk to a lower register while the broken-hearted variation lived on above it, a uniquely ornamented life of its own. "Weakened physical condition—induced emotional dependency on the captor—the Stockholm Syndrome. A classic case. What else would you call it?" He continued to play.

"Well I didn't do it on purpose!"

"Surely," he said, the fingers never stopping their slow, elaborate progress on the strings, "even you have lived long enough to realize—the thousands of degrees or grades of 'on purpose' possible to human behavior: some of us act with malice aforethought—some merely have our predator instincts still intact—"

"Look, what are you trying to prove?"

He shrugged blandly and got up. "Proof is irrelevant." He began to look around in corners. The room was really lined with guitars, propped against things in their cases. More seemed to have come while Tom and I were at the cabin, and now that Tom was gone, even more had mushroomed out of the carpet.

Those jeans weren't very much like Tom's; they were exactly like Tom's. Maybe he'd been cute and torn his to match. But no, he had the bottoms rolled, and the tears and white patches were worn there by longer knees. They weren't exactly like Tom's. They were Tom's.

So what's he doing, daring me to notice?

He'd found what he wanted: a spacey evil-looking black graphite bass. He plugged it in, began to tune it up.

"Nicki's?"

"Mine. I believe you play."

"That's more than I do." Don't know why: it never occurred to me that Harlan owned a bass. If it had, I might've taken up drums.

He wriggled impatiently. "Tom *says* that you play."

"Tom's never heard me."

He handed me the bass. "Well, I'd like to. Come play with me?"

My mind fractured. Part went off trying to recall what age exactly kids get too old to ask their friends to "play" (unless they're talking dirty or mean instruments):

Say, say, oh playmate,
won't you come play with me,
and bring your dollies three?
Climb up my apple tree,
splash in my rain barrel,
slide down my cellar door,
and we'll be jolly friends
forever more?

Not bloody likely. But what the fuck was I going to do? (That was the other part.) Plod and mangle through my pitiful bag of Belshangles tunes, things this little darkness maybe wrote? Out of the inside of his head? What a heavenly, delicious, wish fulfillment opportunity. And be damned if I will. Be damned damned damned damned.

I said "'Louie Louie.'"

"Mm. Easy out."

"Or 'Wild Thing.'"

"Well, they're quite the *same*, aren't they? Your part at least. Probably the first you learned to play."

Not so. My first was "Just Good Friends" off the *Steel Tears* album, and I can *hear* the hump and slide of that bass line in my mind, the part that goes

—White hot immaculate
Noontime pleasure,
Cool black and sumptuous
Midnight treasure,
And nobody says—
What nobody sees—
'Cause they never could see
the forest for the trees—

But if he thinks I'm going to admit that, he's got another think coming. "My teacher claimed it's the one song you can be too drunk to fuck and still get through."

"Having never been too drunk to fuck," he said, "I wouldn't know."

We *Louie-Louied*, not so badly. I was sweating like a horse, but I had a wool shirt on. Maybe it didn't show.

"Right enough," he said. "This time, stand up."

"No."

"What?"

"No."

"I said, stand up."

"I heard you."

"So do it."

"Can't."

"Why ever not?"

"Guess I can't do two things at once."

"That's absurd; do you breathe while you run?"

"That's different from holding up the instrument and—"

"It has a strap to it."

"—And managing my hands, and managing my feet, and remembering the music, and—"

"Why?"

"I guess because I'm no damn good!"

He clicked his tongue. "Don't slag yourself; you'll find others better qualified to do it for you."

I *know* when I'm stuck; just when I thought I'd got my self slag off perfected, a kind of mental firewall against the inroads of the better qualified, I am *utterly* stuck, staring up slack-jawed at a man whose music (say nothing of his person) I have nearly (at times) worshiped.

He is staring back.

Long black hair, long black lashes. Gold leaf eyes in a white face. Not milk white: almonds and honey, the marzipan of mythology. He is enough to scare the socks off anybody.

So which is it to be?

Subservience for life to the Marzipan Martinet? Cave in to him just once, it sets a precedent. *Or*: "Fuck off, you're not my mother; *you can't make me!*" A precedent for lifetime enmity with Harlan Parr. God, I really *didn't* want that. I'd rather cast him as the bad guy than me. I put the strap around my neck. I stood up.

All he said was "One free measure?"

We started "Louie Louie."

Harlan was embarrassingly easy to follow: minimal motion, but he still conducted with his whole body. After several measures though, he turned it into "Wild Thing." Well okay. My part truly was the same. I thumped along. By a kind of relentless crystal logic, "Wild Thing" turned to "*Eine Kleine Nachtmusik.*" And either I was too distracted to notice, or I wasn't messing up. A moral or immoral victory for somebody, as "*Eine Kleine*" gathered to itself melodic bits of "Get Off of My Cloud," "The Sloop John B," "The Star-Spangled Banner."—Then came to the solo. Jimi Hendrix versus "The William Tell Overture." And it was close, but Jimmi won.

The last power chord popped his hands right off the strings as if they'd shocked him. He raised his eyes.

I thought I'd try a small shrug of my own. "The Kingsmen it wasn't."

"Was it supposed to be?"

Hendrix jogged my memory. "By the way, the kid from the coffee shop: was he any good?"

"Who?"

"The one Tom invited up. 'Hendrix was a spastic.' You know, the guitarist kid with the tapes?"

Harlan pouted. Slowly shook his head.

"He did come up?"

Shake turned to nod.

"Pity."

He gave me a long, strange look.

I said, "Tom hoped he'd be good."

"Thomas was charmed. Thomas charms easily. Pity, I agree, but charming doesn't necessarily play guitar (as his own came off over his head), any more than long practice necessarily makes perfect. So," he yawned, "take me out." A contained, luxurious small-animal stretch. "*Entertain* me."

"Where do you wanta go?" New trial. At least a change of venue. He had the guitar neatly away. I handed him the bass.

"Anywhere. Ah, except for Castro Street. I refuse to do the Castro again. Everyone who's shown me San Francisco has, in some misguided assessment, deposited me there. I find ghettos unacceptable, and am repelled by clones."

I couldn't see him lining up on the bleachers with his popcorn and his beer for "Dynasty Night" at your friendly neighborhood gay bar, that's for sure.

"—Would you believe, I actually owned a Cuir Noir jacket at one time? I fear it haunts the hind parts of my wardrobe still. Once I'm home, I will donate it to OXFAM. Promptly. Unless some more—imaginative—disposal can be thought up for it."

At last, an opener for a plain old conversation. "I was at Anarchy Bookstore once," I said, (a hesitant opener), "when these like, real doctrinaire-type punks walked in: the shredded denims, and the tartans, and the holocaust hair, the whole post-nuclear tribal trip. And one of them had honestly just found a biker jacket in the street. They all got talking: what was the baddest thing he could do with it. What he decided was, slit the leather up all over, and pull through strips of plaid from the inside—"

"Like German mercenaries in the Hundred Years' War?" He looked amazingly relieved and enthusiastic. "You know the story goes," he went on brightly, "under their combat rags they put on silk shirts looted from enemy officers, and teased out little puffs through all the tatters; it set the cultivated style for half a century." A pregnant moment passed. "Anarchy Bookstore?"

I said, "Haight Street."

"As in Ashbury?"

"Uh-huh."

"As in the 'Summer of Love'?"

"Only different. You haven't been anywhere, have you?"

"That," he said, "is what I hoped I had made plain."

So we went there.

After all that jazz about Cuir Noir, Harlan wore his black leopard fur jacket over the Levi's, and a haze of beetle-wing green shadow around his eyes. "Don't worry," he purred. "I'm safe on the street."

Harlan had never encountered Zippy the Pinhead. He was openly delighted. He bought all the Zippy books they had, and a Zippy *"Yow! I'm having fun!"* pin, which he fastened through a belt loop on the front of his jeans. Tom's jeans. We ate piroshki from a place down the block; we laughed and walked in the sun, eyed the vintage clothes and records.

Hard to help eyeing *him* (covertly). He didn't look like a gay. He looked like a guitar wizard. Line him up between, well, say, Jimmy Page and Eddie Van Halen—anyone with eyes would recognize three masters of the same far-out arcana.

Generic gays look light years straighter and more up to date than that: neat, conformist sporty clothes, trim non-threatening hair. Manly little moustaches. The hairy lip trip may be declining, but for the longest time, if I were gay and wanted to be sure no one suspected, the first thing I'd have done was shave the moustache.

Harlan was just an order of magnitude prettier, is all. Eddie Van Halen, hang your head. Jimmy Page, eat your heart out. In that same Anthology of English Verse which yielded me *Bermudas* was another little piece. Straight, as written, it didn't show me much. Ah, but sex change it:

He walks in beauty, like the night
Of cloudless climes and starry skies,
And all that's best of dark and light
Meet in his aspect and in his eyes—

I could never make it dry-eyed past the first four lines.

· — ·

DINNER: pretentious, meager, and overpriced, in the farthest confidential nook of the nouvelle trendy hotel restaurant.

Harlan curled a polite lip at his mesquite-broiled sturgeon in sorrel sauce, and poked the last of it in circles 'round his plate.

He'd gotten a mental hammerlock on the wine steward, twenty minutes of esoteric vintage notes, and what must have been the finest bottle of California Chardonnay in the hotel cellar. Even I could appreciate. I was raised on good wine, just never too much of it at once.

A glass for him and a glass for me. Another glass for him. Regret. I said, "No more for me, thanks." Harlan and the steward glared. I stonewalled. Getting all sloshy and moth-happy under Harlan's acid scrutiny fit my every last criterion for risky business.

So Harlan passed on the dessert and doggy-bagged the Chardonnay. As he unlocked our door, the phone was ringing. Without a word, he was on it. After a while he started to giggle and bop like a kid with hot rock on his Walkman.

"Sorry, love," he murmured at length. "Not that easy. No, *No*. Nothing fatal. Bit of hardship establishing her identity, that's all. Oh, Christ, no. You have the only papers proving her right to your name. Yes. No. No, don't. I take it the ones you have aren't certified. Fear not; wheels are in motion. Certainly. We'll keep busy. Well what did you expect? Building her a wardrobe. She's nothing at all. A wedding dress for her to marry in? Having her hair done, her face done, her nails done—"

I wanted to poke him. I would have poked him, if I could've done it without touching him.

He mouthed, "There's an extension in the kitchenette."

I flew at it. Tom, on the far end, said "—have her looking like *you* before you're finished—"

Harlan stiffened. "Is there something wrong with the way I look?"

"Yeah, you're better at it. I got one of you already. Her hair's straight now; you leave it alone. You'll only make her look all older, and I don't want that—"

"How old do you want her to look?"

"Fourteen."

"What?"

"Well? I took to her the first I saw her; does she have to look so different? I happen to like young girls."

Harlan giggled. "Pervert."

"*Oh!* Oh you! Six thousand miles away, you think you're safe!"

Harlan said, "I'm counting on it." He giggled again. "Child molester."

"So you want me on the next available to San Francisco? I'll child molest you!"

"Is that a threat or a promise? Thomas, you can't come here. You have your jig to organize: five hundred randy bands, five thousand London bobbies, the Department of Public Works, ten thousand famine relief volunteers—"

"—And a partridge in a fucking pear tree," said Tom.

"Exactly. So you can't get *at* me, really. And I can't—quite—get at you. Do you truly want this child to look fourteen?"

"Yeah," said Tom. "Fourteen. And forward in her ways."

"Define your terms."

"Get her to do it for you."

"Can I put a word in here? What's wrong with Levi's? The stuff I ordinarily wear?"

"Nothing." Harlan looked up mildly: "If you want the London media to eat you whole. And doting Thomas with you."

I could hear Tom on the other end going, "What'd she say? Harlan, what'd she say?"

"Levi's."

"So make it Levi's and a hockey mask. Levi's and chain mail. Levi's and lizard skin boots. C'mon, you two can figure it out. For that matter what do I get married in? Ha? What about me? Have you thought about me at all?"

Harlan laughed. "What can I say?"

"If I knew, I wouldn't be asking."

"You want me to play arbiter elegantiae and list your options for you?"

"How you usually do, ain't it?"

"Well." Harlan considered. "You could go the morning coat and striped trews route. The old school uniform."

"I couldn't."

"Why not?"

"People'd say I'd sold out."

"All right then: rock soigné, lavender tailcoat, lavender ruffled shirt, lavender—"

"Turning myself into a Duran clone is *not* what I signed up for. Now don't bother telling me to do it naked and dipped in orange glitter either. I'm not into mocking the sacrament of matrimony, I'm only trying to contract it in public, according to my lights."

"And you want my judgment."

"If I'd wanted somebody else's, I'd've asked."

"Then I think you should wear the 1830s frock coat and breeches from the *Andy* video. They're in your wardrobe and will cost you nothing, time or money. And they're certainly according to your lights. Suitable in every way."

I thought he'd been disconnected.

"Are you suggesting I should wear white to my wedding?"

"Yes," said Harlan, a calm little French aristocrat before the guillotine. "Assuming that I've understood the rationale behind your grand display of identical engagement rings and wedding bands, I quite believe you should."

Tom said, "Thank you."

I set down the phone, and got away from it.

Harlan was back to laughing. Listening and laughing, turning rosy. "Oh," he whispered. "Oh, oh oh, it washes out. It really does." The giggle turned into a tune under his breath, sung to little wordless syllables. I hungered to pick up the phone again, to hear if Tom was singing harmony, to hear if his half had the words, to try and figure what it was—an old shared joke in melody, and I didn't know the punch line.

Maybe I ought to leave the room. Go down the elevator, down the street, and not come back. It was Harlan's room. And it wasn't just fear on my part, but certain knowledge: Tom was the medicine of life to him, body and soul.

Harlan held the receiver in the air.

"Here," he said. "He wants you."

Instead of picking up the phone under my hand, I saw myself go, trancelike, to the one offered. "How's the child bride?" said the far side of the world.

"Just fine."

Harlan trailed off contentedly into the kitchen. I saw him pour a nightcap of the Chardonnay, hesitate, and pour the last of it into a second glass.

"Y'know, I miss you."

I said, "I miss you."

"I'm used to having all the company I care to keep. Now I get married, I'm in bed by myself. Not the way it was to work out, was it?"

"I'm sorry."

"My fault, mostly."

"I love you."

"I love you. But please come soon."

"Okay."

"G'night."

"I thought it was morning where you are."

"I got the curtains drawn. C'mon love, tell me good night."

"G'night."

I listened to the dial tone for a long time after he was gone, wondering what it was that washes out. After that, I collected the glass of Chardonnay Harlan had poured me from the counter end, and went to bed.

· — ·

SO we were in the restaurant at Needless Markup, Union Square, recuperating from the wedding salon. The place doesn't call itself Needless Markup: Papa and his friends do, relentlessly, consistently. It was years before I knew it was Neiman Marcus, or there was any joke at all.

You don't buy a wedding dress off a hanger at Needless Markup. The wedding salon *has* no hangers. It has soft lights, a little stage, an elegant desk for the wedding consultant, and sink-in-to-your-hip-bones chairs. The wedding consultant has albums of fashion design photos, fabric swatches bound in sumptuous books, and compendious catalogs of laces and embroideries.

Back at my craziest (age thirteen or so), Mama had, in a fit of terminal frustration, tacked a quote from Revelation to a bare spot on my wall between the Belshangles posters. Such unauthorized additions got torn down and garbaged usually. But this was rather different and it stayed:

> *I saw the holy city New Jerusalem coming down from heaven, prepared as a bride adorned for her husband—*
>
> *And I heard a great voice out of heaven saying, Behold the dwelling of God with men, and he shall dwell with them, and they shall be his people, and he himself shall be their God.*
>
> *And he shall wipe away all the tears from their eyes; and there shall be no more death nor sorrow nor crying, neither shall there be any more pain; for the former things are passed away.*
>
> *And he that sat upon the throne said, Behold, I am making all things new.*

She thought the key phrase was the bit about the tears.

But that's what I knew—basically, all I knew—about the adorning of brides. Now here I was, standing in the Needless Markup wedding salon, with my jaw hanging. It was like special ordering a car from the factory. For exactly *the* dress, with all your options added to the sticker price, racking up a $10,000 total was easy. A girl was in there with her mother, doing it.

At some point, I turned around very fast, before anyone could ask me what I wanted, and bolted. Head on into Harlan standing quietly behind me.

Harlan smells.

It was his scent that filled the hotel room when I first came there: never cheap or overpowering, delectable. Until you began to suspect it was hallucinogenic, and he was your hallucination. Like Moorish palaces: musk and bitter herbs and incense resins, blended with some kind of very subtle excellent sweet food.

Running into him produced a good giddy OD; I retreated to the restaurant. Harlan ordered lunch.

I was beginning to get a fix on him.

All his days began the same. On the bar in our suite stood his electric coffee grinder, his electric orange juicer, and his French filter coffee pot. In its refrigerator was a giant sack of oranges and a small one of Arabian Mocha coffee beans, the real old $20-a-pound kind Mama never bought because they cost too much.

Harlan's Arabian Mocha could have powered a Saturn rocket. His fresh orange juice wasn't any slouch either. He'd handed me mine this morning with an announcement: *we* were shopping for a wedding dress.

I said, "I have a wedding dress."

When he realized I meant the white cotton knit mini, his scorn was total and mirthless. I explained its special qualities carefully, how it was one of the very few dresses I'd ever really liked, how I'd personally pulled it from the bottom of the five-dollar bargain bin at the Esprit factory outlet store, where they toss all the damaged stuff, the ugly stuff that didn't sell, and the occasional nifty one-of-a-kind sample; further, it was sanctified. I'd gotten married in it once already.

He countered: it was hideously out of keeping with Tom's white damask 1830s frock coat.

It was still my wedding dress. My piece of the real.

He asked if I thought Esprit might replicate it for me in finer fabric and full length.

So I took him to the factory outlet, right down in the warehouse district on the edge of the windy, skittering bay. He saw my point at once. The place is a supermarket. Nothing *wrong* with that, the clothes are fun: its just no place to look for individual service. All their stuff is Fabriqué à Hong Kong anyway.

And the Muzak at Esprit is select solid vicious rock (with the Belshangles admixture prominent), played non-stop loud enough to cook the brain. The effect on teen female better judgment is very dependable: buying frenzy, like a feeding frenzy of sharks. It never worked that way on me; it made me mad: like the songs were being whored with and I was being bribed. I loved the music so much better than the clothes.

So we wound up back at Union Square.

First at Gump's. Their street-level boutique had a special on furs. Black ranch mink. Half price, only $6000. Almost out the door, I saw the bomber jacket: white ermine with the little black tails on, flippety-floppety, one to a fur. That was a proper giggle, and I *almost* took to it: traditional royal drag transmogrified. The quintessential rude girl thing. And I've got no qualms about fur; I eat meat too, and I wear leather shoes. But the tag said $3000.

Then at Sak's. The clothes were 100% rayon, and they all had shoulder pads. I don't need shoulder pads. I have shoulders.

Then at Needless Markup, first the wedding salon, then in the restaurant, empty handed. Doing what the Stones' song said: "sitting, drinking (mediocre Chardonnay for him, ice tea for me), superficially thinking—" If I could *tell* Harlan all about the Holy City New Jerusalem, and the tears wiped away from the eyes, might he possibly understand?

Did he have any religion?

Maybe he didn't, and that was the problem.

Maybe he did, and that was the problem.

How much did I know about him, anyway? His father was an Anglican priest, a bishop's confessor. Wow. As stunning an argument as I could think of for the celibacy of the clergy.

Oh, and I'm so deadly tired of watching him order food he doesn't enjoy.

At last he said, "You know, you have three thousand dollars. You have thirty thousand dollars." So that was what was on his mind. The ermine jacket. No rude girl thing is worth three thousand dollars; it's a contradiction in terms.

"Look," I said, "I'm the kid whose belt buckle always slid around under one arm, whose blouse was out of her skirt, whose nails broke off, whose socks came down, whose hair was parted crooked, and whose shoes had horseshit on 'em. There's only so much you can do."

His look of honest frustration, fierce and innocently rumpled like some big black-feathered bird of prey, is more appealing than I care to admit.

I said, "Did you ever dress up a kitten?"

"What?"

"A kitten. A baby cat. In doll clothes.

"Whatever for?"

"Cause you were a kid and didn't know any better. They turn out silly, stuffed, lumpy, frumpy, scared, mad, smelly, undignified, and shaped wrong!"

"Well none of this morning's exercise was *my* idea!" (His lashes are black kohl smears below his wide gold eyes; you want to wipe 'em off, only they aren't mascara) "I call the whole of it a thundering, provincial snore: if *that's* the all your San Francisco has to offer—"

Now he's hit me where I live. What could he have been *doing* here while Tom and I were in the mountains, hanging by his heels from his hotel ceiling like a bat?

"If it wasn't your idea, whose was it?"

"I'm following you, as per instruction."

"I wouldn't be caught dead buying clothes in this place!"

"Nor elsewhere, by the look."

"This is ridiculous. I like thrift shops," I said, "and vintage clothes shops—"

"So do I. We dressed from them for years: they give one at least a chance to substitute intelligence for money."

"—I like weird old things there never were too many of, and now there's only one!" I flopped my hand and rings smartly on the table. Day-Glo orange diamonds, half a weird old thing there's only one of. The other half's in London.

"Although," he said, "given my head, in your case I might proceed quite differently—"

"Such as?"

"Mm—trot you 'round to Hermes of Paris, say, and have them dress you out."

"Harlan, 'dressing out' is what you do to *game* you've shot—"

Didn't he know. He was the utter mischief, and I'd called him by his proper name. Damn. A first. It just slipped out. He grinned at me sideways, and his hair fell in his eyes. Tom's gesture. He had it down exactly.

WEDNESDAY, AUGUST 27

Trouble is—

Sex is addictive.

After only One Week's Free Trial Offer, something awful is happening to me. I'm losing my grip on fantasy. Love has left me dreamless. I pulled the extra pillows off my closet shelf last night, and made a pillow husband for my bed. Tom was my hinge pin and pivot of all dreams anyway; now he's gone and gotten real. Absent lovers, absent lovers.

I could dream myself in Harlan's place once. He's real too. I *think*. I don't know what Harlan's place is anymore. Stuck with me, incognito in San Francisco? God. Okay, I'll humor him. We had our mocha and orange juice; we had our guitar session. I started out standing up:

da dump, da dump, da-da-da
da-da-da-da dump, da dump
da doodi dadi doodi da—
doo wah, doo wah
doo wah doo waah, do wa-a-ah!
Don' wanna be your sla-ave!
(da dump, da dump),
Don' wanna be your sla-ave!

I didn't bellyache and he didn't comment.

Suppose he knows *anybody* here? Lots of music types around San Francisco. Huey Lewis, The Tubes, The Grateful Dead. I'm *sure* he knows Bill Graham. Suppose he'd ever introduce me? People call him on the phone and make him laugh. Except for Tom, I don't know who they are, or where they are. Tom's the only one who makes him sing. And if he has any amorous night visitors in that bedroom next to mine, they're supernaturally quiet ones.

Wonder if he makes pillow lovers in his bed.

I took him to Britex on Geary street, which displays more fabric per cubic inch than any other store on earth. That's what he'd determined we were after, a rare exotic legendary white silk: and we'd have some local extrapolate an upscale copy of my dress.

Just to look helpful, I wore the dress. He wore a black velvet three-piece suit, and looked like nothing earthly.

Britex's back door lets out onto Maiden Lane, and the silks are next to it. And they were all for dated little Chinese cast iron yuppie-matron cocktail dresses: the kind they wear to high school awards night when their sons win first in everything. Nothing legendary. Prim pale damasks, with peonies on 'em.

Nah. I can't afford to look disappointed.

We wandered on down Geary. There is another little shop, advertising "Unusual Fabrics." And they sure were, in the Cyndi Lauper sense. Being weird is not enough.

It wasn't precisely that I didn't believe in Santa Claus. Hell, I even believe in faeries. I was embarrassed. I didn't believe in *me*. That was all there was to it. I didn't pray for anything at all. And if Harlan had his own list of Tings 2 Pray 4, I didn't want to know about it.

Of course, the Psalm says, "I prayed: because You answered." Answers prove the prayer exists. They're all that does. So the real world must be crowded, jammed, and littered, in fact, made up of the interlocking artifacts of other people's prayers. I don't think I'm alone. Do I? Like the old joke about the guided tour of Heaven, and the quarter the tour bus has to cross in total silence 'cause it's where the Roman Catholics are, and they think they're the only ones there.

Here I am, poking idly through bolts of synthetic glitz and fringe, of eyelash acetate and Lurex leopard skin, a Holy Lonely Roman Catatonic Church of one, socked in by spiritual fog of my own making, while—

"May we use your phone?"

—Salesperson, fortyish, sharp, and Asian, is saying to Harlan, "I don't promise—" She checks her privacy, and writes on a slip of paper she first tears from the pad, "—but it should be entertaining." (In come two young guys with moustaches.) "You'll find a pay phone, I believe, in the lobby next door. Good day, sirs, may I help you?"

· — ·

HARLAN stuck the receiver between my ear and his: the phone booth was too small for comfort, and smelled of Moorish palaces. A little surge of gagging panic came and went as his dark hair swept my cheek.

Steady. Look at the paper in his hands.

Look at his hands. Look at the muscles in his fingers, the way the cords rise across his knuckles. *God, I don' wanna look at his hands!*

Above the number on the paper in his hands is written "How Sam Wah, Silk Merchant."

Business hum and traffic noise. A brisk man's voice (abandoning the middle of another conversation) chirps, "Sam's. C'n'I help you?"

"I am calling a Mr. How Sam Wah, is this—"

"Moment sir, put y'on'nother line, c'n'y'hold? Thanks."

My eyes are shut, so I can't see his hands. On the wall outside the booth was this big red-black-and-white poster for an AIDS support group: testing, lectures, counseling hotlines. A new tomb, and more getting laid in it daily. An entire city crying with Tom's voice, "I don't want to die of that stupid, goddamn ignominious disease! I don't want to die at all!" I kept the eyes shut, and prayed that Harlan wouldn't notice.

At least there was no canned music. Don't think I could stomach "Greensleeves." Or "Moon River."

The other line, responding, bore an accent, rich, female, quiet as luxury: a Chinese plum sauce voice.

I whipped across the street, ultimately glad to be delivered from that phone booth, and bought a map. We're looking for 17b Dalton. Dalton is an alley not so far away, tributary to Grant. The darkest heart of Chinatown. Our appointment with the silk merchant, if the woman with the voice, and we, have understood each other (neither certain), is at two o'clock.

Harlan's watch says 12:33.

Just off Union Square is a place that makes real, true sandwiches, sandwiches which *are*. Avocado, bacon, and sprout sandwiches on thick sweet slabs of fresh-made bread. With an hour to kill, and a sudden heartfelt need to see Harlan eat California and like it, I ordered for us both.

Delight. He ate his with a look of quiet wonder. He picked the last sprout and bacon crumb out of his plate. He even asked about dessert. I tried to get him on sliced pears and yogurt, but he shuddered politely. Back outside.

We had to pass a street entertainer on the downhill corner of the Square, a kid getting out of chains, padlocks, and ropes he bullied his crowd into fastening on him. A crew of friends passed the cap and managed to wring out three collections while he strutted, bragged, claimed he was starring in a movie on Houdini, and showed himself off naked to the waist. Brassy and skinny and limber as a snake.

At last all possible pigeons were milked; his bondage was firmly in place. He raised one shoulder high, dropped the other past the limits of anatomy and started to shimmy. Chains began to hit the sidewalk. He moved exactly like Tom. Sandy-haired. Tawny. Fifteen years younger.

As we left, Harlan tossed a small green spindle into the cap. Maybe, I thought, he'd stuck his name and phone inside the money, like the bold chicks do at concerts.

Half a block later I'd guilt tripped myself into a vigorous stomachache. *Ow*. Harlan's watch said 1:45. We hiked up Grant street. Ow *ow*. Lower than stomach. A sharp pang, like runner's cramp. Guilty-gut ulcers, the worst kind. I was the one who'd thought the kid was sexy. *Me*. Harlan only gave him money. He and Tom had worked street corners for a living once.

Crowded shops and Chinese hustle pass me in a haze. Off Grant, the crowds thin out. One-room factories make fortune cookies; strange trash ferments in gutters, and steep old stairways go to joss house temples on the second floor. One more turn leads into damp, pungent solitude.

17b is a door with nothing on it but the number. 17a was

bricked up in the last century. It's plastered now with old concert bills (one for the Belshangles tour), old politicians, old agitprop, and most recently, the AIDS support group poster. In Chinese.

Harlan leaned on the buzzer. It sounded (if at all) so far inside, no rumor reached the street.

No "Greensleeves." No "Moon River."

Trouble *is* (ow), sex is addictive. Eighteen years I've done without. Eight days, and it seems like the real old natural order, indispensable. OW *ow ow*.

Somebody unbolts the door, one of those perfectly sleek young Asian women who's about four inches at her thickest, front to rear. Her dress is tiny black silk, slit at the sides and fastened on her shoulder with curled black satin frogs.

The glimmer of her flawless nylons and dainty black silk heels precedes us up a dark, canted staircase, along a hall, through a door. Inside, a buzzing office full of skinny little men at desks are answering phones, typing, keeping ledgers. Across the room, a jagged hole is kicked out of the wall, four feet tall by four wide, maybe. I can fantasize Godzilla's big green toes protruding through it. Now, I didn't pray for this. I've never thought of anything remotely similar. But at last and at least, here is my city: not Act III of *the Masque of the Red Death*, and not a thundering provincial snore.

Our guide glides on between the desks. No one glances from his work. She dips and bows through the hole in the wall like a Chinese dancer, and we have to follow, around three sides of a balcony or mezzanine above some industrial operation (old-fashioned looms? or presses?) clattering away a floor below.

Down a second dark, sagging staircase. Down a hall. Into an exquisite little office, with a deep blue carpet, low chairs, and lacquer tables, and sliding doors to a garden (stone lions on boulders above a dry stone stream), laid out with wit and nerve in the strip of shadowy waste, six feet narrow, between one warehouse and the next.

There is an old man at the far desk, black dressed, black-eyed and moth fragile. The girl introduces How Sam Wah the Silk Merchant, in the voice we heard on the phone.

And Harlan starts to talk.

He takes about ten minutes explaining who he is, who Tom is, who I am, where London is, why we're here not there, and exactly the sort of silk (white fantastic) we need (He needs? I need?) for a wedding dress.

The girl listens, dutifully dazed, and turning, makes Chinese of it for the old man, in about half the time. It did occur to me, they both might understand quite well; she might be saying something else. He replied, about a sentence worth: a voice as soft as caterpillars in the mulberry leaves.

She turned to us. "He says, no white."

"What?" said Harlan.

"He says, in China is the color of—how we say." She made small puzzled shapely gestures. "The dead are in white, and those who—"

"Mourning?" said Harlan.

"Yes." (relieved) "Is color of mourning."

The old man spoke.

"Also, he says, is only the rough, the raw silk: is not the fine silk used for mourning."

"Well, scratch this plan," I said.

Harlan shook his head, an almost imperceptible "no."

"Do you deal exclusively in China silk? What about silk from Japan, or Thailand, or—"

The girl had already begun her translation.

"He tells us, is all same. In all part of Asia, white for the dead." She smiled helpfully and said, "Color of mourning?"

Back where I started. A new tomb in which no one had been laid. White for purity. White for deprivation. I would feel a lot more comforted if I knew what the difference was. Harlan is still *talking*, about comparative symbolisms of color. And I have paranoied myself into a stomachache bordering nausea.

At the old man's ring, waiters come with steaming pots of jasmine tea, and cups and plates and trays of Dim Sum. Egg rolls. Pearl balls. Tiny little pork buns.

Personally, I prefer my pork buns large.

Harlan has hobbit blood. Harlan has a hollow leg. Dude, he's barely finished one big lunch; I'm having to defend my territory, or he'll get all the pearl balls.

Harlan can be an awful bore.

I guess enough exposure to anyone'll demonstrate they aren't the Fourth Person of the Blessed Trinity after all, but *now* he's arguing philosophy of art or something: about *synthetics*, and why they can't ever be esthetically *pleasing* as *natural* fiber, as if these people even knew the words: what a crock—And the tea was all poured—and the food was all gone—

Even Motormouth Parr appeared to have run down. The silence grew embarrassing. Then painful. Nobody moved.

The old man spoke.

"He asks, if still you wish to view the silk rooms."

Wearily, warily, Harlan tucked his head and smiled.

· — ·

IT was a huge room, cellar-dark. Each length of silk lay loosely wound between fat lacquer poles in horizontal racks so no crease formed. As Harlan and the old man passed, the girl put out one lamp, switched on the next, over colors and colors, like the exotic moth collection of some grand museum.

There's nothing at all like what we want. They know it, I know it, Harlan knows it.

Harlan missed his calling; Harlan was cut out to be a Southern Senator. He's on his second wind now, rapping on in that exquisite, intolerant little voice about the French silk industry's decline since the war, about the annual fabric collections at IdeoComo, about sportsmen's thermal underwear, and antique parachutes, and Papal vestments—

I wandered away.

Closed doors are a challenge. The first I opened was a janitor's closet: concrete sink, mops, buckets. The second was a toilet.

The third was pay dirt.

Chinese carpets rose toward the dark center of the room in heaped-up, layered luxury like a dragon's horde. Around the walls stood tall cabinets, wardrobes of the sort you climb through into Narnia. All the light came in the door, one dim shaft with my head in the middle of it, picking out a cabinet on the far wall. Gleams of colored lacquer and moon-pale carved stone.

I tiptoed up across the rugs; it wasn't locked.

Fright of a lifetime. I didn't quite run screaming. Somebody in there: a mannequin in gold brocade court robes and headdress, escapee from Chinese Narnia. Faint cold sweetness flooded out, like Harlan's perfume only far older, more forbidding. I shut the door on it.

Most of the cabinets were dead dark. But the first on the right—was visible *enough*—to make out three fat poles of horizontal fabric. The top one, black as Harlan's hair, melted into shadow. The bottom one was red as Tom's, no shadow disguised that. I drew an end of the middle stuff out to the light; white raw silk, rough and plain.

Something fell back glittering underneath.

· — ·

FIRST, they said there was no other room. Then, that it was all antiquities, no silk. Then they said the antique silks were for museums, not for wearing; fourth (of course) there was no white; fifth, it wasn't what we wanted. Sixth, she led us in, switching on the crystal chandeliers.

Two white fabrics housed in that cabinet, on a single pole with the raw silk outside, like a peasant handmaid set to guard a royal mistress with her body and her life.

"This is death silk for an Emperor's concubine."

Harlan's face was a classic study.

"But surely—the last ruler of China was a woman?"

The old man spoke.

"He says, the gentleman is well read. Tzu Hsi, the great Empress Dowager died in 1909, but the last of the Emperors is Henry Pu Yi, who lived yet but few years in the People's Republic. He lived yet, 1927, in the Forbidden City when treasure houses were burned by palace eunuch who wished to conceal crimes; many many treasures stolen and sold over the world, many sold here."

"Ah."

I elbowed him.

"Plausible," he murmured. "I've worn older silks than that, and this piece appears never to have been cut, or even left in the light."

A buzzer brought silent men, who unrolled it on a table in the silk room, one piece and perfect. And the pattern, what was that? Some places swirled, nebulous, thick textured; were they clouds? Places were almost sheer, twined with sinewy satin flows, what were those? A river course half hidden in mists? A huge scaly body too vast to comprehend? But in between it all, an emblem shone recurrent, like a great sign in the heavens. "What does that say?"

"The Dragon's blessing, it means 'Ten Thousand Years.'"

"How much?" said Harlan.

"Ten thousand."

"No. What is the price?"

The old man spoke.

"He says, is not what you wish. Is for the dead."

"But *is* for sale?" Harlan persisted.

"It is three hundred dollars for the yard; thirty yard; he does not cut."

"That's nine thousand dollars?"

The old man spoke.

"Plus tax," said the girl, smiling.

"Will you accept my check?"

I saw it for sure this time, the glitter of satisfaction flash across behind the old black silk eyes. But the girl still translated. He replied. She said, "Cash."

Chapter 6

THE WAY OUT was not the way in. Godzilla had booted more boltholes than one. We waited quietly in a door with no number, until a black Mercedes spun into our alley, tires squealing. I saw the girl interpreter was driving.

The merchant was in back, swathed in a great coat, black cashmere to his shoes. Harlan got in beside him. I perched on the jump seat. The bundle of silk lay in my lap, warm and heavy as a sleeping child, tied with its raw silk companion in rice paper and scarlet cords. An end stayed open to show it was the same stuff; they had tied that last of all.

We parked at a yellow curb in front of Barclay's Bank, while Harlan sprinted in. I sat facing How Sam Wah. Take my eye off that one for an instant, he and his silk might vanish in a thunderclap. Maybe it was faery treasure anyway, and fell to ashes in the morning.

No cops in sight. Glad of that, somehow. I get to watch Harlan count ten banded packs of ten one-hundred-dollar-bills, meticulously, from his big Italian shoulder bag into a nearly identical one belonging to the girl. Now we're out on the curb.

"Could you recommend a local designer competent to work such silk?"

The old man drew a black address book from his breast, consulted it. The girl produced writing materials. His little book was all Chinese. But her note read (in English) "Seven Blows" and an address on Liberty Street. The black Mercedes and its occupants disappeared, not into thin air, into traffic.

The cabbie Harlan flagged knew Liberty Street, but it was map study time for me. By now he'd dodged and cornered onto Market, headed west. Our quest was turning into a cosmic scavenger hunt. Hustling south now on Valencia, I located Liberty. Its coordinates were—it was a cross between—Oh crud. No use trying to hoodwink Harlan; he had laser eyes.

"Is that too close to Castro for you?"

He said, "I'll let you know."

· — ·

IMAGINE a narrow old Victorian, wooden second story on a stucco storefront; and between the two, reading right across in brass letters on a red lacquer panel, "SEVEN AT A BLOW." Around the words perch big (about a foot long), brass, 3-D houseflies. Seven of 'em. The window, done up in P.T. Barnum lettering said, "TIM THE TAILOR."

The coin dropped. "The Brave Little Tailor!"

"So it seems."

A phalanx of striped sword plants stood guard inside the window, then there was a bench, a red tile floor, and a counter. The door jangled a bell in back.

Noises. Chair scraping.

Through an archway lay an airy workshop, sewing machine, cutting and pressing table, neatly cluttered tools of a tailor's trade. But what rounded that archway looked less like a Castro Street tailor than Harlan did; he looked like Sinbad the Sailor. Barrel-chested, not tall but *wide*, he moved with the rolling swing of a storybook sailor, and wore old Sinbad's big gold earrings. I guessed he was Hispanic or Mediterranean of some kind, and he wasn't very young. Either one was hard to tell: he was the most exquisitely made-up person I have ever seen, so well done it was almost natural: shadowed, lined, and glossed into an icon of male vitality and Technicolor health. His hair (dark I imagined, but it might have been gray) was frosted gold.

Harlan's recovery was flawless: "How brave are you?"

The man looked him over, intelligently, impudently, took in his last detail, finally leaning forward on the countertop to check his feet. When he straightened up again he said, "What did you have in mind?"

"We need a first-rate designer to copy her frock, or extrapolate from it—but full length, and in silk."

Tim the Tailor evaluated my five-dollar Esprit mini: the same unhurried once-over he'd given Harlan. "Why?"

"For a wedding."

"Yours?"

"Hers."

"But not to you?"

"To my partner."

I rested my silk load on the counter. A blue and white bowl beside the cash register held a pile of glossy ovoids, mottled appetizing shades of brown. Now I knew what those were, they were Chinese —

"Tea eggs," said the tailor. "Have one."

Harlan had one. I wasn't sure he'd meant me, but I had one. Tim the Tailor had one. "*You* remind me," he said, waving his at Harlan, who had handkerchiefed his hands and started to work on the knots of the silk package, "of the rich Arabs in Paris."

"I beg your pardon?"

"Prince Ibn Hobnobbi views all the collections, see, and smiles 'How excellent, how fine,' and I buy forty of this fashion in different color; *but*: you must make the few small changes: the hem must be to *here*—' (pointing at the floor), 'and the sleeve to *here*—' (just below his wrist watch)." It was an LCD calculator job, Grand Prix race car game and all, on a gladiator-width black leather band. With studs.)

"I am Arabic," said Harlan, softly satisfied. He helped himself to another tea egg.

That stopped Tim the Tailor dead, in sassy open-mouthed appraisal. "Well I hope you're not *offended—*"

"No. Oh, no."

"—They also want the necklines up to *here—*" pointing to his throat. His shirt was open to show off four gold chains nestling in the chest hair, a high school class ring worn like a charm on each.

"I'm not that Arabic."

"But they're ruining Paris: like rich Texans in a way; the finest houses for leather in the *world* are in Paris: so what do they show this year? Elegant, exquisite jackets with a goddamn fist and falcon hand-painted on the backs."

Harlan flicked the last memento of tea egg from his fingers and unrolled the contents of our package. Tim the Tailor blanched, gazing from the shimmer of silk to the shimmer of Harlan in honest, unconcealed awe.

"How Sam Wah."

"Quite well," nodded Harlan primly. "And you?"

"*No. You* got *around* How Sam Wah: do you mind if I—"

"Not at all. As—I believe it was Samuel Pepys—once remarked: 'Pretty thing, what money will do.'"

"I once offered that old—well, everything I could think of: money, drugs, rare erotic manuscripts—for that length of silk—"

"Perhaps he didn't understand your language."

"His English is as good as yours. He runs Sam's Video out on Taraval. That's his legitimate business, at least. He did the whole show for you? With the interpreter and—"

"Exquisite interpreter. Exquisitely fractured diction."

"Number one daughter. She's a psych major at Cal."

"Why did you want it?" asked Harlan suddenly.

"I imagined I had the proper use. The proper use since moved back to New Jersey. That's neither here nor there."

Harlan's murmur was pure reverence: "White silk pajamas, white silk dressing gown, white silk—"

"Oh you are a live one, aren't you?"

"You don't know who I am?"

"The lost Dauphin?"

Harlan snickered.

"The Twelfth Imam?"

I'd been peering up at the wall above the front door. A small, dark object hung there under glass. Curiosity triumphed. I climbed Tim's waiting bench. Then I could see what it was. I hopped down and went out onto the sidewalk, out in the gathering evening. The conversation didn't seem to require me. I felt an embarrassing advent of tears.

All down Liberty street, as it dropped east toward the Mission, I could make out those AIDS posters wreathing lamp post and telephone poles: festive, red-white-and-black. Half the ones out here were English, the rest Spanish. Defiant jaunty mourning bands. People were strolling the warm twilight. Guys, mostly. Lights were coming on. I saw Saint Francis's city, gearing up to glitter.

Oh, he doth hang upon the cheek of night,
like a rich jewel in an Ethiop's ear—

Come on now, this won't do. Breathe deep. Smell the salt air and the eucalyptus. Do some stretches. Slight pain in the gut still. Go inside past the jangling bell. Tim and Harlan have taken the silk in back; Harlan's given Tim his card, and is digging VHS cassettes out of that bottomless shoulder bag.

Tim's on the phone. "Richard. Me. Go downstairs—Well, tell him to stop. All right, so give the phone to Cody. (pause) Cody? Yeah. Okay. Go downstairs. (pause) Go into my room—*my room.* You there? Okay—"

"Long cord," I whispered to Harlan.

He whispered back, "Cordless."

"Look on my dresser. The blue glass—Yes. Run them over to

the shop, would you, son? Well, tell Danny to *hold* dinner, or I don't care how legendary he makes it, we won't be there." Then, apologetically to Harlan, "Just a block or two."

Sure enough, in no time, a blond black-leather boy undulated past the front window with the stomping over-long stride peculiar to skinny young guys in motorcycle boots.

The blue glass was an old-time covered icebox dish. It was full to the top with pearls. And what pearls. Lumpy blue, bulgy silver, warty gold, long and narrow rose pink, not a one was white or round.

"Flawed pearls. My friend collected them. Now of course, they're styled 'Baroque' and they're not to be had, but then nobody wanted them. He'd been all over the Orient.

"He sold everything else, but not these. He spent the last months, while he still had use of his hands, drilling them. There's another safety deposit full. I was left to find them a good home."

I scrambled past Cody in a hurry, on my way back to the street. Cody was small and smooth and pretty, a little older Calvin minus Hobbes, trying so hard to look scary in his leathers, one ear bristling with silver death's heads, axes, crucifixes. I fought off a dreadful urge to hug him, and stopped short of the front door, embarrassed to make another big bell racket going out. Harlan was saying, "Can you recommend a shop for vintage clothing?"

"How vintage?"

"'Thirties. 'Forties."

"God, the vintage people do their buying in the thrift shops and flea markets. I had a friend in the trade, he'd take me buying sometimes. He had a list—Cody, dear, in the file cabinet, would you, under 'Charlie's Trap Lines.' See? Pages of it. All ye need know. Addresses and what's hot at each. A vintage buyer's itinerary for the Bay Area—days of the weekly half-offs and the monthly flea markets—Charlie was organized. Little out of date, I'm afraid. We do seem to have an embarrassment of dead men's riches—" That put me out the door, bell or no bell.

I was born in 1968. I suppose I must have bought the '70s moonage daydream, and in some way, I still do.

If all the "holy" I know about comes from desert saints and Latin chant, all the "City" I know is San Francisco: not Rome, not Constantinople, not even Jerusalem. I am a citizen, a high-visibility member of that Babylonian merchants' and sailors' guild who stood afar, heaping ashes on their heads and weeping, when none were left alive to traffic in their wonderful stuff.

> *Alas, alas, that great city!*
>
> *And the merchandise of gold and silver and precious stones and of pearls and fine linen and purple and silk and scarlet—*
>
> *And cinnamon and odors and ointments and frankincense and wine and oil and fine flour and wheat and beasts and sheep and horses and chariots and slaves, and the souls of men—*
>
> *And the voice of harpers and musicians and of pipers and trumpeters shall be heard no more at all in thee, and no craftsman of whatsoever craft he be shall be found anymore in thee—*
>
> *And the light of the candle shall shine no more in thee and the voice of the bridegroom and the bride shall be heard no more in thee—*
>
> *Alas, alas, that great city.*

I didn't have that one by heart. Like Rocky Raccoon, I got back to my room and found it in Gideon's Bible. I just knew where to look, one page before the Holy City New Jerusalem.

Oh God, I've got no sense of proportion! I never could keep scripture and nursery rhymes and dumb rock lyrics separate! And the tears are coming, too fast to hold off now. This is the kind of thing I have by heart:

> *Granfa' Grigg*
> *Had a pig*

In a field of clover.
Piggy died,
And Granfa' cried,
And all the fun was over.

If I could only wipe away the tears from the eyes and see the working out of that great promise: No more sorrow, no more death, I am making all things new. Not just some things new, the safe respectable things, but all things new.

· — ·

A TAXI cruised up Liberty street, to Harlan's summons, doubtless. I went back through the bell.

"There she is. What's your size in 501s, dear?"

"Guys' 28s." Shock. My own voice.

"Sooper. We'll need to part you from your dress." Tim had this shelf *full* of new black Levis, tags still on, like at the store. He produced a guy's size small white dress shirt too, and when I exited his changing curtain, traded my dress for a black velvet jacket (Harlan's, from the scent,) and a silk tie draped around my collar. "Love it."

There was Harlan, in the velvet pants and weskit, white shirt, open collar, pouting voluptuously at me like the King of the Cats. "So take me out," he said. "Entertain me."

He glanced above the door as we went through it, at the small round item under glass. "Something of interest?"

"Don't be *too* entertaining," Tim called after us. "We do expect your bodies in the morning—"

I whispered, "Purple Heart."

"?"

"War medal. Wounded in battle."

"His?"

"No name." Crossing the sidewalk, I said, "You really think that stuff was woven for an Emperor's concubine?"

"Does it matter?" He flashed this wonderful, cool bland smile. "Shopping for the stuff of legends, weren't we? If it's plain, verifiable history you want, get it from People's Textile Cooperative

573, or IdeoComo, or anyone. I think we ought to celebrate. I, for one, would enjoy a supper commensurate to the occasion."

"Okay." Filled with a sudden overweening confidence in my ability to deliver legends on short notice, I ordered our cab across the Bridge to Berkeley and Chez Panisse. One of the three best restaurants in Paris is in Berkeley.

The food upstairs is every bit as fine as downstairs, and it doesn't cost an arm and a leg and a reservation to get in; you eat right in the kitchen, where you can watch the food dance through the chefs' quick hands and bask in the enormous sunny breath of ovens uttering calzones.

The bread was warm too, sweet euphoria-scented as the side of Tom's collar. And the salad had orange and gold nasturtiums in it; the pasta had cream, smoked trout and scallops from the Great Barrier Reef, not your ordinary anonymous white flesh punchings, but with the whole little succulent nasturtium-colored animal attached. And Harlan ordered off the downstairs list what must have been the hugest Chardonnay in California.

I'm wondering what war yielded Tim his medal. Not sure he was old enough for World War II. With all the makeup who could tell? The point, I guess. He was certainly too old for Vietnam. Maybe it was someone else's. I had a friend once.

I had a friend.

"The French—" Harlan eyed the glass hump in the bottom of our empty bottle somberly, "—have a name for that, they call it 'the Mound of Despair.'"

Didn't look too despairing: the image of surfeited luxury, more like. I thought he was going for seconds. And he was: seconds of the almond tart, a rendered gold essence of nuts and cream fit for the Twelfth Imam.

"'Come home looking like the Pork Pie Faery at this rate,'" he said. "'Can't have that, now.'" Tom's delivery. He had it down exactly. "Where do you run around here?"

"I don't."

"Thomas says you run."

"Not around here."

He drew a great breath and shut his eyes. Then he said, very carefully, "Where—does—one—run—here. Pardon. Not *here*, San Francisco."

"Golden Gate Park?"

The eyes flicked open. "Are you asking, or telling me?"

"People—run—in—Golden—Gate—Park."

He pushed himself slowly from the table. "Very well. We'll both go there in the morning." Then he grinned at me. "But this has been a *day*."

"All that California in one place, huh?"

"I wouldn't have believed it."

I said, "Welcome to my home."

THURSDAY, AUGUST 28

I said, "I've got no shorts; all that stuff is down at Stanford." Should've stalled him? Wrong. He came out of the bedroom in his coal black jogging suit, and flipped the matching black jersey and shorts at me.

I put them on. Moorish palaces. My mouth began to water, and I didn't want it to; it put me in a fury. Did he have extras? Was he naked now under those sweats? I'd be secretly peering for panty lines all day, didn't he know.

The labels said "Hanro, Reine Seide, Pure Silk, Pura Seta, Soie Naturelle."

Hanro of Switzerland makes expensive lingerie. If they make guys' athletic stuff, it's news to me. For Harlan maybe, anyone made anything. Maybe, like the poison tunics of mythology, they'd eat into my flesh, corrosive, unremovable.

On the bathroom counter was a little mother of pearl box of cloth-wrapped elastic hair bands; they were ink black, every one. All the cloth-covered hair bands I ever saw at Long's or Safeway come in assorted kid colors—you know: red, yellow, blue—and when those all break, you're stuck with the Girl-Scout green ones. Now here's Harlan Parr, with unlimited black satin hair bands. Sure, I could use a hair band, but not one of those.

Have to draw a line somewhere.

We took the Rent-a-Sentra. It bucked and farted like an evil-minded pony, seaward to the park. Behind the Academy of Sciences we dumped it, and we ran the bridle paths down to the misty, thundering beach. Fog twined through the cypress and the eucalyptus. Dripped from the rhododendrons and the ferns. We rounded the Dutch windmill, passed the monument where Roald Amundsen's brave little ship that made the Northwest Passage stood for sixty years, moored up to its plimsoll in sand. Passed the little green duck ponds and the bison paddock. Back to the car.

Harlan went under the hood (yet another equivocal view of his Hanro black silk rear), diddled the carb and got it to leave off farting. It still bucked.

I have the stomachache again.

Across town to the south and east, all the little inland valleys drowse behind their hills in as sheltered and unreal a hothouse sun as the remote Bermudas in the Ocean's bosom unespied. A narrow old driveway sidles past Tim's narrow shop: twin cracked ribbons of concrete snuggling in Bermuda grass. Harlan pulls in like he owns the place. The sign says CLOSED, but the door's open. Old Pirate Earrings is grinning at us from his archway. "Salaam, Effendi."

Harlan acknowledges, does his mini-bow.

"I put in some research," says Tim the Tailor, "among my younger acquaintance."

"Yes?"

"I now know who you are. Or claim to be."

"Which is more than I do of you," says Harlan.

"True. But good God, are you sure you want me for—that flaming red-head creature in the video, that's—"

"My partner, yes. Her husband."

"Tommi Rhymer."

"Quite."

Sadly, "There are things in life I've missed."

"Culturally deprived," said Harlan.

"Now, now. But his *outfit*, the white silk coat, and the weskit, and the pantaloons, they look for all the world like they were worn to Queen Victoria's wedding—"

"Don't laugh. They were."

"—by Prince Albert!"

"No one quite so grand, I'm afraid. The kidskin breeks are modern, the originals were all to bits, but the rest was tailored in 1832."

"And the outfits on the band—"

"Modern."

"Done in London?"

"Paris, actually."

"Mr. Parr—do you ever have illusions that you've died and gone to heaven?"

"Frequently."

"I feel as if I owe you some assurance of quality. I haven't been pegging pants on Liberty Street all my life; my career was in theatrical costume; I *have* worked Broadway; I *do* have references—"

"The reference which led us to you should be adequate."

"Sam Wah has a bizarre sense of humor."

"I'm sure of it," said Harlan. "So have I."

The front bell clamored. *"Yoo-hoo! Me! Valerie!"*

We'd made our way in to the workshop. "—index my fees to the cost of raw materials," Tim was saying, "thusly, whatever figure Sam Wah accepted for that fabric I will charge to tailor it, plus as much again for expertise and overhead and N.R.E.—"

"One quid fer 'ittin' it wif a 'ammer, and firty fer knowin' w'ere t' 'it," said Harlan.

"Quite."

The woman bustling toward me juggernautical as a cable car has got an old green cashmere coat on, a little black hat on her '50s poodle-cut hair, a huge black handbag, and three bulging string-bagsful of food, and she wants to hug me into the middle of it.

"And the pearls?"

"Considering their origin—"

"Can't be sold," said Harlan.

"But for full London publicity, plus agreement that, if the gown is ever disposed of, I have first option—"

"—Valerie Lagomarsino! I'm Timothy's assistant. Are *you* the little girl I'm s'posed to measure? *Oh Sweetie!* You're the *bride!*" (Tim's left off negotiations for a quick plunder in her string bag, handing deli cartons out to an appreciative Harlan.) "Sicilian olives and Kalamata olives, marinated prawns and feta—" "Oh dear, this's so *wonderful*; we've never had a wedding! He's done Gilbert and Sullivan and Children's Theater, and Renaissance Pleasure and Dickens Faire, but never a *bride*! *Come on, you!* Out of the cheese! I'll *cube* it for you, honestly! And I've got toothpicks—my late husband always used to say—he was a doctor you know, and he used to say—*Out! Oh, honestly!*"

She recovered her groceries with minimal loss. In an apartment out the back (I gathered she lives there) I could hear her batting and clattering around, warbling old Broadway show tunes in a girlish voice. Tim and Harlan, meanwhile, had rumbled grandly up the stairs at one side of the shop on a mechanical lift: a scene from some bizarre old opera, two unlikely saints on a diagonal ascension into second-story paradise.

Valerie reappeared, her goodies cubed and tooth-picked into blue and white bowls. Some went out to the counter. She trotted the rest upstairs, stood tiptoe, yoo-hooed, and set them on the edge of the lift. Then gathering tape, pen, and measurement chart (a guy's, I note, with inappropriate points scratched and the female equivalents marked in) she came to work on me. All I had on were Harlan's shorts etc.; she measured over them.

"Hips, 38—"

"I do not have thirty-eight inch hips!"

"Well, it's *all right*, dear, those inches happen before we know it sometimes. Bust, 38—"

"I do *not*!"

"Don't get excited! Now look, here's the end of the tape, and here's Valerie's thumb—"

"You're starting at the wrong end!"

The doorbell clamored again.

"You're starting from the wrong end of the tape! You're gonna have me with a forty-eight-inch waist!"

She clicked her tongue at me and bustled out to the young guys at the desk. "Oh Sweetie! Hello there, we're closed for the week, I'm 'fraid. Pickup only, no new stuff.

"Oh, he's got a really *big* job. Something *so* exciting, I'm not s'posed to tell. Really famous people. When you come back, I'll tell you *all* about it—"

"Hello below." Tim's black leather legs stood at the top of the stair. "Seventy-two minus forty-eight," he said quietly, "is twenty-four, *n'est ce pas?* I can subtract, so long as she doesn't change ends in midstream."

I'm sitting here wondering what a sharp old buzzard like that could want with a really dumb cluck assistant.

Her old purse is sitting here too. I see familiar items sticking out the top. The plastic rosary case. The tiny black mantilla. The old Saint Joseph's Daily Missal, utterly useless for following the Mass since before I was born. But I bet I know what it's there for. The book bulges pregnantly, held to with rubber bands. Sure enough. Holy cards. All the usual: novenas to Saint Jude, Saint Anthony, the Little Flower, Our Lady of Carmel, Our Lady of Perpetual Help, Saint Martin de Porres. Then the antique gorgeous lacey ones handwritten in Italian.

Then the funeral cards your Catholic mortuaries still hand out. Lots of recent ones. Pious pastel picture on the front, guy's name and a prayer on the back. Birth date, death date. Young guys. Prayers to ease their trip through Purgatory. All from Most Holy Redeemer in the Castro.

I bet Valerie walks to 7:30 Mass each morning. Wow. Talk about "safe from priests' and prelates' rage." With that saddle-bag of pious intentions to pray through, no wonder an outdated missal serves her fine. Poor dude at the altar might as well be reading her the NASDAQ quotes. Talk about your Modern Church and survival tactics. I had to feel a kind of admiration. Nevertheless, I didn't want a 48" waist.

"Hello Sweetie!" More young guys at the counter.

The lift is blocking the stair top, but I can still swarm up the banister, to an upstairs bright and vacant: only cutting tables, storage cabinets, other tailor gear. Valerie's blue and white bowls hold toothpicks mostly, and Kalamata pits. I get the last three prawns, spaced with Sicilian garlic olives and feta cubes.

"—The Privileged Peasant or Twiggy goes to Afghanistan effect," Tim says. "Sorry, am I dating myself?" They had my mini on a hanger and were looking at it. "Esprit is clever that way: everything cut from squares and rectangles. Those big bat sleeves are squares folded diagonally. Triangles actually, but I'm putting my seams up the top of the arm, so mine are squares.

"I don't believe in seams one's supposed to ignore. No patience with that kind of piety. *Tim's Law*: 'If you can't *hide* it, decorate it.' And," he went on, "Corollary One of Tim's Law, should you *ruin* it, transmute the damage to a central design concept. Amazing what debacles become triumphs of creativity."

I wasn't sure I found his philosophy of art a comfort.

"So I'll run the trim up both sides of the seam—even better, there won't be a seam. Leave it open and button it across with silk loops and pearl clusters, wrist to shoulder—then straight across the collar bones, and down that big V-back. I take it (to me) you *are* fond of white leather? Should hope, if your intended's intending to get hitched in those britches. God, what an apparition. Hard on an old man's blood pressure."

Harlan dimpled modestly. Having never realized Tom's video-britches *were* leather, best I can manage is the dry grins. Like an unobservant teenage twit.

"Now *you* (to Harlan) said, 'same, only floor length—'"

"Ibn Hobnobbi."

"Exactly. But I assume (to me) *you* take a stride; you didn't want a straight skirt did you? Dropping that width straight to the floor's like the old song about Mabel, '—nice to hug and she's nice to squeeze, but you can't get her hobble skirt above her knees,' neither practical nor very rock'n'rolling—

"*So, my* skirt is a half-circle. Since the silk's only a yard wide, and we'll need a radius for the waist, you'll *still* have your mini length in front, see, then it sweeps out wider and wider as it goes, to any length train you choose, no seam in back either, closed above with pearls and loops. A little risqué and a little military, little like your old dress, little like your husband's coattails—unconstructed, unconfining, simple and sexy and bare, and all *you* need, is good legs, which you have in abundance, and a good tan back. Go lie in the sun, sweetheart, Ol' Uncle Tim is gonna fix you all, all up."

"Timothy!" Valerie hollered up the stairs, "Genji's here!"

The guys rode down the lift, Tim still waving his arms at Harlan. I used the banister, thinking what an unexpected load of souls' comfort there was to having this outrageous overbearing old character, so cock-secure in his talents, graciously willing to accept twenty thousand dollars to close his little business for a week and fix me all, all up.

Genji was a delicate looking kid, pretty, except for very bad skin plastered over with a coat of flat ivory makeup. Highly dubious the name was real, but he was Japanese from Japan; his fractured English was no put-on. "Levi's" were "Revi's" for him.

"I try it?"

"Oh, I insist."

What Tim had done for him: altered a pair of 501's, removing the button-fly off another and running it up the seat. The two sides were totally breakaway now, one long continuous button-fly, down the front through the crotch and up the back. Yuk yuk. Where Levi's patch used to be, Tim put his own: two giant houseflies hitched to a pair of jeans and pulling, with the slogan SEVEN AT A BLOW.

Genji hopped around the shop in them, crowing "Ta-Da!", "Banzai!", and other such fitting remarks to the blushing amusement of two friends, ordinary young S.F. guys, who seemed shyly gratified someone was doing what he was doing, and relieved as hell it wasn't them.

Wonder what could be his expectations: to have that super-fly unbuttoned for him as frequently as possible? Or was it "all for show and not for blow," as the saying goes?

Pathetic, kind of, either way, like a poorly informed tourist, come looking for the fancy dress ball five years too late. His flat white Kabuki face made the oddest contrast to old Tim, with his perfect fashion makeup.

And Harlan, whose skin was flawless ivory anyway.

And Valerie. Her lipstick wasn't on too straight. Her eyebrows were pencil, and looked like pencil. She was wearing base; it gave her peachy orange facial hair and an orange line in front of her ears—perfectly respectable middle-aged lady, in other words; nobody'd look twice. And me. A hole in the air. A brain with eyes. No matter what the makeup, nobody'd look twice.

· — ·

ON the way out, Harlan used Tim's phone.

"Mr. Pfau—" I'm eavesdropping again. Papa has an engineer buddy named Ed Pfau. Obviously not the same. Then he giggled and said "Is it so. Raoul Falconer gave me yours also. You've a 356 Speedster you wish to sell?"

He cowboyed the Renta-Sentra south down Interstate 280, swearing mildly in Arabic.

The Pfaus have a rambling '70s ranch house on a knoll, formerly prune orchard, above the freeway west of Stanford. They have four boys I used to play with, till they discovered girls weren't guys. They all play guitar now and are into motorcycles, the Grateful Dead, other good things like that.

Harlan wore his brown cord pants and tweed coat with the leather elbows. He stood around the driveway, chatting up Ed Pfau in the very primmest British sporting fashion.

As he was getting out his checkbook, and about to buy the car, which was virtually rust free, perfect to restore, and all those other nice things, Ken Pfau (14) wandered through, spotted him, did an enormous double take, and split.

Harlan wrote the check.

Ken reappeared with Dave (17).

Dave seconded his identification. They went away.

Ed dug out the pink slip, spare parts, maintenance log.

Ken and Dave came back with Ron (19). Ken had an electric guitar. Dave had a tape recorder and a practice amp. Ron was paying out three long, bright-orange electric cords.

Very slowly, Harlan turned to face his public.

"Mr. Parr," whispered Dave Pfau, "sir—"

"Yes?"

All were absolutely tongue-tied.

Harlan gazed gravely. "Which one do you want?"

The boys looked at each other, Dave whispered, "Solace."

He asked for a metronome. They had a Casio toy synth, the cheapest one with auto accompaniment. He made a quick survey of available rhythms. I couldn't have begun to set "Solace" over any of them. But he selected, turned the temp and the volume to the lowest click.

And played. "Solace," all right. Only he had Tom's vocal translated to a guitar part and was playing the two at once. Until the solo came. Here came the solo.

Music towered up from the middle of Pfau's hilltop. The breeze died, and the freeway's ocean roar grew hushed. From the dusty and rototilled orchard surrounding, two covered race cars, a parted out hulk, assorted motorcycles, and a tow trailer listened as attentively as ever ox and ass to angelic musicians. No jets whined down the landing pattern to SFO. No dogs barked. No birds sang. When it was over, he lifted his hand. All that sad glory slid back down the sky and vanished in the guitar pickup. He turned it all off. And I'm standing here, trying to hide the tears.

"That's not the solo off the album!" gasped Dave Pfau.

Truer words were never spake.

"Why, you wanted it the *same?*"

"No, no sir. Only, God, that's not same as anything, I've got all the concert—"

Harlan waited brightly for him to say "bootlegs."

Dave messed his Doc Martens around in the gravel. "—I mean, it wasn't that way on this tour—"

"Of course not," said Harlan severely. "Its yours. One off. Record it yourself some day; I'll remember you."

"I'm not much good."

"Get good. I'll leave you to it."

Ken and Dave and Ron went off with their prize to phone every guitar-playing kid in Santa Clara County.

Ed came back with the last of the parts.

Finally Harlan turned to me. "I understand you drive."

"But of course."

"Of course. You shovel this load of old codswallop back to airport rentals; I'll do rearguard in case."

The renta-Sentra put on its best show of bucking and farting. In vain. Thirty minutes saw us rid of it at SFO. Harlan signed it off, paid for it, grabbed my hand and cantered jubilantly out toward his new old Porsche in the parking. I cantered with him.

"Chez Panisse?"

"But of course."

He'd sequestered his little car in a well-defended corner, and had to hand me in through the driver's side.

"Thought you might—want to try—new things."

"Oh, God no. My Americanism for today—" Having me settled, he settled himself, (tucking my hand he still held firmly in between the seat and his warm brown corduroy thigh), dug out his key, stuck it in the ignition—

—And froze. We both sat and thought about it. I felt, but avoided, his long slow look. At last he sighed. "My Americanism for today:" and turned the key "'If it ain't *broke*, don't *fix* it.'"

So my hand stayed where it was, passively appreciative of the flex and dance of muscle as he heel-and-toed Ed Pfau's bottle-green Speedster north up 101. At the first good cloverleaf, he took us round the *whole thing*, gearing down and standing on it, making the little Porsche squat and drift the turns, 360 degrees.

Papa's driven old Porsches all my life. He never raced

himself, just pit-crewed buddies like Ed Pfau. We used to go to Sears Point and Laguna Seca for the vintage races; his friends'd sometimes tour me round the course at speed.

Lots of talk, when I got my license, of putting me through Bondurant's performance driving school. It was just talk, of course. I'm from the Bat-Out-of-Hell driving school strictly. But I know all the mannerisms. Over the city and across the bridge to Chez Panisse we go.

Chapter 7

FRIDAY, AUGUST 29

"LOUIS VUITTON SUCKS. Four hundred dollars for an itsy-bitsy carry-on with somebody else's weird initials all over it?"

"Then solve the problem. You desire luggage—"

"I can't see flying to London with that wedding dress in my hand."

"—You desire luggage which is out of the ordinary, cannot be mistaken for anyone else's. What will you have?"

"Steamer trunks."

He fell silent at once, and made one lap of the carpet. Two laps. Head absorbed in concentration, hands absorbed in pockets. "Ah. Too bulky. The airlines should cooperate for a fee, but I doubt they'll cram into the limo. Being met at Heathrow by a lorry wouldn't do at all."

"*Very small* steamer trunks."

"From what source?"

"We-Buy-Junk-We-Sell-Antiques shops."

"Ah. Mold. Mildew. Dry rot. Fragile handles—" Harlan's "fragile" rhymed with the river Nile. He pronounced it with infinite relish.

"Look," I said, "old steamer trunks are what you call 'collectibles.' There's like, this social stratum—of crafty women in California who make their entire income off restoring old steamer trunks, or antique dolls, or whatever. Strip, paint, shine the metal, new canvas, kill the bugs, new fancy paper, new handles—"

"Show me."

"Okay, Missouri." I didn't think he got the reference.

· — ·

I FOUND one lousy lonely steamer trunk, big and gringy, like the hatchet murderer'd use to ship his victims. I said, "No thanks: just looking." The man at the antiques galleria followed us around anyway. I could feel Harlan's superior gaze. Modest. Attentive. Insufferable. Right through the back of my skull loud and clear.

But the man says, "I know what you want, and we aren't it—" He's digging out the phone book: good sign in this business, as I recognize already. "There is a shop—" He has it open. "—out in the Fillmore—" Visions of bay breeze and Italian stucco; meanwhile he's cruising down the page. "—A shop called Pachyderm. Their entire business is restoring trunks." Vindication is a very sweet commodity.

· — ·

IN the window: a white ceramic elephant, waist-high, potted cymbidiums blooming from its howdah. Against it: two elk hide portmanteaux the color of oyster bisque, perfect: loving hands put them away in tissue a hundred years ago. And on them, just casually, as if the owner tossed it at his bags, a Knights of Columbus cocked hat, splendid and blue-black, smothered in braid, gold couched work crosses and a froth of ostrich plumes.

Ms. Pachyderm is slim, modish, vague, intense, and cross-eyed. Human version of a Siamese cat. Whichever eye you choose to talk to, the other points over your shoulder. She has some vintage clothes as well as luggage, one tall ornate brass rack of them, labeled April 14, 1911. The question, of course: *why*? And Harlan makes the big mistake of asking.

"*Oh*," she says, "that's the date of the sinking."

I can tell he's headed for deep water. I head for the back of the shop. Trunks and trunks standing open, trunks of romance, trunks of mystery, trunks full of dreams.

"You mean you don't *know* about Titanic Parties?"

One is coffin-shaped, and standing upright on the flat end, has a hanging locker to the left and drawers for nameless treasures on the right. Beside it is a gloriously handsome little trunk, its inside and its several trays done in rose-sprig paper, flyspecked just enough to be original.

"—*Well*, on the anniversary of the sinking, we charter a Bay Cruise ship, and everyone comes in 1911 outfits; there's food and champagne and dancing all night, people who get really into it want period luggage so they can change from their deck clothes to their evening wear—"

Inside the high, bowed lid a label says,

NATHAN NEAT & CO.
MANUFACTURERS, WHOLESALE AND RETAIL DEALERS
IN THE FINEST QUALITY OF
TRUNKS AND TRAVELING EQUIPAGE

SARATOGA TRUNKS, EUGENIE, CONTINENTAL,
BEACH, IMPERIAL, FRENCH,
SOLE LEATHER PORTMANTEAUX, SOLE LEATHER VALISES,
HAT BOXES, EXTENSION BAGS,
RAILROAD, MACKINTOSH, SHOPPING,
IN RUSSIA, GRAIN, SEAL,
AND ALLIGATOR LEATHER

TRUNKS AND BAGS REPAIRED AND MADE TO ORDER
AT SHORT NOTICE.

It's *me* this time. *I* want it. Nathan Neat indeed. I'd love to set him up with Joshua Sweet, on whom I laid my extra Belshangles ticket. Nathan Neat and Joshua Sweet'd make a classy pair of Rap MC's. I'd love to order out *one each* of *everything* in Nathan Neat's hundred-year-old catalog, all held together with alligator leather.

"—So popular," she's saying, "we've added another in November and tickets are left for that one—" (Harlan nods in all the right places but his eyes are beginning to glaze.) "—only fifty dollars, everything included; such a *sensational fun* value for these days—"

· — ·

I TOOK the coffin, Nathan Neat and the two portmanteaux from the window; Ms. Pachyderm looked quite disconsolate at the Titanic Party's loss.

But Harlan broke her heart. He paid her price, and took away her cocked hat. Poor bare window: only its elephant and orchids left.

We belted the coffin in the passenger seat, Nathan Neat sat on the floor, the huge portmanteau eased into the boot (as Harlan called it), much newspaper safeguarding it from jack, lug wrench, and spare tire's rage. I crammed myself behind the seats, hugging the smaller one. Harlan wore his Knights of Columbus hat. We Porsched home through fog and sun and other San Francisco traffic.

A bellhop helped us port our treasures: big tall girl in monkey-suit. Long gold hair. Then I checked the shoes. It was the same pretty guy who'd tried so hard to lavish Tom with almond tart. Harlan stopped digging for change, and glancing up sharply, gave him much the once-over he himself had received from Tim the Tailor.

"What's your name?"

The boy shuffled and studied his feet, shyly as any sweet child. "Christopher."

"Christopher what?"

"Grantham. Most people call me Chris." Small hope raised his eyes.

"In which case, I shall call you Kit," said Harlan (and owned him for life). "I need someone for errands—"

"Can't sir, during hours—"

"My name's Harlan. When are you off? Soon enough. Come in, I'll give you money; here are the things I need—

"—now these you can have from a cleaners' if you ask politely and offer to pay; the sewing thread should be of the following shades; this is from the market; and this—may have been sold. If not, lay it away and cash the second check. Should the bank give you difficulties, call me."

· — ·

SO Harlan called Tom this time.

We'd been ransacking the hotel newsstand for hype on Rhymer's Jig. Tom told him where to find the good stuff. Harlan wrote down titles and issues.

He lay on his back on the couch, telling stories that didn't need ends, giving cryptic rebuttals to undecipherable questions. He giggled and sang. Tom's part sounded just the same. Private accent, private grammar, private words.

Twin language.

Then Tom puts on some English for my benefit; Harlan leaves us privacy. Look at me: another poorly informed tourist, a stranger in their strange land.

Damn.

They don't need anyone to leave them privacy, they secrete their own, like an octopus does ink.

And now I have a yet worse guilty conscience. I've written Tom's London phone number in ball point pen on the palm of my hand while Harlan wasn't looking.

"I take it you do like white leather?"

"Women who bought silk frocks didn't do elastics."

"So why didn't she hand it to her dressmaker or her lady's maid or something, if it's such a treasure?"

"She could afford a new one."

"So what am I supposed to do?"

"The elastics."

The item in question was crinkled, yellowed, enormous in the waist as some old lady's baggy underwear. Harlan found it in a basement Salvation Army Store by his usual method, running a light hand and a jaundiced eye down the shoulders of the garment racks.

The woman at the register was also old and yellow.

"Whazzat fabric? Ha? Whazzat? Zat *silk*! Ha!" She looked at the tag: $2.99, marked down to $1.99. "Those girls in back," she said grimly, "they don' know *nothin'*."

I heard her, as we left, vigorously upbraiding the back room in whatever language they spoke.

"Elastics is *all*?"

"Wash it."

"All the silk tags I see say dry clean only."

Harlan gave his chin that haughty little tilt. "Do you believe everything you read? Washing old silk is a sensual experience. Run your hands through it. Cleanse it of its care. Think about the brown silk moths in their mulberry trees, and the summer moon in old China."

Some of the stuff our new liveried retainer Kit was buying vanished, unopened and mysterious, into Harlan's room. But a scary large amount of it was for me: packaged elastic in several widths, assorted needles, thread in off-white, beige, black, navy, midnight blue, pearl gray, and red—why those colors exactly? Plastic dry cleaner bags, vinyl drip-dry hangers, padded hangers, bottles of Ivory Liquid.

I hauled the crackly attenuated old elastic from its casing, using it as line to pull the new one in. I sewed it up. The old dress gained a whole new shape, all the sags and bags departed. I dumped it in the sink, as per instruction, with a shot of Ivory. The water turned dirty orange. About ten sinkfuls later, the silk had lightened to the color of dead skin. I hung it in the shower. It clung to itself and shivered.

"Shake it," said Harlan.

"What?"

"The frock. Repeatedly. Until it dries. It reduces the necessity for ironing." Like they say in the movies, I got a bad feeling about this.

But sometime in the night the silk faery came and made a changeling of my withered washee. The top is like a guy's shirt now: cuffed sleeves, pearl buttons, breast pockets. Only the collar's long, I can make a small tie of it or let it flow down smoothly on the breast. Then the nipped-in waist with loops for a tiny belt. Kathryn Hepburn could have worn this dress. The skirt's a half circle (like the one Tim's making) that shimmers and glimmers around my legs and swings and clings, curls and swirls, shines and twines—Lauren Bacall could have worn this dress. And maybe she did.

· —— ·

TIM has the skirt of the wedding dress deployed like a parachute, engulfing his upstairs worktable. Stacked around, all over everywhere like giant communion wafers, are circles or discs of white kid leather. About 2½ inches in diameter, fine, thin, flexible, rich, alive to touch.

Here I stand, with my little bag of silk stuff that wants mending and pearl buttons, wondering where the merchants live who deal in magic leather. Are they more good friends, and all Tim has to do is call and they deliver? Have they died too, and left it to him? Wondering how Tim cut the piles of discs so cleanly and so round; how long it'd taken him to do it. He must sit up all night at home, working on my stuff.

I wonder where home is.

A house within walking distance. Inhabited by him and four boys. I've heard its genial uproar on the phone; I've never seen the house. I haven't been invited. Haven't spied on Harlan's every move, but I don't think he's been invited either. Would he be invited if I wasn't here?

I've seen the boys, one at a time.

Cody's a motorcycle mechanic. Cute cute cute.

Danny's going to California Culinary Academy and trails this wonderful aura of onions, garlic, lemon, and sweet basil behind him. Makes me drool whenever he walks in.

Neil. There's a priceless one. Neil wears the surplus of several armies, lots of pockets pulled wrong-side-out into flapping tongues, a yellow shower cap with a big pink button asking "What's Innuendo??" and answering (fine print underneath) "Up your ass in Italian!" and condom packets on earring wires in both ears.

That's a game I know well: Cut-Rate Hideous, your most outrage for your least outlay. The kid is obviously with some rude boy band. Bet I could even guess the name of it.

Richard is a bank clerk and dresses as straight as the Golden Rule.

Tim calls all of them "son" and "dear," but they aren't his sons. Or are they? They aren't all his lovers. Are they? What's he keeping? A boarding house? A harem? A sanctuary for rare and endangered youth?

"*Yes,*" I said, "*I do like white leather. Very much.*"

He'd turned the hem outward by an inch and a quarter, flattening and distributing the extra cloth along the curve. Over it went the leather disks, tangent to each other and the finished edge. The raw edge vanished. Then in all the valleys, as if they'd sifted down, a rain of precious hailstones, lodging in every depression between the white leather moons, went the pearls.

"There. Now that's how it's going to look."

He had the partly finished top already on a hanger in a bare closet. The remnant silk lay carefully re-rolled, enthroned in imperial darkness on the shelf above.

"I was reading in a paper," I said, "where this—like, soap opera heroine? —got married in Texas; it took four people three whole months to sew the seed pearls on her dress. Now, I hope that I don't have three months."

"Larger pearls," said Tim.

"More people?" queried Harlan.

"Smaller people."

"I beg your pardon?"

Tim had enlisted the services of a seamstress, or rather, seamstresses to sew them on: a tiny smiling Thai woman, Lourdes Ng, and her daughters. She spoke no English but introduced them anyway: Lorette, Salette, and Fatima. The Pearl Ladies.

"I do hope she's not past the age of childbearing," Harlan whispered in my ear. "I can hardly wait for Garabandal."

"And Medjugorje," I whispered back. We shared a good long giggle over that.

Religiously as any surgeon, Tim washed his hands, then spread the long silk semicircle on the cutting table. "I want to do the leather part by machine, and I'll do it myself." He'd hefted a portable from another room. Now he positioned it and eased the silk hem into its metal jaw. Gently, he immobilized the discs with hairdresser's tape. "Stronger tape'll mar the surface; no pins for the same reason. Can't re-stitch or alter anything, so—we'll just have to do it right the first time." With a tiny regular stitch, he edge-sewed the first disc: from its left, where it covered the raw edge of the silk, in a right-hand arc across its top; then he smoothly pivoted the cloth, punched "reverse," and sewed the bottom sector backward, arriving where he began.

I understood, intellectually, what he'd done, sewed a full circle without screwing the silk full circle through the machine. Skill of that kind leaves me cowed and speechless. All sewing machines hate me on sight. Needles shatter, bobbins jam. Gordian knots form in their insides.

Tim broke his threads and positioned the second disc. Then the third. After about the sixth, he washed up again.

I saw Harlan absorbed in working with him, easing and expediting the flow of cloth into the master's hands, deftly as an apprentice of many years.

Curly Locks, Curly Locks, wilt thou be mine?
Thou shalt not wash the dishes or else feed the swine,
But sit on a cushion and sew a fine seam,
And feed upon strawberries, sugar and cream—

My inner voice and I are not always on speaking terms. I got out, quick, through French doors at the back of the shop, onto the sun deck (tar and gravel inside a solid wooden parapet). I was now on top of Valerie's apartment with my dumb plastic sack of mending.

She was still singing in her kitchen down below.

A giant eucalyptus overshadowed me, dropping shreds of bronzy bark, green sickle leaves, drifts of bloom and woody seed pods onto gravel, a few dusty metal chairs, and a chaise. Big redwood planters filled the corners, man-high jade plants thriving in them. Next to the sunnier one was a cardboard carton with an arch scissored in its side.

Somebody'd taken felt pens and written in a rainbow round the arch the name "Shadrach." From the arch, the front end of a large land tortoise eyed me placidly.

My inner voice, completely unrepentant for "Curly Locks, Curly Locks," sang "O-o-oh, they all walked around in the *fiery* furnace, *Shad*rach, *Me*shach, *Abed*nego-*o*—"

The boook of Daniel's "three children in the furnace," walking up and down and singing praise, with that shadowy fourth, "like an angel to God" to keep them company. Add the bass line to their harmony. Keep them from burning up. I think all the grown-up children of this town are walking in the furnace, with no asbestos angel anywhere.

Shadrach rose high on his legs and surged to meet me, sedately grand, a miniature colossus. He solemnly checked each Eucalyptus dropping in his path, ending with the toes of my shoes. The eyes that looked up into mine were gold as Harlan's. *Oh, look out.* Suddenly there's no place safe from Beauty Incarnate.

I said, "Hold it right there," to Shadrach, dumped my mending, zipped in, across the room, and down the banister, averting eyes from Harlan and all his works.

Old city houses have kitchens like ships' galleys, narrow, wooden, and dark. Valerie's isn't hard to find. Just follow the Rodgers and Hammerstein.

Sure enough, right above the sink is an antique picture of the Sacred Heart, one of the disembodied kind the New Church banned as heresy. You wouldn't expect her to pay much heed to that.

Mama had its double—flaming with love made visible, rose-wreathed, wound with thorns and dripping blood, in sweet, faded nun's embroidery on padded silk—stuck behind our own front door at home. Where we'd have to deal with it going out, but visitors wouldn't have to coming in. It always fascinated me, even before I knew it was anything radical. I remember being very small and asking, *"Is that a heart wrapped in barb wire?"* Mama said, "Yes."

"'Scuse me, Mrs. Lagomarsino, who feeds the tortoise?"

Took her a moment to catch up. Then she turned this most amazing smile on me, big, silly, sloppy-loving as a dog. "Why *dear*," she said, "*you* do!"

She fixed me up a blue and white bowl full of lettuce and tomato. I knew exactly now why old Tim hired her.

SATURDAY, AUGUST 30

"Well, it is fun," I conceded. Ms. Pachyderm and her Titanic parties filtered uneasily through my mind.

Harlan nodded sagely.

White silk isn't white.

It's beeswax color: new wax comb nothing's been laid in, no brown honey, no orange pollen, no white bee-grubs.

They used to melt that virgin wax for church candles.

Candles the color of white silk. Work of insects, both: the bee queen's nursery, the caterpillar's shroud. They have to kill the worms to get the silk off. Wax and silk and candlelight, all the same magical-mystery color. (Don't look now, I think I'm being seduced.)

Some thrift shops harangue and flirt and giggle in Spanish. Some buzz Vietnamese. Some operate on Island time, weighty, bright colored and Samoan slow, while some are witty black as Africa. Some keep the books in Tagalog. Some hire the handicapped. And their wares? Oh. Just everything, from K-Martian ticky-tack to Paris originals. Come in, friend, and see if you can tell the difference.

And add to those the tribe of vintage clothes shopkeepers and the flea market and antique show gypsies with the wonderful shady gauderies they buy and sell, you have the whole City of Man on parade. Parade, nothing! *For sale!* Come by, come try, come buy! Tim's old Charlie, the vintage clothes guy, must have enjoyed one incredible fun life while it lasted.

I don't just *think* I'm being seduced, I *know*. Like an insect victim with one or two more seconds of thrash left, before the spider poison gets me.

"*However,*" I said. "However, there is something still just basically, morally unsatisfactory about spending all day every day shining myself and playing games."

He looked perfectly shocked. "Humankind was designed and placed here for the express purpose of playing games! The fate of the universe hangs upon how well we do it! Holy Wisdom—" he waved a finger at me, "'Holy Wisdom says:

The Lord possessed me in the beginning of His ways,
before he had made anything from the beginning—

I was with him forming all things: and was delighted every day,
playing before Him at all times;

Playing in the world: and my delights were to be with the children of men—

So the Devil can quote scripture.

I surveyed myself in the mirror again, full length front, back, and side, in my latest vintage clothes shop treasure, bought with wild excitement, washed and pressed and mended with endless loving care at Tim's this morning. A midnight blue silk '30s dress, a print of small gold clockwork spangled over it like innards of a watch.

"No, this is absurd. I look like shit."

"Why do you say that?"

"I can *see*."

"Thomas is a lover of beauty, and I mean a lover, not a critic. His taste in human flesh is kindly (as he is), and eclectic, but excellently high. Thomas doesn't bed ugly people. And, since he is, first and last, a slippery bugger, ugly people don't bed him—"

Feeling more and more bitterly at risk, I sneered. "Not even the rich ones?"

"The rich are seldom ugly. No, I assure you, keeping close check on Thomas's activities yields an almost frighteningly formidable catalog of human beauty. In which your own is, to date, the latest entry—

"If your self-evaluation is so lacking, shouldn't you honor his? You're built like a thoroughbred filly; most all Thomas's women are. You could do high-fashion modeling. In an era capable of fueling its fantasy on Princess Stephanie of Monaco, you could rule the school. There is *nothing wrong* with your looks: you just weren't properly brought up, that's all."

What I wanted, what I wanted very badly, was to punch him in the mouth. "I was *very* well brought up; I was *raised to use my head!*"

"Ah," he said, "That is exactly how you look. And I do understand: for so was I. Fortunately, such things are—not past remedy. Every mutually agreeable bargain wants a buyer and a seller, hmm? Buyer says 'Here's my cold cash, serve me one of *those*.' Seller strikes a pose and says 'If you want my services, *bid high*.' And you *do* want your services to be required, don't you? Buyer sees, and makes advances, seller advertises, and, when the desired offer is received, accepts. With grace. You've been taught so far to see, and make advances—"

"'Worked, hasn't it?"

"Granted. *But now you intend to marry*—"

"*Have* married," I put in.

"—You *are marrying*—" He paused to check my expression.

I nodded. "Better."

"—What is known in the common parlance as a Rock-and-Roll Star. You are about to *be seen.*"

"Look," I said. "I told you, I'm the kid whose blouse was always out of her skirt and whose socks came down, but I was a great two-miler. There's only so much you can do."

"You're the kid married to Thomas."

"Well maybe I *shouldn't* be married to him! Is *that what you're trying to say?*"

"No. I'm asking what he saw in you."

"I don't know!"

"Think!"

"Whatever it was, I'd better not *mess* with it, had I?"

"Ah. Which you are in constant proximate danger of doing, just as long as you don't know what it was. In order to defend, you must evaluate—"

"There's bound to be more to self defense than learning to keep your clothes straight!"

"Quite possibly so, and when we've accomplished the matter of the clothes, we'll turn our investigations in that direction, but—"

"Clothes first?"

"Clothes first. Well, who ever told you there was anything wrong with 'shining' yourself? It's only the most human and humane of pastimes, even for the sanctified: one of the Fathers (Bernard, I think) said, 'You wouldn't want a Bride of Christ to be *dull?*' Games are the stuff of life.

"Oh, and *you do* play them; only the name of *yours* is 'Unobserved Observer,' while I say: in order to observe, or know to the full, one must oneself be known, seen, observed. Choose your term. You've loaded all the world's glamour onto poor Thomas and kept none for yourself, a form of self-denigration he'd be the last to ask for or approve. You'll have to stop it soon; you'll make him dreadfully uncomfortable, and you *don't* want that. You want the Parr Short Course on Grace and Advertising. Let's have a look at you."

I stumped around in a blind fury.

"Ah," he said, "problem. You need shoes."

"I have shoes."

"Heels."

"I can't wear heels."

"Why not? Have you trouble with weak ankles?"

"Certainly not!"

"The paper-thin flats young stylists are affecting, aside from enriching the shoe men by being unrepairable, are nothing in origin but witless imitation of our Princess Diana, who has, after all, extraordinary reasons for wearing them. Standing taller than one's mate ain't politic, when one's mate is the future King of England. But you are *not* five-foot-ten, and Thomas (thank God) is not the Prince of Wales. You should dress in two-inch heels. They convey authority."

"Bull*shit!* They convey sore feet!" Going barefoot always was my mode of choice. After that came the best running shoes I could torque my near-and-dear into buying for me, and after that, the cheapest canvas tennies going: good honest things according to their kind.

But force me to look civil, it was paper-thin flats, and even those worn in—to the point of worn out—before they felt acceptable. Princess Diana never entered the picture. And I kept on wearing them, till mere fragments of sole remained between my grubby little toes and the pavement and the uppers looked like spats.

He practically bum's-rushed me to a dancer's supply store. "There," he said. "Sturdy, sensible, old-fashioned, wicked all at once: athletic gear for medalists of stage, boudoir, and silver screen: a genuine, authentic pair of Fuck Me Pumps."

Character shoes. Tap shoes minus the taps. Suggestively displayed on a Lucite shelf shaped like a grand piano, with blue sequin shorts, a top hat, and a telescoping cane. I would gladly have killed him. He had the shop girl snickering already.

"How many pairs of her size have you? In the white, that is?" They came in black, white, and tan. Harlan took one pair each of the blacks and tans, and all four whites. "Three white pairs we'll have dyed. One red, one blue, one—you name it?"

"Lavender," I said.

"Lavender it is."

"I really don't care what color you have 'em dyed, I don't intend to wear 'em anyway."

"I think you will."

"Nobody makes *you* run around in heels!"

"Perhaps not, but I can. Thomas is quite elegant in them."

Feeling almost unendurably spiteful, I said, "Just too slow to catch the boys, huh?" God, what a mistake.

"You don't understand. Thomas doesn't chase 'boys.' Thomas chases girls. 'Boys' chase Thomas."

"Do they catch him?"

I got an amused look out from under that mass of hair. Just a trifle mocking. "Well that depends, doesn't it, on whether or not he runs—"

"Does he?"

"—And how fast."

"Does he?"

"More often than not."

"Not in stupid uncomfortable old heels!"

The sales girl had come back with all the boxes.

"What's the largest size in these?" asked Harlan.

"We have tens, I know."

Harlan had his sock foot on the measuring gadget. Dumb girl was giggling up a storm now. "Good *heavens, tiny* feet! That's a ladies' nine and a half! (giggle giggle giggle)."

"In the black, please," he said. And when she'd gone, "I'll wear them just as long as you will. Is it a wager?"

Damn. His shoes were a full size bigger than mine. So why should they seem so small? How, in fact, did *he* get off seeming small? He was exactly the same height as I was. *Exactly*. And *he* got off being this elegant little creature. He didn't have to wear panty hose: he had plain masculine socks, little tweedy ones that bagged around his ankles. They looked just darling. I saw no justice in that.

I longed to promenade him by some flock of Japanese tourists with their cameras out. So fixated on his shoes, I hardly noticed my own: only the sound we made together coming briskly up the sidewalk: clop-clip, clip-clop, like the two ends of a horse. Fairly sharp thoughts I had, too, about which end was which. I wondered if there'd ever been such a phrase (or such a concept) as an *"homme fatal."*

It was his face. Nothing human deserves a face like Harlan's—not the perks or the burdens of it, either one.

Women with beauty like Harlan's warm the beds of princes and tycoons and presidents; their faces hog the covers of the magazines. People want to know the last small thing about them, how they live and love, and how they die. And if they drug or drink themselves to death, if their lovers bash or their husbands divorce them, when they get fat or go crazy and die young, well, everybody's interested, but not too very much surprised. It had to be paid for someway. People are obsessed, fascinated, and scared as hell of a woman with looks like Harlan's.

But what about a *man*?

I knew this guy at school who kept a poster of The Doors' Jim Morrison on his wall. He said, "I thought I was an atheist, but whenever I look at *him*, I'm not so sure—"

Morrison was the ultimate Black Romantic, all doom and gloom, but, supposing you don't fall for it completely, just a hair—(Say it in a whisper) stodgy. Even before he wasted it. Harlan had it over poor Jim Morrison every way. And he was anything but wasted. Drugged out, at one time, he may have been (I wasn't sure I understood that, even now): his face was still a museum piece of ivory and ebony and gold inlay, a treasure out of Tutankhamen's tomb. Perfect preservation.

Damn his eyes.

The rest of the day I spent sneaking my own eyes shut, times when it didn't matter, pretending I was blind. Wondering how it would be simply to enjoy Harlan's company. Wondering how it had been growing up inside his face. He couldn't've ever spoken with a person, male or female, not for a minute—before he'd see their eyes begin to slide around his face like melted butter.

And my husband said the rest of him matched it.

· — ·

WE spent the afternoon on Polk street, the place to go for bootleg music. Whenever a shop gets busted, a better one takes its place. Where we went had the good stuff individually priced in racks up front. After it sat there long enough, it was half-priced in boxes underneath. The truly high mileage crud was banished at a buck an album to the back room and finally, tied in newsprint, forty or fifty to a bundle, was disposed of, ten bucks each, as "Mystery Mounds."

But with the really, *really* interesting stuff, only the cover was in the rack: you asked for the vinyl at the desk.

Young guy behind the desk was the kind who couldn't stand still very well, and practiced drum riffs on everything. So Harlan found himself a Belshangles bootleg, *Hard On Belshangles,* plain white jacket with the oddest contents list you ever saw, 129 of a limited 500 edition, on clear orange vinyl. And he wanted to write a check.

"Could I see your driver's license, please?" Then the guy saw the license. Then he saw Harlan. Unlike Tom, all he had to do was tack his hair back: nobody knew him. But today he had his shades on, and his hair was looser than Medusa's.

Holy shit.

Oh my God.

Could I take you to lunch?

The Hot Szechwan place next door was closed for the lull between lunch and dinner, but he hauled us in there anyway. Food began appearing. A whispered word, a phone call, and weirdo music guys began appearing too, like so many dwarves on Bilbo Baggins's doorstep. They spent the rest of the afternoon enthralled, listening to Harlan pontificate. And he could do it for hours without telling *anybody anything.*

Food came in three speeds, brewed mild for American taste, hot, and lethal. I went for lethal, as usual (as did Harlan), and had the usual disappointment. "Lethal" was only mildly warm. "I wish," I whispered in his ear, "like just *once, somebody'd* lead me to *something* that's genuinely too hot."

Harlan turned on me that long, warm, gold-eyed look that

can raise your internal body temp from the center out, like microwaves.

"I meant *food!*"

The look broke down under pressure of a grin. He whispered, "Okay, Missouri."

When the restaurant should be opening for dinner, and everyone was full of Princess Beef and Kung Pao Chicken, and the guys were mostly full of Tsing Tao, Harlan slithered away amid loving farewells.

He had all their phone numbers. Nobody had his.

Down the street, at a lingerie shop, he found what he'd looked for elsewhere, China silk-knit panty hose, brand-named archly (but not inappropriately) "Queen's Wear." They were twenty bucks a pair, and came in twelve colors. Harlan calmly bought me all twelve colors, three pairs each. $720 plus tax.

I was flabbergasted.

They also had silk-knit bikini briefs from China.

Harlan, again, prepared to go for all the colors.

I said, "*Wait a minute,* I happen to prefer white pants." (Scared too many times by a hemorrhage of paisleys.) So white was what I got.

They had all sorts of frisky stuff for guys, this being Polk Street. Silk knit briefs cut for the male crotch, black satin briefs with studs. And the most obnoxious joker jockstraps of pink satin; the pouch for the balls was an elephant face, complete with button eyes and ostrich-fluff forelock, and a quite unnecessarily large satin tube trunk poking out in front.

Harlan bought something for himself. I didn't want to know. I stayed as far away as possible. I mean, what if it was one of those elephants?

And it could have been a giggle meant for Tom.

SUNDAY, AUGUST 31 11:00 AM

We motored down to Palo Alto and sang with the Saint Ann's Choir.

Marc Swann is a professor of early music. Marc Swann is also my godfather. He has directed Saint Ann's choir since before I was born. The choir rehearses an hour before Mass.

MARC: "What part do you sing?"

HARLAN: (meekly) "All of them."

MARC: *"Soprano?"* That got a big laugh from everybody. Marc put him on tenor. He sang it, sweet and clear. He sight-read perfectly.

MARC: "What about bass?" He had three tenors, and only himself on bass. Harlan switched. His bass was accurate but unexceptional. Marc squinted and glowered at him: you could see that Harlan had him just intrigued as hell. Next motet, he said, "Okay, alto."

Harlan's alto was a natural extension of his tenor, full, rich, and *loud*. The rest of the women sounded like breathy kids.

"All right! Soprano!"

Out came this glorious blazing falsetto. Nobody was audible but him.

Marc said, *"Where did you study?"*

"King's College Chapel Choir. Cambridge."

"Oh."

Harlan sang bass with Marc, neat, straight, I almost said to myself "inconspicuous." Hardly the word for him. Every woman, girl, female whatever in the place cozied up to me in turn, goggling and gushing.

"Why didn't you *tell* us?"

"Ooooo, *he's wu-uhnderful*!"

"That's Harlan Parr? The rock star?"

Pray harder, and field his compliments for him. Try to keep my teeth from showing. Pray for insight. Some Holy Wisdom from the Mass to help me keep my shit together.

> *When you are invited by someone to a wedding party, do not sit in the place of honor in case some greater dignitary has been invited. Then the host might come and say to you, 'Make room for this man,' and you would have to proceed shamefacedly to the lowest place—*
>
> This is the Gospel of the Lord.

I got out. Just cruised out the side door at the homily, and lay on the sunny lawn between the chapel and Newman House. My pain in the gut was there in force. I felt queasy, bloated, and weird. Infected. And it *wasn't* all in my head: things were noticeably swollen out; I could feel it with my hands. Maybe I'd lie here till the Mass was over. When my parents found me, I'd say I was sick.

Shadow fell across my face. The pastor's big gold furball of a collie came, panting solicitous dog breath, darkening the sun. When he started to drool in my eye, I retreated to the house. Harlan found me.

Harlan asked me no questions, I told him no lies. He took me away instead, and fed me jalapeno fettuccini. I scarfed it down embarrassingly fast, seeing as it wasn't my first square meal in weeks. Gut pain still with me.

Well, I could be getting my period. How about that?

Quick hike to the ladies' room. Nothing.

On to the thrift shops.

Silk blouses.

Oh wow. Some kid's junior ROTC Marine's dress jacket. It fit me perfectly. Midnight blue with red piping, brass buttons, and epaulets. Stick daisies in the epaulets, I'd look like Sergeant Pepper. Get myself a jarhead haircut, I'd look like a Marine. A very small Marine.

It also fit Harlan. He didn't look like a Marine.

I am the Monarch of the Sea,
(my inner voice suggested)
The Ruler of the Queen's Navee,
Whose praise Great Britain loudly chants—

I went and found myself an item he couldn't wear: a shirt-waist frock in Thai silk, very proper with a self belt and self buttons, blue and white all over pattern like Tim the Tailor's Chinese dishes.

I took that back, and he said "God, *no*. Sorry, but it's strictly Princess Margaret."

Princess Margaret is known to have a penchant for rock stars. Going off to the Caribbean with 'em. Shit. Harlan might *know* Princess Margaret. I wondered how well.

· —— ·

SUNDAY night dinner.

I ate, and didn't hear what was said to me. Everyone who knew my family must have been there. They pushed the two long tables together and had to bring another from outside. People were eating off their laps in the living room. Every damn Stanford musicology student came to hear Harlan hold court: those intellectual Ph.D-bound women especially, simpering and dangling on his every word.

I got my *Choosing the Wrong Side* glass full of milk, and went off.

Mama has a little bookcase by her side of the bed, all favorite stuff, some of it kid stuff, like Milne's *Now We Are Six*. Something in there I'd wanted to remember, about dressing a bride.

Here. A poem called "Shoes and Stockings." I got to the part about all the old wives "weaving gold stockings for her dainty feet," and put the book back where I'd found it.

Unreal. Totally. My feet are very practical, nothing dainty about my feet. And as of yesterday I am the owner of enough Polk-Street silk pantyhose to last for life.

You can't mend anything with sugar frosting. Nothing quite so unpredictable as anchoring one's whole world view to half-remembered poetry. And I wanted cosmic glue so very badly.

Finish the milk. Back to the bookcase.

Now here was input of a different kind, *The Lost Books of Eden*. Hokey title, but the contents aren't: all the early church stuff that didn't quite make it into the Bible. Here was the *Gospel of Mary*, and the *Protevangelion*, with the stories about Saint Joachim and Saint Ann.

I did the random access trick. Close eyes, open page, finger in the middle, smack.

What I *wanted*—was where Joachim met Anna in the city

gate, and they kissed (so nothing would fall, like the song says), and both lived (like the other song says) happy ever after in the marketplace. And that's not the way to *do* it, need I say; you can't go looking for what you *want*, only for what's *there*:

—At this Anna was exceedingly troubled, and
having on her wedding garment, went about
three o'clock in the afternoon to walk
in her garden.

And she saw a laurel-tree, and sat under it
and prayed unto the Lord—

And as she was looking toward heaven she
perceived a sparrow's nest in the laurel.

And mourning within herself, she said "Woe is me,
who begat me? And what womb did bear me that I
should be thus accursed before the children of
Israel and that they should reproach and deride
me in the temple of my God: Woe is me, to what
can I be compared?

I am not comparable to the very beasts of the
earth, for even the beasts of the earth are
fruitful before thee O Lord! Woe is me, to
what can I be compared?

I am not comparable to the brute animals, for
even the brute animals are fruitful before thee,
O Lord! Woe is me, to what am I comparable?

I cannot be compared to the waters, for even
the waters are fruitful before thee, O Lord!
Woe is me, to what can I be compared?

I am not comparable to the waves of the sea,
for these, whether they are calm or in motion
with the fishes which are in them praise thee,
O Lord! Woe is me, to what can I be compared?

I am not comparable to the very earth, for
the earth produces its fruit and praises thee—

I roosted on the edge of my parents' bed (which Papa regularly told me not to do for eighteen years because it breaks the mattress down) and cried in the dim bedroom.

Both my wedding garments are hanging in a gay tailor's shop in San Francisco. It's nine o'clock at night. I don't have a sparrow's nest. I don't even have a laurel tree.

Papa, instincts firing on all cylinders as usual, came looking for me and told me to get off the edge of his bed.

I got into the middle. Still, what a ride I was embarked on. Not the product of my own imagination this time, but, as A.G. Bell said when he produced the telephone, "What God Hath Wrought." I am an observant flotsam in the fierce throes of reality. Praying like crazy, Lord: that I may see. *Lord: that I may see.*

And while You're at it, heal me. *Please.*

Papa stuck his head back in. "What nationality did you say he was?"

"Who?"

The head jerked toward the laughter in the dining room.

"I've carpeted this place with fan mags for six, almost seven years, and you haven't got that much by osmosis?"

"Not required. It's fairly obvious."

"What?"

"Spanish aristocrat. I went to Berkeley with a couple of brothers like that."

"Nope. *Wrong.*"

"What d'ya mean '*Wrong*'?"

"He's half English, half Arabic."

"Well? Doesn't that about describe what I said?"

My mind strayed momentarily down the genealogy of Spanish princes, Northman and Saracen bred into one, like the night of southern climes and starry skies, with all the best of dark and light met in their hair and in their eyes.

PAPA: (unflapped) "So which side are the nobility on?"

"The Arabs, I think." Horribly sober thought: the English might be as well; Parr is a super old name, after all. Like Catherine Parr, the wife who outlived Henry VIII.

"You sure you married the right one?" said Papa.

MONDAY, SEPTEMBER 1

"This," he said, standing in the middle of the living room carpet in the hotel suite, graphite bass in hand, "was the basic movement of the minuet. I trust you've done some dance?"

I'd have to lie to say no.

"Levé—French for 'up', a step on tiptoe—Plié—"

"French for 'squat'?"

Didn't quite break him up. His face shimmered, but stayed straight. "Relevé—up again, and stand. Up, down, up, stand—" All the while he's holding that bass and circling the carpet slowly to the left. Freaking eighteenth century must have had the strongest thighs in history.

Levé, plié, relevé, stand,
Levé, plié, relevé, stand—

The bass began to speak in rhythm:

Dum di-dum-dum
Dum dah—
Dum di-dum-dum
Dah—

"Also familiar, I trust?"

Not the minuet for sure, any more than this is Kansas.

It was the bass to "Holy Names."

"Holy Names" was off the *Sundog* album. All it said on the lyrics was, "Since the Names of the Almighty are infinite, no one knows them all."

Even wordless, it was several shades more exotic-erotic than "Calling Sister Midnight" or Led Zep's old "Cashmere." Even with the amps down, "Holy Names" should be meaner than Ravel's "Bolero." We've been playing electric rock for two weeks in this hotel room; either they've got totally great insulation, or total indulgence with the rich and famous.

It's the first Belshangles piece he's chosen. No excuses, I've survived the rest, he has me cornered. He hands me the bass, and settles into the Morocco strap of his electric Oud.

One-and-ah Two-and
(Rest) and Four (and)
One-and-ah Two-and
Three (and-rest-and)

step left, behind, left, point—
right, behind, right, and point—

My knees shook. My pelvis gritted. Round and round we went, rhythmic follow the leader, like the old camp game Ali Baba and the Forty Thieves. Like the old joke: "Know what happens if I unscrew your belly button? *Your ass falls off!*" My belly button's not just loose, it's gone. All my insides, from the ribs down, are gonna drop out on the floor.

My friend Mimi was a volunteer, answering phones for the VD Hotline. Said some guy called in and told her he had things dropping out of his rear, like grains of rice, only they wriggled. He was scared to death.

"So what did'ya tell him?"

"I told him he didn't have VD."

"You dummy! The poor guy had a tapeworm! Those were tapeworm sections! You mean you didn't recognize he had a freaking *tapeworm?* You got his number? Call him back!"

Maybe I have a tapeworm.

Keep the beat. Keep the spare, bony faith:

One, ( ), ( ), and-Four,
One, ( ), Three, ( ),

For Harlan's guitar line to wind in and out of, purr and rub its sides against in endless orgasmic variation: cough and moan, wheedle and hyperventilate like a tigress in heat.

I hurt all day.

· — ·

"WHAT say," said Tim, "we lower the V back."

"It's down to my shoulder blades already." Tim and Harlan, side by side, no response. "Any further and I can't wear a bra!"

"Pardon my ignorance: why should you?"

"Cause I look like a fourteen-year-old guy if I don't."

Tim and Harlan, side by side, fixated on my chest in thoughtful silence. "Slip the bra from under that and show me," said Tim. "You can do it in the next room."

"This silk's got show-through places."

"Mmm," said Harlan.

Tim said, "Clever, those Chinese."

Next room, hell. It's full of giggling Pearl Ladies. Downstairs I go, to the claustrophobic bathroom.

The bathroom is full of Thai food memories: *"Garlic,"* says Tim. "*Fish sauce.* Call it by its rightful name: *Nam pla*! We eat it and thrive, we also wash it off." After their meals, he washes his Pearl Ladies' fingers personally. By now that sink has a Nam Pla ring.

Jettison the useless little bra. Slip the unfinished top back on. What an amazing thing it is already: elegant, priceless, and funny all at once, not the least bit like my old dress. Tim's security works; it doesn't smell like Nam Pla. It smells like Sam Wah's treasure room. Like Harlan, only older.

Harlan's taste.

Me and mine getting all made over to Harlan's taste. I want

to scream and fling it, like a spider I've picked up by mistake. Yet what a flaming hypocrite I am. I'm head over heels in love with Harlan's taste, always have been.

How much of Belshangles was Harlan's taste?

How much of Tom was Harlan's taste?

Harlan's taste infected and infested everything he touched. Rare luxury, cheap luxury, found luxury, hard-won luxury, awesome luxury, funny-as-hell luxury, exquisite and down-at-the heel dirt-comfortable luxury sprouted around him like a garden of delights.

I started out of the bathroom, leaving the bra on the floor, and heard Tim's voice above say, "I still have the sense I'm missing something."

"Oh, assuredly."

"It isn't a joke?"

If Harlan said anything, I couldn't hear.

Tim persisted. "He *is* marrying this child? I'd hate to butcher Sam Wah's silk and find the whole thing wasn't on the up-and-up."

"As up-and-up as Thomas gets."

"If you don't mind my asking: *Why*, O Wise Effendi?"

And that would be the question, wouldn't it? The very thing I wanted most to know.

And sure as I was that Harlan knew, I was even surer that I didn't want to hear it. *Scared to, scared to, scared to!* The bathroom was suddenly unbearable. I was going to get sick. In the top half of my wedding dress. I pounded up the stairs to sunlight and fresh air. I made as much noise as possible.

Tim and Harlan. Side by side in grave inspection as I spun slowly before them, a jeweled Imperial treasure above the waist, Levi's below. "Hormones and silicone away from any boy I know," said Tim.

"I know."

"'If you can't hide it, decorate it!' Corollary Two of Tim's law: 'If the truth hurts, wear it.'"

Harlan choked on his piroshki.

Tim had me stand facing from him, while his big bright shears took another three inches off the back neckline.

· — ·

I HAD a dream that night about the hem of my dress. The white leather discs became all the full moons of summer inherent in the dragon's blessing; the pearls, an August meteor swarm of strange sky wealth sifting down among them.

TUESDAY, SEPTEMBER 2

My Harlan problem, I decided, was a guilty conscience. I took him to the beach, across the Golden Gate and out to the headlands of Marin through windy green valleys like the Braes of Scotland. We stopped at Rouge et Noire for a Brie, a French bread, and a bottle of Chardonnay.

Drake's beach. Long, straight, almost empty on a weekday afternoon. Behind us, the chalky bluffs that had made Drake homesick for the cliffs of Dover. In front, a mile or two across a placid sea, the fog bank lurked. In the narrow sea alley between fog and surf commercial salmon boats tended their wet business, back and forth. A queue of gulls screamed hopefully after each.

Harlan drank most of the wine and was going on about the press and countermeasures (a favorite topic). Things I Needed to Learn. He was quite emphatic with his bread and cheese.

"—So when they enquired about sexual matters, you see, I merely said, 'I sleep with my guitar.'"

"Plugged in."

"Exactly. (You've done your homework.) Noncommittal, you see, but memorable. Put them off, but give them some tidbit for the daily column. A technique to be mastered early.

"Actually some time elapsed before one of them had presence of mind to ask if I *still* slept with my guitar, to which I answered, 'Yes, and since I own over a hundred of them, it gives me a very rich emotional life. But busy.' Since that time, that's all they remember."

Just look at him now: white shirt, white slacks, white canvas jacket, white cap, white shoes. If Tom was like the classified ads for thoroughbreds, you know, the dressage and three-day event hopefuls "Athletic, willing, *spectacular* mover—," Harlan brought more to mind the listings on collector cars: "World-class racing performance with classic luxury. One owner. Lovingly maintained." Wow.

It didn't matter how he was gotten up, it was always done with the same whimsical, delicious care. He was just ultimately desirable. It was equally obvious he belonged to no one present. Look. Don't touch. I knew what Tom meant when he'd said he looked "expensive." I would have called it more like "unaffordable."

We were sitting on the sand below the cliffs at Drake's Bay, and the wine was all gone and the Brie and French bread almost were, and things had gotten very quiet except for the waves' long, lazy arch and dump against the sand, when the question, which had been baying at me now since yesterday, slipped out like a dog under the fence.

"Why did he marry me, Harlan?"

He loaded up the last of the bread with the last of the cheese and ate it. Dusted off the crumbs. "Why do you think?"

"I don't know."

"You never asked him?"

"Scared to."

"Ah. And he never said? I assumed some conversation took place on the matter."

"He said a lot of stuff."

"Par exemplum?"

"Like, kids have a right to know they were conceived in love."

"Ah. Such a romantic." He clicked his tongue in contained mirth. "Having not the slightest doubt one was conceived in love is *not* the bower of roses Thomas fantasizes."

"Like, if one or the other of you had sex change surgery, he could've married you."

Done it at last. The man is shocked. Eyes as round as Krugerrands. "He didn't!"

"He did."

"He lied to you!"

"He said he'd rather have it done to himself than you. He cried a lot, Harlan."

"That was most unkind of him, seeing there's no truth in it. What a wretched wedding day he must have given you."

"Don't know; it had its up side."

"What's more, he's left me guilty by implication; I feel obliged to set your heart at rest. No such matter was ever discussed; you can't realize how contrary to his nature that would be. Thomas never, *never* considered sex change surgery. Be assured. Why, the procedure adds five years to one's looks at best, or so I'm told."

I gaped at him.

I'd been had. Intellectually, emotionally strung along. Bested. Or worsted. Stung beyond endurance, overcome with the urge to do something ignominiously physical to him—I scored a fast hit on his immaculate little shirtfront with a double scoop of sand. I hoped it went inside! I hoped it got in his underwear! I hoped it chafed!

He was laughing, scrambling backward.

"*You!* You—you—you—"

"Go on! Think of a word!"

"Poop!"

I arced another great gout of sand at his head, his dark blowing hair. He was running down the beach—"The word is *poof*, dear—"

"The word is snake!" He should be like an Arab horse, longer on endurance than speed. What I hadn't known, but was finding out—he could also dodge and change directions faster than Joe Montana.

"My favorite is—*catamite*—interesting derivation—look it up sometime—Means—a pretty lad—kept for—immoral purposes!"

The idea Joe Montana brought to mind: I'd always wanted to try tackle football, but never found a social opportunity. I launched myself arms first through the air, like a cartoon superhero.

Talk about beginner's luck. I hit his back and grabbed. Then he was going arms first too, both of us sailing through the air. Into the wet sand Harlan plowed, with me on top of him. The next wave, a big, foaming pile of gritty, icy, gray-green Pacific broke waist deep over us.

The water drained through our clothes—mine into his, into the sand, sucking and sliding away below us. His hair streamed out over the departing water, black foam tendrils.

I was lying on him, full frontal contact, like a heavy breathing scene out of some movie, a sex-reversed *China Girl* or *From Here to Eternity*—looking down into his face, and he was a shipwrecked sailor whom lascivious mermaids thought far too pretty to let drown. The expression on his face was unmistakable. He *melted*. What used to be known as "sweet surrender."

I'd been had again. Yet. Still. Conned into setting him in his position of greatest strength. This was his game, his gambit: he was master of it. He'd taken Tom with it a thousand times.

I got off him as fast as I could.

I walked up the shelving sand to where the dry began, and sat down with my arms around my knees and my head in my arms. Under my elbows I could see a billion sandflies streaming by, all in one direction, absorbed in their own affairs. The waves dumped quietly. Arched over, broke, and retreated. After a while, Harlan was sitting there beside me. We sat in silence for a long time. I heard him sigh. "Learn something new every day, don't we?" he said.

"Speak for yourself."

"I was. Miranda. Look at me."

"Nobody's called me Miranda since third grade: a bunch of guys made it 'Miranda Salamander' and I had to kick 'em all repeatedly in the shins to make 'em stop."

"You might have been more gracious. The salamander lives in fire."

"No they don't. They're little and wet and they live under rocks."

"Legend," he said softly, "has them native to the fire. So don't look at me, then. But listen. I want you to know that Thomas never contemplated sex change surgery. Third World butcher shops are not his venue. And together, we are the last, the very last thing on earth that any legitimate clinic wants to see come prancing through its doors. A five-minute evaluation of his personality profile, or of mine, and with any professional conscience they would say—"

"No way, Jose."

"Not my words, dear, but certainly my drift."

"Don't call me dear." The waves came in their order, pouring over heavily. Sighing back out again, playing with the sand. "Unless you mean it, that is." I had to take my head out of my arms to look at him. "*Do* you mean it?"

"Yes-No. I suppose."

"Make it a hundred percent, and you're welcome. You are covered with sand from head to foot, know that? You are a sight!"

He grinned wickedly. "At last we match."

We were too filthy and too far away for our regular evening pilgrimage to Chez Panisse. We found an oyster-market-cum-café on the east side of Tomales Bay, serving oysters and oysters, and very little else but oysters. We each put down a dozen fried, and when that didn't seem to do the trick, we split a third dozen between us. All there was to drink was American beer, which Harlan didn't fancy. We went home very sober.

"Thank you for a wonderful outing. You should consider going into business: the finest tours of San Francisco and environs."

"C'mon, you: I wouldn't do it for just anyone."

He went into the bathroom. I heard the shower start.

What if he burst out wet and naked and pulled me into the shower with him? Nothing. The shower went on running. Some night I'd go inside my room and shut the door, and only then I'd notice his hand was still in mine, and he was on the end of it. And then. And then.

I went to the phone in my room, found Tom's London number that I'd cribbed off Harlan when he wasn't looking. I got an operator, asked for England, asked for the number. I imagined him answering. Imagined everything I had to say—

"Tom."

"Well, well."

"I've got a question for you."

"Unusual time."

"I wanted privacy."

"Oh yeah?"

"I'm worried about Harlan."

"You two not getting along?"

"Contrariwise. I'm afraid we are."

"Oh?"

"Tom. You know how attractive he is."

"What are you trying to tell me?"

Then I could say, "I practically made love to his picture when I was thirteen, just like yours—" No I couldn't. I could say, "We're getting closer and closer. We're living together: falling in love with him would be so inanely *simple*—"

"Christ, I understand that, but is he doing something to provoke it, outside of just breathing in and out?"

"I don't know. Sometimes I think not, others I get myself convinced he's moving in."

"He wouldn't. God. Maybe he would. Is he trying to get back at me? I'm really getting what I've earned; that's what you're trying to tell me, isn't it?"

"I simply want to know what I should do if he winds up in bed with me some night!"

Even thinking it I felt stupid and miserable, like the jerk who's just yelled *"Fire!"* in a crowded theater.

Then Tom—the real one—answered the phone. "Rhymer."

"Hello, love."

"Well, telepathy works."

"I wanted to hear your voice, that's all."

"Getting cold on me already? Here I was wanting you in bed. Or the shower, or the living room or—What'd y'do, give Harlan the slip? Wondered how long that'd take."

"He's the one in the shower."

"Is he now."

"I took him to the beach. Got him all sandy."

"God. Don't mar the finish."

I had to laugh; I knew just what he meant. I told him about Harlan on the first day, in his black leopard coat and eyeshadow, saying, "I *am* safe on the street—"

"He is, too: nobody takes liberties with Harlan."

"You do."

He chuckled. "Look closer. He issues the invitations. All I do is RSVP." Then he said, "Is he being happy?"

And here was the place to tell him. "He's running around raising my consciousness on vintage clothes and vintage cars and vintage wines, and playing guitar and dancing at the same time, and jogging Golden Gate Park and eating better than I ever dreamed was possible, and—"

"Oh, Harlan's fond of his comforts, all right. *I'm* fond of his comforts. Keep on loving me, that's all I ask. Any sign of your papers?"

"No. We'll be on that plane the minute they arrive."

"Certain he's not doing a number on you?"

"Who?"

"Who else?"

"What do you mean?"

"About the papers, and how long it takes."

"I was right there in the passport office with him—"

"Every time?"

"The only time. Why would you ask that?"

"Thought I caught a whiff of where he'd been, that's all." Almost as good a jab as the one about the finish.

"Tom?"

"Still here."

"What's the name of it? The perfume he's soaked in."

"Seraglio."

"What? *Oh no!*"

"What I call it. Well? Don't you think he smells like the Sultan's favorite?"

"Favorite *what?*"

He giggled. "I won't tell. Seriously. He's very territorial, like a dog fox. Anything that's his, he puts his scent on it. You couldn't borrow his shirt and forget for a moment whose it was, now could you?"

Another item of the class "things I can't tell him": I'm wearing Harlan's silk jersey and shorts for pajamas.

"Ah—" said Tom, "I guess it's got no name but his."

"What?"

"I had it blended specially for him in Paris."

"His own private perfume? People can do that?"

"Lots of old-time stars have had their own. Famous men have done it. For their lovers.

"I fancy that old master parfumier wasn't so surprised. He asked me what I saw in Harlan. I told him, too. He did some tests to see what his skin was like. Then he squired him around Paris for a night or two to see what *he* was like. Quite a scene. And that's what he came up with."

"I think he got it right."

"Yeah. I'm proud. One grand gesture I thought up that worked. Harlan's got a million tricks like that, all swarming in his head; but I, well I've never been so fertile-minded. I'm in luck if I come up with one. Find one right gesture for him." He drew a breath. "So now, how about yourself? I owe you a wedding present. I bet you're thinking about that."

"No I wasn't."

"Has to be something really special. Think about it."

He was up to something.

I suddenly remembered Madame Hoang's bracelet. I knew that was it: I'd been so dense, I thought he'd bought it for himself.

And teasing me to guess was going to be half his fun.

Chapter 8

WEDNESDAY, SEPTEMBER 3

I REMEMBERED READING something, some dignitary's address to the British Medical Society, how we need for health's sake to change the image of our heroes: how James Bond, if he were real, would have a hundred illegits by now, and every venereal disease known to man.

And that was before AIDS.

Well, I didn't have AIDS, I knew that. AIDS takes much longer than two weeks to show. But some things probably don't. I wondered what things.

I remembered all the pills in Tom's suitcase.

We went jogging anyway. From the Academy of Sciences, down the bridle paths to the beach. And back. Pain. Not quite like a knife in the gut, but too much like to make it any fun. How long was I going to ignore that I was sick? Tender, bloated, painful, queasy sick.

Harlan never got tired. And he never sweated. Not at all. The bones in my pelvis gritted with every step, like my joints were beginning to rot out. My damn old hair was in my face. I actually longed for Harlan's hair bands.

Bet he had 'em made to order. Welcome to the world of unlimited money dispensed with unlimited nerve. I bet he did. His very own custom hair bands, black satin, like his heart. Scared to put one in my hair, all sorts of legendary precedents came to mind, like the Wicked Queen's poisoned ribbons zapping poor Snow White.

That's ridiculous. If I'm spiteful enough to typecast Harlan as the Wicked Queen, it's a pretty sure sign Snow White I'm not.

· — ·

LORD God, Father Almighty, I don't *want* to love him.

Lord Jesus Christ, *do not let* me love him.

Lord God, Holy Spirit, *please make me stop* loving him.

Dona nobis pacem.

Dona nobis requiem.

Dona nobis cold showers. Navy coffee. *Something.*

· — ·

AFTERNOON already. We're in a big old smelly thrift shop in San Jose. "Harlan. *Harlan!*" I'm bouncing up and down so I can spy over the racks. I see Harlan shoot out of the book section, his fingers still keeping place in the middle of a volume called *The Wines of California*. "Look, look look Harlan, Harlan, Harlan, Harlan—This *is* what I'm looking for? This *is* one! Isn't it?"

All he says is, "Does it fit?"

Oh God. What if it doesn't? What if it's too small?

Dingy plywood booth. No lights. Lank dank curtain. Piles of sweaty musty clothes people hadn't hung back where they found 'em. A fringe of price tags (unacceptably high ones) stuck behind the edges of the mirror.

Out of the running shoes, the Levi's, the shirt. A sweet dry benediction of antique withered silk over my head. The moment of truth. I don't fill it out like Mae West. But the shoulders cling honestly to my shoulders. The waist is in the vicinity of my waist. The hem lies demurely near the concrete floor. Hot Damn. The shirt, the Levi's, the running shoes. Out into the light. Harlan's still poring through *The Wines of California.*

"It fits!"

He looks me in the eye for a moment without speaking, just the kindest, quietest smile.

"Thomas will love it. Very much."

"It doesn't match the top thing." The gown is a waxy-hued mosaic of small random wrinkles spaced with shriveled, crowded lace. The peignoir, shades lighter, has acquired big square creases like a road map.

That got one of his little shrugs. "So the gown made it into bed; the peignoir spent its youth in the hope chest, poor thing. There are ways to minimize such differences."

The two together cost $2.99, the same as Harlan paid for *The Wines of California.*

Good fortune to ponder in silence: all the way home from San Jose. The gown and wrap are such a treasure. $9.99 would have seemed an amazing error. $19.99 would have seemed a steal. By now, I can make a fairly accurate estimate, the vintage clothes shops would have wanted $99.99 at least. $199.99 wouldn't amaze me.

But it was too old to be content labeled. If the collar has a tag saying 100% SILK, DRY CLEAN ONLY, the girls in the back room can relate. If the label's in French or German, 100% *seide* or 100% *soie*, forget it. And they never know raw silk at all: be it heavy and rich and labeled; it could lap your skin and cling to your hands like the living essence of love, they wouldn't know what it was.

Most people never do know what something is, if they—first off—don't expect to see it, and it isn't plainly labeled on the collar.

· —— ·

YOSH for hair. Just before closing. The tall young man assigned to me had perfectly sculpted golden curls himself. Harlan leaned across, and whispered in his ear.

He let out a very unprofessional squeal. People turned

around and looked. I bided my time until the hair was all wet down and he was snipping away, I asked him what Harlan had said to make him laugh.

"Nothing," he said. "Your friend was being witty."

"What?"

"Really, nothing."

"Come on, or I'll think you were talking about me."

"He suggested a name, and I didn't expect it, and it struck me as funny, that's all."

"What was the name?"

And he must have thought it was really hilarious; he was giggling again.

"Theda Bara."

I had only the vaguest idea who Theda Bara was, and no idea at all what made it funny. I clammed up. Spent the rest of the time vigorously loathing Harlan, whom I could still see perusing French glamour mags on a divan out front.

But the hair worked, Theda Bara to the contrary not withstanding. When I was finished and dry and the guy put the mirrors around, it was minimal, durable, sculptured smooth and close to my head, a helmet of sleek seal brown.

Harlan could take his black satin hair bands now, and stuff 'em.

· — ·

BESIDES, I now knew how to get away from him. Ha. Wait'll he's in the shower, and split.

There was a really opulent bookstore a few doors up from the hotel. I strode in there and found what I wanted almost at once. Books on Hollywood, movie history, *Glamour Gods and Goddesses of the Silver Screen*.

Find the index. Look up Theda Bara.

And there she was.

Dark hair, bangs. Eyes like two enormous smoky blazes consuming half her face. Shapely little mouth and a steel jaw. Impossible: I knew I couldn't look like that; old Harlan passed for Theda Bara light years easier than I did. Incongruous. That's why the guy at Yosh had laughed.

Or was it?

I found three pictures, and a short blurb on her: the original vamp (as is vampire), the "v" also standing for the vengeance of her sex, she was the woman who used up men, wrung them dry and threw away the rind. Could that be what Harlan thought of me? Maybe he wasn't being funny. I had got his lover, and was set to suck him dry.

It wasn't funny at all.

One other thing, though. She was actually this proper Midwestern Jewish chick named Theodosia Goodman. The studio promo guys concocted "Theda Bara." It was an anagram for "Arab Death."

Now *that* was funny.

THURSDAY, SEPTEMBER 4

I woke up, got up. Threw up. All over the bathroom. I wanted to mop it up, but I was too sick. Harlan found me trying. He rang for the maid. I rang for the Marines.

Doctor Eldridge Curtis. OB Gynecologist. First saw him years ago; Mama panicked because I didn't have periods. He said it was because I ran. After that I saw him once a year. A sandy, skinny, weathered, down-loose man, with a funny laugh not unlike Father 'Chi's.

He was standing outside his suite in the courtyard of the medical building when Harlan and I slid past. He was showing some expectant couple the plant.

In among the tropical wonders growing in the long court is this big-leafed *thing:* it extrudes a bloom like one year in five. It had one now, a man-high jack-in-the-pulpit, or when open, dick-in-the-pulpit: an amazing shameless green phallus, like Audrey II with a hard-on. "How about *that?*" cackled Dr. Curtis. "Is that the sign for a gynecologist's office *or what?*"

I got the exam room I liked best, with the paper mobile twirling from its ceiling. There was the symbol for "male," and the symbol for "female," and two silhouette people, frank and primitive like Bushmen made them. The little guy was bowlegged and his penis was a tab sticking down. The little woman's breasts sat out in cones, one to a side, and her crotch had a round paper-punch hole. The guy's tab fitted perfectly.

You could just tell: the nurses each time they tidied that room would routinely tear off the paper on the exam table and roll out more, pitch the used gown and sheet and set out clean folded ones, and take the little paper guy's tab out of his little wife, letting him dangle free so the next appointment could have the secret satisfaction of reinserting him before the doctor came.

Funny. Lovely. Wonder what minute percentage of women didn't think to do it. *Gloria in excelsis Deo.*

Memory pulled the plug, and all the fun drained out. There was that tiny sparkle of pain in my guts again. I hadn't quite started to cry when Doctor Curtis came in.

"There she is," he said. Did his usual little double take. "They tell me you're infirm."

I told him. I told him good. He didn't say anything.

He lifted up my sheet and pressed my soft parts solemnly all over, leaning his weight into his hand, first down the right side, no problem—

"Ow."

"—That would be your—left ovary—" Then over in the middle, his entire attention centered in the kneading pressing fingers, while his eyes bobbed forgotten on the ceiling.

"Find anything?"

"Your uterus."

"Is it all right?"

"It's—quite hard—and a tad enlarged. Let's go inside and have a look." He warmed his little stainless instrument of torture in the sink—still that shock when he stuck it in and opened it, *Whoop! Click!* Like an umbrella going up inside me.

On my last exam I asked him, just hypothetically of course, like rhetorically, for curiosity's sake, whether anything he saw in my anatomy might make sex difficult. "If I can put *this* in all right—" *(Whoop! Click! Yeeow!)* he said, "your husband shouldn't have much problem."

Now I was married, and here was Dr. Curtis again, looking up me with a flashlight. "Noticed any unusual discharge?"

"What?"

"Itching? Burning? Bleeding?"

"No. No. No. Only a little—"

"Juicy."

"Right."

He took a swab for evidence, saying, "Hardly need to do this, but I'll send it to the lab anyway. I think I can make a visual diagnosis. Classic symptoms. Madam, you're pregnant."

"You mean I'm all right?"

"Assuming you like being pregnant."

"But what about the pains?"

"We feel you're entitled to an ouch or two."

"You mean I'm not sick?"

"If you are, it's not in the parts I look at."

"I've only been married three weeks!"

"Come on, lady, you know where babies come from—"

"I was only with *him* one week! *Part of one week!"*

"So what d'you want me to say? A little dab'll do ya? Your husband's a good shot?" He reached for my file again. "Let's see. Your last period must have been—and counting fifteen days (about) from there—When did you say you were married?"

"The seventeenth."

"Gotcha the first night out."

"He's in England!"

"Give him a call. Get dressed."

In the office down the hall, white starched rumps swaying in unison, nurse and receptionist leaned across the desk, peering out through the receptionist's window at the little lobby with its cozy colonial furniture and baby magazines.

"Can't be, that was a month ago."

"Don't care," whispered the other, "That's *him.*"

I knew just what they were seeing.

"Well he must be with *some* band, it's the only excuse I know for looking like that—"

"Marta," said Dr. Curtis in the direction of the prone nurse and receptionist, "Have you got Andy's billing here?"

I tackled him again. "Don't I need some special diet?"

"Do you eat meat once a week?"

"Come on, be serious."

"Do you drink a lot? Smoke? Do drugs?"

"No!"

"Young lady, you are a perfect physical specimen. You obviously know how to take care of yourself. Pregnancy is a natural condition. An ultimately natural condition."

"I run a lot. Shouldn't I stop?"

"Probably harder on your bod to stop abruptly than go on cautiously. You've got good sense. Your own comfort is the surest guide."

"What about sex?"

"Same goes. The final week or so when things begin to open up, there's some increased risk of infection, but I've seen lots of healthy overdues induced into the world that way. Why, it's better'n climbin' in the ol' pickup and ridin' down the railroad tracks."

"I'll need to find a doctor in England, won't I—"

"*Pas de problème.* It's a civilized country."

Doctors, it's claimed, have the same speech defect as Las Vegas women, all they can say is "One hundred dollars." My billing was all typed out, laid out on the desk.

I went, "Sssst," at Harlan through the waiting room door. He, being never slow, came through it wallet in hand. "That *is* Harlan Parr, by the way," I breathed to the nurse, behind his back.

"Oh God," she breathed back. "Oh God. You're—*not?*" (I shook my head.) "They said you were married, I didn't think to check your record—" (doing it) *"Miranda Rhymer?"*

· — ·

HARLAN had me outside already, next to the plant. From its tip, at eye level, hung a fat round drop of nectar. The whole world looked bright, flat glittery bright, like I was going to faint. "Harlan."

"What?"

"You didn't hear what he said."

He searched my face in quiet alarm. "I assumed from their manner—No, I heard the doctor say you were well—"

"I'm pregnant."

Everything went black.

At last I was inside Harlan's charmed circle, with his hair over my eyes and the rest of me glued up against his warm rough linen suit. He was just like Tom, he kissed with his whole body. Tom said Harlan hadn't known how to kiss very well the first time, but it was terribly sweet. That second part was true even now. Tom said they'd taught each other how to love. They sure were each other's star pupils. I thought he said, "Now I understand—" (against my right cheek) "why—" (a kiss to the mouth) "I've felt Tom's hand when I took yours." Implausible as a dream he should be saying that, and convincing instantly, as dreams are—

Then he backed off a little and said, for real and for sure this time, "Promise me, promise me you won't tell Tom until the proper time. Please promise."

I was sure he said that. "When's proper?"

"I'll tell you when the time comes." He seemed so pathetically earnest. "Please trust me. I'll show you how it works."

"Sure." I would have promised him almost anything just then. Amazing how reasonable it all could seem. I'm well and I'm pregnant, God bless me, Tom would be kissing me, exactly the same if he were here: exactly the same—exactly the same—in the cool of early evening, presided over by the exuberant protuberant greenness of that enormous phallic plant, in the sweet smell of the blooming courtyard.

· — ·

SOMEBODY cleared her throat, and queried in a genteel whoopy dowager's voice like Julia Child's—"Your first?"

We were holed up in the next door down from Dr. Curtis, which was, in fact, the entrance to a dentist's. An elderly lady in a red suit and hat was waiting to get past. We let go of each other and faced her in as total alarm I'm sure as if she'd caught us fucking in the bushes.

"Er, yes, quite!" said Harlan, blushing and bobbing, doing an excellent job of looking young, flustered, upper class and English. Which, of course, he was.

Hat Lady smiled benignly. "Well, I wish you many *many* more," she said, patting his arm, then mine. "Small families may be modern, but the world *needs* beautiful people."

We abandoned the Porsche in the medical suites' slowly emptying lot, and hiked around the corner into Stanford Shopping center. Gaylord's of India. My hand that wore Tom's rings traveled tightly enclosed in Harlan's small, hard, comfortably warm one.

We tried to rev up our old discussion about hot food, but talk kept lapsing. When the split of Chardonnay he ordered was almost empty, Harlan eyed the Mound of Despair and ordered another. And finished it.

But his touch with the car felt smooth and sure as ever.

I curled up in my bucket seat. The pain in my insides wasn't. Oh, something was still there, but it wasn't pain. Just something. Short ride.

I was still half asleep when Harlan unlocked the door to the suite. He ducked into his room and came out with a small manila envelope. He handed it to me. It was addressed to Miranda D. Rhymer c/o the hotel. In the upper left corner it said U.S. Passport Services.

"Harlan?"

He was already on the phone. "Want to place a transatlantic call to England, please. London, England." He used the delay transferring his body to the couch. "Yes, thank you. The number is—" he gave it.

"Harlan, how long have you had this? When did you—"

"Twenty-four hours after our visit to the bureau."

"But, they had to get my records from—"

He had the phone to his ear, decorating the couch in lithe, half-potted patience; he wasn't looking at me. "There are four wedding chapels in the street behind the licensing office in Carson City. They read me the numbers, I called them one by one. You were married at seven o'clock in the evening, in the Garden House of Serendipity Square, by one Reverend Milton Pritchard, Episcopal, retired. One hour to locate the right chapel and the

Reverend Pritchard, one half-hour of genteel conversation to convince him that I hold Tom's lasting power of attorney—"

"You do?"

"Of course. As he does mine. How else?"

"I understand," I said, "around here some guys adopt each other—"

He flopped his head back over the arm of the couch, to regard me upside down. "What—adding incest to injury?"

Somebody must have asked the number again; he repeated it, with emphasis, and continued "—then he, being a gentleman, walked across to the State offices, expedited the issuance of a certified copy; a local courier service carried it in a sealed official envelope to the passport office in San Francisco, which had this issued and delivered to the hotel desk in twenty-four hours."

"How long would you have hung on to it?"

"Until I knew if I could live with you."

"What if you'd decided that you couldn't? Harlan, *answer me!*"

Tom said Harlan had tried his hand at suicide. I found that hard to believe. With all his poise and self-assurance, he was the least suicidal-looking creature in the world. Still, Tom said Harlan had come for *him* with a knife, and that was even harder. But what did I know about crimes of passion? Wasn't it all an act, a gesture? You know, fling himself bodily over the edge, force his lover to catch him, save him. Hot stuff: kissing and making up in hospital emergency. That was more the Harlan style, I guessed, but oh God, what if I was wrong? So who would it have been this time, himself or me?

"Maggee." Both halves of the name so evenly accented, you couldn't tell if it was "Maggie" or "McGee."

He giggled. "I know." Sinking to an ominous guttural, he rasped "*A voice from the dead!* Listen, have you a pencil handy?" The person hadn't, evidently. "I'm coming home. Yes. That's right. I'll have Thomas's new bride with me. As soon as I have the flight details, I'll let you know.

"First. I want the lads at Heathrow. I've tried Thomas. He's not to be found. That's right. With one of the Mercedes. Make that both the Mercedes.

"Second, Thomas will want to be at Heathrow. I have no idea. Somewhere between London and Norwich, like as not. Locate him.

"Third, Thomas will want the world to be at Heathrow. Tip the fan clubs. Oh no, of course not. Anonymous will do. You have the numbers. (Pause) Those are indeed the ones. Next. Reservations: a suite, or better still, two, in one of the larger, more impregnable tourist hotels, Strand Palace, or the like. At least through the first of October.

"Right. Expense no object. We'll make a grand pretense of installing the lady there. They'll do for her family later." He giggled again. "Nothing but the finest red herring. Yes.

"And lastly—that's right. Lastly, Thomas and his bride will be coming home with me." Whatever was suggested on the far end, Harlan looked perfectly aghast. "*Oh no*, it *isn't* that *at all:* you're to make as much of them as possible, or he'll be terribly hurt. It's not the other bit at all. Thomas is well and properly married; give the dear boy his money's worth.

"No, his own room. But do turn it out for a bridal chamber. A fire in the grate, lavender between the sheets. Well, whatever you think appropriate. That's the ticket. The office should know when they open. It *is* six o'clock in the morning. Five-thirty. Thank you, Maggee. So, goodbye, dear. Much love."

Whom does Harlan love? Besides Tom. That's what I'm thinking now. Who loves him, lives with him, does his errands for him? Laughs and jives with him at five-thirty in the morning. Older or younger? No clue. Male or female? Female, I imagine somehow. Oh God, I hope that's not just prejudice! It might be like Tim's boys.

Before ringing off he's smiling anyway, murmuring again, "Much love."

I'm off to sleep with both hands under my pillow, and my official U.S. Passport, issued to Miranda Dolores Rhymer, in both hands.

FRIDAY, SEPTEMBER 5

Harlan has taken to the phone already, and I'm not out of bed. *Remedy that.* Two glasses of orange juice this morning, and an almond tart Kit delivered from the coffee shop.

The first available fight to London is a red-eye with a plane change in New York. That gives us one long day and most of an evening to get packed.

Trunks. Bags. Tissue paper. I spread it out one last time and looked at all my wonderful collected stuff. And it was certainly my stuff, all right. No one else's.

Dead people's clothes.

Rings from old ruined marriages.

Mourning silk for an Emperor's concubine.

Castoffs lovingly restored by outcasts.

Luggage off the *Titanic.*

As if I'd picked up every last thing I could find that was bizarre, offbeat, ill-omened and was trying to drag it bodily with me through the sacraments of Christian Grace.

Tim appeared at the door, just after dark, and behind him four giggling black-leather guys. Black caps, black jackets, black jodhpurs, jack boots. A matched set. I'd seen them all severally at his shop, but not together, and not in uniform: Richard, Neil, Danny, and Cody. They were carrying my wedding dresses.

Tim had another shirt-box-sized package, done up in white rice paper shot with silver foil. "For you, blushing bride," he kissed my cheek, "To be opened on the morning of your wedding, *before* you put your stockings on."

He rolled on past me into the suite. Utter shock. He walked with two canes, those metal orthopedic kind with braces up the forearm. I'd only seen him moving around his shop. No wonder his arms and chest were so built up; his lower body was crippled: thoroughly, and miserably. I cornered Harlan when I could.

"Shot through the hips at Pork Chop Hill," he whispered. "Pelvis largely reconstituted from bone chips and bits of metal—"

How embarrassing, that I hadn't seen, or realized or asked. And Harlan obviously had.

Harlan boxed most of his stuff, including the guitars, for Kit to mail at leisure. Some, like the orange juicer and coffee machine, he simply gave him. Also in Kit's pocket: (quasi indefinite loan?) the pink slip, maintenance log, and keys to the green Porsche.

· — ·

AT last it was time.

Pulled up grandly at the curb before the revolving doors, was an antique London taxi, huge, upright, and black as death. Kit and the boys strapped my steamer trunks into the open cargo bay. Driving was a guy I hadn't seen before, an amiably weird old German by the name of Constantine.

Kit crammed inside with the rest of us, holding Tim's sticks respectfully. The leather boys hopped on motorcycles and we pulled away, tight formation.

Halfway to SFO Harlan said, "I like your entourage."

Tim sniffed. "Footmen on the running boards are a nice touch too, but it tends to get the CHP a skosh excited."

He left us at the airport curb. "You'll *pardonnez-moi* for not walking with you? Just remember me, Lord, when you enter into your kingdom." He kissed Harlan on both cheeks.

He did the same for me. Kit stayed with him, holding his sticks. The boys took my trunks and Harlan's to the counter.

First Class. First time in my life. In the front door of the plane, and turn left instead of right. I feel like the newly made archbishop who said, "Gentlemen, from now on I expect never to eat a bad meal, nor to hear an honest opinion."

Still a stifling metal womb. The womb begins to move.

Look down from a window seat by day, you see a variegated pavement taxi by gray and black, green and yellow islands set with little lights. But now it's night.

Noise swells from soft ventilation to a whine, a shriek, a whistling roar. Wheels lope purposefully over the cracks in the pavement; tires take the rhythm of the cracks, faster and faster. Pause at the end.

A sense of incredible muscle, gathering up behind the small

of my back and hurling forward: a walk, a trot, a lope, a gallop, freeway speed. Now faster than any freeway ever. The plane rears back on titanic pneumatic haunches and lofts itself. Thousands of tons of steel and glass and rubber and plastic and carpet, compressed air, fabric and jet fuel, bad food, magazines and human flesh. The rapid-fire stutter of tires along the pavement is gone. And so are we from San Francisco. The fog below us is a wrinkled sea. I see a ring of small islands, the tips of the Coast Range, Mt. San Bruno, Tamalpais, the Berkeley Hills—all the rest of San Francisco Bay lies in between, submerged, invisible.

Food arrives, not very good and too much of it. Temptation is to eat it, because, like Mt. Everest, it's there. Harlan looks at his with undisguised contempt. I eat all of mine. I'm riding warm and passive in my airline seat as that other unseen passenger inside me.

Most of my girlfriends' parents spent two years of middle school and four years of high in a permanent screaming flap their daughters'd get pregnant. (None did.) My friends were fought with, mistrusted, grounded, locked up, stuffed through family counseling, shipped off in tears to distant boarding schools. Nobody gave me any of that stuff. Had me worried for a while, whether it was an insult or a compliment.

Imagine Papa engaged in his favorite occupation, "Monkeying with the Computer": brooding in a darkened room, over the little green terminal screen, Palantir fashion. I've been filling him in (unsolicited) on the vicissitudes of my friends' home lives, leading up to the real, intense question: "Why aren't you ever scared that I'll get pregnant?" I figured he hadn't heard.

A few more thoughts got punched into the PDP-11. Then he said, "I don't believe in abortion." In agreement so far: neither did I. *Then he said,* "So *should* you get pregnant, guess you'll just have to share your room."

That was the only lecture on the subject of teen sex I ever got at home. Now here I am, sharing my most intimate inside room. Some other minute stranger alive and well inside me. My pelvis a living cradle of delicate arched bone to rock it in. Her in. Him in. Seems that I should know this person, thrown together in a lottery of Tom's dear stuff and my stuff. But I don't know anything. What a jolly comic miracle: do-it-yourself build-a-person. Here we go, there's one from you, and one from me, and one from *you*—and one from *me*—

I learned human reproduction off of educational TV.

Channel 9. NOVA.

Body fluids. His stuff, part of him. Think about how he is, all composed of swift energy. His sperm a jostling horde, so many microscopic marathoners at the start of that great race, each one carrying all his information.

And the course? Where Alph the Sacred River ran through caverns measureless to man down to a sunless sea. Such caves, not Mammoth Cave, Carlsbad, or any other famous cavern could vie with them in beauty, if only they were big enough for guided tours—my female insides. Think of that. More beautiful than any National Park. Stalactites, stalagmites, alabaster grottoes, passages, translucent walls and curtains, hanging traceries of every hue.

And somewhere, waiting like the pirate's treasure in the very inmost recess of that maze of little twisty passages all alike, my own genetic contribution. Round, smooth, pearly, featureless. Motionless, unmotivated. Helpless. The junction of all riches and all poverty. The future is in eggs.

In the midst of death
we are in life—
The Lord taketh away
and the Lord giveth—
Blessed be the Name of the Lord—.

Baby and me, and Harlan makes three. We flash over the top of the world toward a bright sunrise.

L'envoi

SATURDAY, SEPTEMBER 6

AFTER OUR TWO-HOUR layover in New York. Still flying.

They set the in-flight movie up, and it was *Drake*, of all things. Harlan looked so smug, I wondered if he'd arranged it. He whipped his little white guitar and dubbing deck out of the garment bag he'd carried on and patched it all together so we each had an earphone to the movie and an earphone to his toys. Imagine the last third of an intercontinental flight spent listening to Harlan Parr play rock continuo to the whole soundtrack of *Drake*. Easily, as if that witty jazzy rollick of music was the machine language of his mind, and everything else, even his English speech, was a poor translation.

When the movie was over he packed it all away and silently showed me his watch. The flight was on time, an hour out of Heathrow.

My failure of nerve began and ended: I couldn't deplane in Levis. With my little portmanteau from under the seat, I went and found an even smaller metal womb to hide in. A restroom, bright Formica-colored, well lighted and coffin-small. I washed my gray and smudgy face, drew on raccoon eyes. Wondered about Theda Bara. Out of the Levis and T-shirt and jacket, into the streamlined little white silk '40s dress and much-despised white heels.

I stuff my real clothes in the bag: amazed at how it feels to give in, sell out, be intimidated this way. I consider keeping out the Levi jacket. No, if I freeze my ass in Heathrow airport, I can at least hate Harlan for it.

Back at the seat now. Watch him never glance up.

The airy whine, which has grown natural, lowers pitch. "Ladies and gentlemen, would you please return to your seats. Please make sure your seat belts are securely fastened—"

Sense of lagging, dragging, holding back, deceleration, like a dropping elevator, only diagonal, interminable. Look out the window. Nothing. *White*. Cut off from all the living in a featureless world of cloud, we could meet another speeding plane in this pale secrecy, and never see it. Death would come faster than fear.

No warning. The fog shredded. We were scudding out beneath it. Night; and the ground a thousand feet below, jeweled and ablaze with lights, as far on every side as I could see. Hung here and there among the strings and ropes of diamond light were huge flaming-green brilliant oblongs, like unimaginable emeralds.

"What are those? Harlan? The green things?"

"Football matches, love," he said brightly, craning to see. "Bread and circuses, and all that. Those would be the circuses. Pretty from the air, what?"

"Ladies and gentlemen, please be seated. We are beginning our approach to Heathrow International Airport; seat belts must remain fastened until etc. etc. Thank you for flying Pan Am to the British Isles, and enjoy your stay in London. Before leaving the aircraft, please check your immediate area for items you may have brought onboard with you."

Harlan went again into the garment bag where all his music electronics were stowed, and pulled out three more orderly packages. First: the Marines ROTC dress jacket, folded neatly. He put it on. Then the Knights of Columbus cocked hat, boxed to save the plumes. He put that on too. Some deft hand, I noted, had hot-glued Belshangles patches over the KoC emblems. Okay.

The third bundle he plumped into my lap.

"Heathrow is notoriously frigid."

Inside the Gump's logo cloth bag was the ermine bomber jacket with the flippety-floppety tails.

· — ·

"MR. Parr, sir—"

"Have we problems disembarking?"

"I understand there's a small crowd—"

"Is my partner—ah. Yes. Are the—? Oh God, the police as well? But they are on the other side of customs? Of course. So ought we to go first and let the rest get on with their lives?"

"'We understand there's a small crowd—'" he mimics as we take the gray baize tunnel hand in hand. "Should hope there's a bloody great riot with that much advance notice, or it's time we cashed our winnings and retired to the South of France—"

Customs sized up Harlan and shunted us to a private room. He seemed to expect it as his due. When their drug-sniffing dog turned up her nose at us, they started on our clothes.

Out of the bag came Harlan's black leopard coat.

He flipped it open. Inside the left front, exquisitely made into the lining, was a clear vinyl window. Inside that, a document certified that the leopards went to glory in India, 1933–34, well before the establishment of protected status. Their pelts were exported to France, and in 1939 became a full-length coat, made to order for a Frau Anna Davidoff of Berlin, who, due to circumstances beyond her control, never took delivery. The coat hung, black but beautiful as the tents of Kedar, in Parisian cold storage through war, invasion, liberation, and efforts to locate living heirs of Frau Davidoff. Almost forty years later it was auctioned and recut to the specs of a Mr. H. Parr of London.

Wow. To what shall I be compared, O Lord? I think about Saint Ann walking in her garden. I could collect ill-omened treasures for a lifetime and never equal that.

The customs guys, crestfallen, nearly frog-march us out, past rows of the mundane explaining away their liquor and their cigarettes. Then we hit the main concourse, and I can see Tom's face—

His head is as the most fine gold—
—His hands are as gold rings set with beryl—
His legs are as pillars of marble—
His mouth is most sweet:
yeah, man, altogether lovely—

The crowd breaks over us like a flashbulb sea.